LAKEWOOD

LAKEWOOD

A Novel

MEGAN GIDDINGS

AMISTAD

An Imprint of HarperCollins*Publishers*

HarperCollins books may be purchased for educational, business, or sales promotional use. For information, please email the Special Markets Department at SPsales@harpercollins.com.

FIRST EDITION

Designed by Jamie Lynn Kerner

Library of Congress Cataloging-in-Publication Data

Names: Giddings, Megan, author.
Title: Lakewood : a novel / Megan Giddings.
Description: First edition. | New York, NY : Amistad, an imprint of
    HarperCollins Publishers, [2020] | Summary: "A stunning debut novel that
    delves fearlessly into the taboo subject of modern-day medical
    experimentation on African Americans"—Provided by publisher.
Identifiers: LCCN 2019038755 (print) | LCCN 2019038756 (ebook) | ISBN
    9780062913197 (hardcover) | ISBN 9780062913203 (trade paperback) | ISBN
    9780062913227 (ebook)
Subjects: LCSH: Human experimentation in medicine—Fiction. | African
    Americans—Fiction.
Classification: LCC PS3607.I2748 L35 2020 (print) | LCC PS3607.I2748
    (ebook) | DDC 813/.6—dc23
LC record available at https://lccn.loc.gov/2019038755
LC ebook record available at https://lccn.loc.gov/2019038756

20 21 22 23 24 LSC 10 9 8 7 6 5 4 3 2 1

LAKEWOOD

PART 1

1

Lena's grandmother's final instructions were that the funeral should be scheduled for 11 a.m. but would start at 11:17 when everyone would be there and seated. Deziree, if she was well, would give one of the eulogies, and at the luncheon, Lena would give presents and letters to Miss Toni's closest friends and tell them one last time how special they were to her. Anyone who was still alive and didn't attend, Lena would send letters to them within a week. And by 8 p.m., Deziree and Lena should be at the casino across town, the one with the good buffet.

Still in her black dress and high heels, Lena listened to the slot machines' songs, their rhythms and chimes, the excited harmony of one loudly announcing a winner. Her mother, Deziree, was talking to a few of the bouncers and waitresses, accepting their condolences, nodding as one said, "I still can't believe it. Miss Toni. Jesus. I'm thirty and she was in better shape than me." And a year ago, that had been true. "She was more alive than most people I know." Lena nodded.

The day before she'd died, the three of them were in the

hospital room, and her grandmother had said, "What I wouldn't give for one more June day." She wanted to talk with her friends on the porch, eat a bowl of raspberries with whipped cream on top, grill out, stay up late playing cards with the two of them. And the weather would be warm, not hot. Big cloud, blue sky weather. Lena had excused herself, went to get tea, and hoped that at the end of her own life, she would only want one more good, but not special, day.

"Y'all are in my prayers."

"Thank you," Lena and Deziree said in unison. The two of them were so used to hearing variations of that, the response was now automatic.

They sowed coins into Cleopatra slot machines. After losing five times in a row, Lena stopped and cashed out. Deziree kept going. Her face was illuminated pink and blue by the screen and it made the tear stains on her cheeks visible again.

"Stop being so rude," Deziree muttered to the machine after losing a second time.

Lena shut her eyes. It was the first time in hours the two of them had been alone, where she didn't feel like she had to look brave or grateful or think about anyone else's feelings. She was saturated with the day. Her grandmother's face in the casket, so still—Lena could only look at it for a few seconds before having to look instead at the pink carpet of the church floor, the white flowers, or her own manicure, gray. Her mother's voice, so steady, as she spoke about Miss Toni. Watching her and trying to focus on the speech, the goodbyes, rather than worrying every time her mom's hands shook, every time she stumbled a little bit on a word, that another flare-up was about to start. The mixture of flowers, mildew, heavy perfume that only really smelled like perfume—not vanilla or lilies like the bottles probably said—and roast chicken in the church basement.

"I'm exhausted," Lena said.

"Feelings? Or do you need to change your shoes? Or?"

"Everything."

"We promised her this."

"I know."

Lena watched as Deziree went up 10, down 20, up 30. She liked the color blue they used for the scarabs. The dopey cats wearing hats. How the game designers had thrown in some fancy English letters rather than try to do all hieroglyphics. How there was no way for her to understand how to win the game. It seemed to be all great robotic whims.

A pack of Miss Toni's friends turned the corner and descended on them. They were in casual clothes, silky pants and tracksuits, but still stunk of the thick perfumes they probably spritzed on every time they dressed up. "Here you girls are."

"Did she tell you all to come here too?"

One squeezed Lena's left shoulder. The other flicked something off her right arm. Another asked Deziree how she was feeling, did she need anything? And Lena, how was she keeping up with classes? College alone is a lot. I can't imagine being so young.

"Everything is going good at school. All of the professors were really nice and understanding—"

"Do you all have things to eat?"

The kindness was suffocating. So many casseroles, so many cards, so many people dropping by, so many thinking-of-yous. Lena wanted to be good and kind. And she was grateful that so many people loved her grandma. But it was also exhausting to have so many people looking into her face, looking at the parts of it and trying to find Miss Toni.

A waitress carrying a tray squeezed in among them and cleared her throat. "Courtesy of Miss Toni." She passed two

Dark & Stormys to Lena and Deziree. The waitress paused, her face crumpled, and she fled.

"Was she at the funeral?" Lena asked.

"Maybe? In the back?" Deziree held her Dark & Stormy up, clinked it against Lena's. "Cheers."

The women stayed around them, chitchatting about how Toni had done such a great job raising them both, as if Deziree wasn't going to turn 43 that year. Lena turned back to Deziree's screen: She was up 65 dollars now.

"I'll be right back," Lena said. She walked to the nearest bathroom, taking her drink with her. She sat in the stall farthest from the door. Took the deepest breath she could, then let it out slowly. Contorted her face into different expressions—happy, anguished, I'm-going-to-get-you-bitch—and took a long drink. There were two extra lime slices in it like her grandmother always ordered. How many Dark & Stormys do I have to have, she wondered, to feel like you're here with us? A song about being so in desire with someone you felt like you had burst into flames was leaking through the speakers in the ceiling.

"Lena?" her mother said.

She finished her drink, set the glass on the floor, and went out to Deziree.

"Everything okay?" Lena asked. The mirror gave a full view of the back of her mother's head. It looked as if she had been pulling on her hair. Her black bra straps poked out. Her eyes were bloodshot, her fingers trembling. It was hard to tell whether it was because of the poor bathroom lighting or because of illness, but Deziree's skin was now sallow.

"We can go home," Lena said. She smoothed her mother's hair, adjusted the straps back into place. Watched her hands and mouth for tremors. They were still. Deziree's dark lipstick was smudged, but still looked pretty good.

"I lost it all," Deziree said. They paused for a moment, and laughed.

Lena coughed when she was finished. She couldn't help asking, "You took your medicine today, right?"

"I wouldn't have been able to do anything today without it."

They left the bathroom and headed to Miss Toni's favorite blackjack dealer. When he noticed them, he signaled a waitress, who brought over two more Dark & Stormys. "May you have Toni's luck tonight," he said. Then, with a laugh, "Please don't have her luck. I need a job."

They smiled at each other, then did what they always did. Snapped their fingers for luck and clasped hands. One of the first things Lena could remember was her grandma teaching her blackjack. The game's rules, but also things like remembering—as with most individual sports—that it was also a game you mostly played against yourself. You had to be confident, engaged, patient. Don't allow yourself to be polluted by the dealer's silence or the chitchat of the people around you.

Lena leaned forward a little. Focused on counting, paying attention to everyone's cards, watching the dealer's hands and eyes, looking for tells. She sipped her drink slowly, at a rate fast enough to make her feet ache a little less, but not enough to feel too bold. And when she hit blackjack for the first time, she automatically turned to the right, where her grandmother might be, before quickly turning and squeezing Deziree's hands with delight.

An hour later and two hundred dollars richer—an amount Miss Toni would have called "fine"—they shimmied and danced their way over to the buffet to eat blueberry-bacon gelato and lobster and scrambled eggs. As they waited to get served coffee, Deziree kept putting one hand over her forehead and rubbing the spot between her eyebrows. "Don't worry," she kept saying.

Deziree sagged down, her head and forearms resting on the table. She didn't notice the purple gelato drip pattern that she was creating on the front of her dress.

Lena asked the waitress for a double Americano.

"She drunk?" the waitress asked. She was young, probably a college student. Hair dyed purple, a nose ring. She had also been at the funeral, Lena realized.

"Nah. She good."

"This is the best I've felt in days." Deziree was crumpling into illness, grief, exhaustion. Her voice came out slurred.

"She gonna need a chair?"

Lena took off her own left shoe beneath the table and rubbed her toes hard. "We'll be out of here in ten, I promise. She's fine."

Stumbling into their living room, Deziree dumped the contents of her purse on the floor. Dollars, credit cards, lipstick, a mint that looked as if it had already been sucked on and then put back in the cellophane wrap, coins scattered across the wood floors. Deziree looked at the mess for a moment, then fell.

Lena rushed to her side. Her mom propped herself up.

"Smile at me," Lena said.

"I'm fine."

"Come on. We both know you didn't drink that much."

Deziree gritted her teeth. Lena raised her eyebrows. Deziree rolled her eyes and did a big fake grin.

Lena had her mother lift her arms and repeat the phrase, "Pancakes are better with bananas in them."

"They said we had to do this every time you fall."

"You sound just like her."

Deziree sat up and went to her bedroom. When she returned,

she was holding a large envelope that was stuffed to the limits. She tossed it onto Lena's stomach.

"Can we do this later today?"

But her mother was already in the kitchen, opening drawers and rifling through cabinets as if she had stored secrets among the plates and glasses. Inside the envelope were bills. Insurance statements that looked as if they were all disagreeing with each other about the amount of coverage. Folded-over invoices from the cemetery, the funeral home. Electric and water bills. Some receipts. Deziree came back holding more.

"Have any of these been paid?"

"I don't know."

Deziree stooped over the coffee table. She pulled more bills from between the magazines. It felt like an absurd magic trick.

Lena rubbed her eyes and the remnants of her mascara stained her fingertips. She made herself sit up straight.

"There's more bills I can pull up on my phone."

Lena felt all the aftershocks of no sleep, the stress of the past months, and now this. She wanted to go to bed and sleep for three days. Instead, she went to the kitchen, found the least green banana she could, poured a glass of water, and pulled out her mom's pillbox. There were only enough pills in the box until Saturday.

"I'm sorry, Biscuit—" her mom began. Lena handed everything over. "Take these." Her mom's eyes were watering. Lena made her mouth soft, adjusted her posture. "I'm not mad, I'm just tired."

"But—"

"This day has been too long for us to have this conversation right now." She watched her mother carefully, making sure she swallowed her pills, ate at least half of the banana, drank all the water. Lena squeezed her mother's hands when they were free, hoped the gesture was reassuring. "Get some sleep and we'll talk about this in the afternoon."

Deziree stood up and went to her room. Lena picked up the bills and carried them out to the kitchen table. She organized them into categories: house, medical-Mom, funeral, medical-Grandma. Then she pulled out a pen and her notebook from her backpack. Flipped to her current to-do list: an astronomy test the next day that she still hadn't studied enough for, a three-hour shift at her work-study job that night, Spanish conversation lunch about going shopping where she was supposed to lead a conversation entirely in Spanish. Thank-you letters to write. Coordinating with Miss Shaunté about Deziree's home health care schedule. She needed to understand the math to calculate a star's gravity and its effect on everything around it while it was still living. Figure out summer work.

Lena tapped the pile of bills with her pen, flipped the page, and started a brand-new list.

2

The letter arrived in the mail on the day of Lena's third job interview. An invitation to participate in a series of research studies about mind, memory, personality, and perception. The Lakewood Project. It offered Lena and her family health insurance if she was selected to be a participant. Also housing and a weekly stipend for qualified applicants. It was addressed specifically to her: Miss Lena Johnson. A signature at the bottom that she couldn't read. An 800 number to call to schedule an appointment. There was something about it—the lack of details, the thick, expensive paper, maybe just the whole vibe—that made her uncomfortable.

Lena showed the letter to Tanya. "Is this a scam?"

Tanya held the letter up to the light, asked to see the envelope it came in. "I don't know. I'm not—" She scrunched her nose. "What's the word for someone who can tell if things are forged?"

"I think they're called—" Lena took the letter back. "Um, forensic document experts."

"It's probably legit. Didn't Stacy say his brother did these?"

"I can't remember. I zone out most of the time when he talks about his brother."

"He'll be at the party tonight. You can ask him about it."

"No one's brother is as great as Stacy says his brother is."

Tanya pulled out a dress. "What I'm wearing now with a leather jacket, or this?"

Lena looked down at the letter again. If you are selected for this study, you will be well compensated.

"You are going to come out tonight, right?"

Lena kept her eyes on the letter. She knew if she looked up, her friend's eyes would be let-me-take-care-of-you soft. She would offer to put on *Work Spaces*, point to the drawer where their vodka was hidden, start talking about doing face and hair masks. "Yes, we're going out. And yes, what you're wearing now with a leather jacket. You don't want to look like you're trying too hard."

"You know what I think?"

"Almost all the time." Lena folded the letter.

"I think you should call."

Lena was still wearing the pantsuit Tanya called Your-Honor-I-Plead-Not-Guilty. "Do you think I should wear this to the party?"

"You need a backup plan."

Lena watched as Tanya held the red dress up against her body. Their room stunk of the black pepper and honeysuckle candles they liked to burn to relax, and to hide the smell of Tanya's cucumber-scented vaping. Doing a research study didn't sound any worse than the Craigslist ads she had just been looking at—a secretary position for a notoriously terrible cable company, openings at a new, "innovative" maid service where you had to dress as a French maid and say your name was Simone at every house you cleaned. "I'll call in the morning."

They took a shot each. Another. Lena changed out of her pantsuit, put on a shade of lipstick that she couldn't help calling Schiaparelli, though it was five dollars from CVS, though Tanya screamed, "Pretentious," every time she did it.

It brought Lena so much pleasure to call colors by specific names, both formal and made up. Klein Blue, Cerulean, Scarab-From-Cleopatra Blue. It made her feel like she was becoming an interesting adult to know things like that, to get pleasure out of the things her brain squeezed onto and refused to let leave.

At the party, music was playing just loud enough to smooth out any pauses in conversations. People were passing around bottles of fortified wine. A girl Lena didn't know was talking about how her vape pen was the best on the market. Try it, the vapor is smoother, she kept saying. Stacy and his boyfriend were quietly fighting over the playlist. You have ho taste in music, she heard Stacy whisper through gritted teeth. Tanya was texting someone. Lena thought that she could be wearing pajamas right now, a blanket wrapped around her shoulders, blowing heat off a cup of tea. Two girls from Lena's How to Write About Art class asked her if she was staying in Michigan over summer break. They were traveling to Montana to learn about rock formations. Everyone was going to summer camps to teach kids archery and how to be away from home. They were going to Senegal to speak intensive French and cry at Gorée Island. They were interning for their not-rich-but-you-know, comfortable, uncles. College—where everyone was struggling until suddenly it was summer, and all the worries got smoothed away.

"Lena, come meet my brother," Stacy yelled.

"Sure, sure."

"This is Kelly," Stacy said. His brother was average height, bald, but with a very nice smile. He was wearing a black sweatshirt that had neon paint flecked across it. Lena couldn't tell if it was expensive or just the sweatshirt he might've worn while painting.

Lena shook Kelly's hand. "So, your parents were lazy, right?"

Stacy looked confused, but Kelly smiled wider. "Our mom was lazy. Our dad probably still wishes he could name us good, strong man names."

After a pause, the conversation started. Kelly was an MFA student in painting out in the Bay Area. He was interested in portraying the environment as it was, as it is, as it should be. Triptychs. Lena was impressed that he didn't seem embarrassed about his art. She liked that his tone was soft, not loud enough to be overheard so people would think, Oh, wow, an artist is present. People were getting drunk now. Dancing. Tanya was trying the girl's vape pen and making an unimpressed face.

"I've heard so much about you," Kelly said. "You're quieter than I imagined, based on Stacy's stories."

She looked down at her shoes. "Life's been. Well, this isn't a party conversation." He pulled out a cigarette and his lighter, gestured toward the door. "Well, maybe it's a smoking conversation." The night was cold, windy. There were few people out, though it was a Friday. A much louder party down the block boomed out bass. Kelly offered her a cigarette, she shook her head. Just six months ago, Lena knew she would've been flirting with him. Or she would have been back inside dancing. Or at least would have been drinking.

"Why are you so serious tonight?" Kelly asked.

"My grandmother died a few weeks ago. And—" Her throat closed for a second. "Well, she was my grandma, but she was also my mom. Not in, like, a weird way. She just did a lot of the work in raising me."

"Is there anything I can do?" He was so earnest, as if he did have the power to make her life much better, all she had to do was ask. The skin on his hands shone underneath the golden porch light.

"Do you want to take a walk?"

He nodded, offered his arm. She put her arm through the crook of it.

"So, why did your grandma raise you?"

"I thought Stacy told you all about me."

"He did." Lena was happy she couldn't see his face. "But I want to hear your version of it. If that's okay."

She told him that the first memory she had of her mother was of her having a seizure in their kitchen. Deziree had said something that was wrong right before it happened, and she had said to her mother, "Mom, that's not how adults talk." And then she was scared and called 911, then her grandma. And the people at the hospital told her grandma later that it was maybe because her mother fell on the ice earlier that day and some-thing was hurt in her brain. Lena was in the room, listening in, pretending to be focused on her coloring book. She already knew adults somehow thought kids didn't care what they did and said. Or maybe, the doctor continued, it wasn't that—it was some sort of disease. It seemed as if all her limbs were arguing with the commands her brain was giving them. There could be many causes for that. She might be severely disabled for the rest of her life. And what were her plans?

The doctor said it as if he was asking them what time they wanted to go get dinner, but her grandmother clasped Lena's shoulders so hard they hurt, so she understood suddenly that somehow they were talking about death. Lena wished she was tall enough to look directly at her grandma's face, to see what she thought of all this every time the doctors told her, essentially, we have no idea what's going on, but everyone's life is probably different now. But her grandma kept her quiet tone. Whenever they were alone, she would take Lena's hands and start praying. Jesus will get us through this. "I guess," Lena remembered replying. Though her mother was sick, she kept it secret that they never went to church except for when they were with Grandma. "Sure."

As she spoke, Lena was pleased that she didn't sound like crying, that she was matter-of-fact: This is me.

Lena and Kelly walked to the all-night diner across town and ordered hash browns with feta cheese and onions and tomatoes and coffee. Bacon on the side. They were talking about tacos, and she knew she liked him because, when he said it was impossible to get an actual good taco in this state, she didn't want to slap him, only gave him a look that said, Do you hear yourself right now? He smiled. They talked about the most beautiful thing they had ever photographed. Joking at first, she said a pile of French toast with syrup and powdered sugar at brunch. And then, sentimental, her family laughing together. Kelly said it's a cliché, but a sunrise over the ocean.

A song by Davon came on about champagne and missing the girl who was sitting right next to him. Lena bopped her head a little bit to the beat.

"Please tell me you don't like Davon," Kelly said. "He's such a—"

"I like him because 1) he's good at making you think you're the one who could change him. 2) He is cut. 3) He is perfect gossip. You can ask almost anyone alive, 'You hear what Davon did?' And either they'll tell you everything or be, like, 'No, tell me now.'"

She was laughing. Everything she ate, even the unasked-for rye toast on the side, tasted good. Kelly's eyes were dark and his eyelashes were so long, it was rude. And it was more rude that despite the fact that he had been drinking and smoking, she still thought he smelled good. The diner was filling up with punk kids showing up from the clubs down the street, talking loudly about the show, sweaty, touching their dyed and bleached hair and showing off the X's Sharpied on the backs of their hands. Kelly paid and they walked back out into the cold night. All the bars were closing in the next half hour, so the sidewalks were busy again with drunk people finding food, tramping home, holding hands. The streetlights were orange-toned and made everyone look more dramatic. Snow flurries took bites out of everyone's hair and cheeks. The apartment buildings and stores and courthouse looked taller in the semi-dark.

Lena said, "So, I heard you do research studies."

"This is my nightmare," Kelly answered, trying to wipe snow off his head. "The contacts."

"Is it uncomfortable? Or weird?"

"Only when they do experiments where someone else has to take the contacts out of my eyes for me. Other than that, they pay pretty well." He blew out a breath and the tiny cloud hovered and then fluttered away. "Why do you ask?"

She told him about the letter in the mail.

"That's not too weird. It means someone probably just referred you or maybe you signed up for a list or something and just forgot."

Lena shrugged. They were back outside Stacy's house. The party was still going inside.

Kelly paused. "It was nice meeting you," he said.

In response, she smiled, leaned in, and kissed him. His lips were soft against hers. Lena had kissed enough people to know that kisses rarely said anything more than Please like me, or I like you, or Let's have sex. But she hoped that somehow, he could feel the Thank you for helping me not to worry, not to grieve, for a few hours.

"It was nice meeting you too," she said.

Inside, everyone was still drinking fortified wine.

"It's great," Tanya said. "You can drink a cup and stay drunk for the rest of your life."

Lena nodded. Someone asked her again, Well, what are you doing this summer? It had been only seconds, but Kelly was swallowed up by the party. I'm figuring it out, Lena said. She leaned against the wall for extra support. The wine was turning the insides of everyone's mouths black, despite the liquid being pale yellow.

Tanya showed her tongue to Lena and said it reminded her of when she was a girl and a kid kept asking her why her teeth and tongue weren't black. Shouldn't they be? he kept asking. Did anything like that happen to you? Lena rolled her eyes. "Probably, but I'm happy to say I forgot if it did."

"We're dying," Stacy said, staring at himself in the long

mirror next to the front door. His voice was pay-attention-to-me-now excited. "We're dying."

Tanya cleared her throat and Stacy automatically apologized to Lena. She pretended to be confused about why he was apologizing to her until he stopped.

"Let's take a picture," Tanya said. Lena posed and stuck her tongue out as far as it would go.

3

They told Lena that to maintain privacy, all buildings were disguised as part of Great Lakes Shipping Company. The closest intake office to Lena was only a mile and a half walk from her dorm—she recognized the address when they said it. Most of the building had a rich-person-store feel, like the all-wood toy store and a high-end Taiwanese restaurant that Lena always wanted to try but couldn't convince herself to pay $25 for an entrée. Great Lakes Shipping Company, the woman on the phone said, was on Floor 2. When you go up the stairs, walk past the drinking fountains, and it's right across from the olive oil shop, A Living Liquid. It's easy to miss, the woman said, and she was right—Lena's eyes didn't register it the first time, with its gray curtains over the window and the cream-on-white logo.

She walked down to the end of the hall, turned around, and went back. The olive oil shop was brightly lit. Rows of copper dispensers, posters of Italy on the wall. A man was filling up a Styrofoam cup, clearly meant for coffee, with habanero-infused oil. Lena considered going in to try some—there were containers of bread next to each dispenser—and to see if he was truly going to drink it.

It was better to be early, Lena decided, as she walked inside the office.

Inside, a white woman with a haircut that looked as if she had shown her stylist an image of a motorcycle helmet and said, "That's the look," was waiting.

"Your IDs."

Lena fished her wallet out of her coat pocket. The woman was wearing a navy pantsuit with an American flag pinned on the lapel. There was a badge clipped to her waistband. Walking over to her, Lena bumped into a small table and knocked over a stack of magazines. When she bent to pick them up, the woman told her to just leave it. Her tone was as if Lena had spent hours knocking over the magazines and picking them up and straightening them, just to knock them over again, and she couldn't take it anymore. Lena handed over the IDs.

"Looks good. Now we have some forms for you to fill out." She led Lena into what might have been the grayest room in the world. Everything in it—chairs, desks, pens, flooring, wall tile, the fire extinguisher—elephant gray.

The strangeness of the room and the woman's brusque attitude made Lena want to joke, to find a way of rescuing herself from her discomfort. Instead, she reminded herself that now was the time to be pleasant, blank. Don't be weird. Don't embarrass yourself. The woman gestured at Lena to have a seat, handing her a clipboard and a pen.

Page one asked for the basics: address, full legal name, place of birth, how she had found out about the study, email address, emergency contacts, have you ever been a participant in any other clinical studies? No, Lena wrote. Page two reminded her that to participate in the Lakewood Project was to consent to a necessary diminishment of her privacy. If you consent to this, provide all your passwords for social media, email addresses, phone passcode. Also provide any potential answers you can think of for standard security questions, such as the make of your first car, the name of your childhood pet, your mother's maiden name.

Lena coughed. "May I have a glass of water?"

Page four was where the health questions began. Do you have any allergies? When was the last time you had vaginal intercourse? Anal? When was the last time, exact date if possible, that you vomited? Do you have a family health history of strokes, cancer, diabetes? Next to the paternal family heading, Lena wrote, Information not available. Her hands shook as she did it, assuming that when they saw that, it would make her ineligible. What's the longest you've been consistently intoxicated for?

She cleared her throat again. "May I have a glass of water?"

"Please fill out the forms."

Lena stared at the white paper, let the words go out of focus. The woman's attitude, the questions, made a small voice in her own head say you are already feeling weird, get out of here. Her grandma had cleaned houses, pulled the hair and gunk out of tubs and sinks, catered on the weekends, babysat, took odd jobs. Worked for people who she said were proof God had a sense of humor. Your grandmother gave you everything. You're the one in charge now.

She flipped the page. At the top, it said WELCOME in bold, underlined type. "Our most precious resources in this country are patriots like you, those who are willing to give of themselves to help this great nation. Your contribution will help end suffering and unhappiness."

"So." Lena put down her pen. "This is a government program?"

"Keep reading."

"But in my letter it said this was for a survey company."

The woman lifted her eyebrows in annoyance. "Read all of it, especially page nine."

After rigorous evaluations of her mental, physical, and emotional health, the form explained, she might be invited to join the study. Once she signed, all interactions were private.

Lena flipped to page nine. It was an NDA. No questions about the studies and their true nature could be signed until she signed this page. There were $50,000 in penalties if she violated this agreement.

Deziree had texted her earlier this morning to say that the electricity had been shut off and she was going over to Miss Shaunté's. They had paid the electricity with the only credit card that wasn't maxed out. Potential jail time. She sucked her bottom lip into her mouth. It tasted of bad coffee and mint toothpaste.

On their last day together, in retrospect, it seemed as if her grandmother had known somehow that it was the end. Lena knew this was how memory worked; looking back at an important day, everything could seem portentous. The apricity and brightness through her grandmother's hospital room windows. How the hospital coffee tasted. As if they had switched to a better brand whose flavor could almost be described as coffee. The way her grandmother said, "You're already doing a good job helping your mother. I'm so proud of you." There had been a mixture of true compliment sweetness and warning sharpness in her grandmother's voice as she said it.

Lena signed. The woman smiled, took the clipboard, and said, Now we can get started.

While waiting for further instructions from "Great Lakes Shipping Company," Lena continued applying for other jobs. She came close to getting a job as a temporary worker at the post office. But according to her mom, it went to someone's daughter. It was fine, though, Deziree had assured her, while reminding her that the post office is a corrupt institution filled with drug addicts and older white ladies who wore wraparound sunglasses inside. She was only half kidding.

To her interview at Burrito Town, Lena wore Your-Honor-I-Plead-Not-Guilty and arrived five minutes early. She handed her résumé to the manager interviewing her. He scanned it, pursed his lips, and said, "Art History?"

"That's my major." Lena smiled, hoped her voice sounded chipper enough.

"So, what's your greatest strength? Weakness?"

She said that her greatest weakness was probably that she was too hard on herself. Tanya called it a case of the Dumb-Lena-Dumbs. "And my greatest strength—" Lena squeezed her knee. The manager was smoothing his blond mustache as she spoke. His skin was a shade of pink that made him look perpetually a little drunk. "I guess my greatest strength is that I'm good at being task-oriented and getting things done on time."

"Honestly, all I really care about is whether or not you can fit in the costume."

"Costume?"

"I'm sorry, but I don't think you're ready to be a burrito maker," he said. "Stand up."

Lena kept her face blank, pleasant as she stood. The manager also stood and took a step backward.

"You are a very small person, you know that?"

"Oh. I thought five-foot-two was tall."

"Whoever told you that was wrong." His eyebrows were

raised, as if he couldn't believe she knew someone so stupid, or would be so simple as to believe that stupid person.

She nodded, reminding herself there was no point in trying to joke around with an old white man who thought you were an idiot.

On the walls were large prints of burritos in the style of different artists. An Andy Warhol screen print, Van Gogh's sunflowers with burritos instead of flower petals, a Lichtenstein burrito that was crying a single tear, a burrito with Frida Kahlo flower crown and eyebrows that Lena thought someone would complain about within a day of the location opening. The space smelled good, like sautéed red onions and fresh dough, though the restaurant wouldn't open for another few weeks.

"There's no way you can be the burrito. But maybe you would be a good Ms. Blue Corn Chip. Smile, please."

Lena bared her teeth.

"Bigger. People need to see you from their cars. Come on, I know you have it in you."

Lena smiled.

"Smile like you're looking at your best friend."

She pictured an alligator plotting against her enemies. A large, openmouthed grin.

"People like to feel invited." He gestured at her mouth. "Keep trying."

She stretched her lips the widest they could go, knowing she was making more of a welcome-to-my-death-house face than a spend-all-your-money-on-these-burritos face. Her cheeks ached after 10 seconds of it. Lena held it another five, another 10, felt her cheeks trembling, and stopped.

"Your teeth are a nice shade of white," the manager said. He wrote a note on his clipboard and underlined it. "We would only need you three days a week, during the first two months after the grand opening."

The manager ran his fingers over his mustache. He tapped the side of his face, then spoke as if offering Lena a hundred-thousand-dollar salary with unlimited vacation time. "And if you do well at this and can prove that you're reliable, we can talk about you moving up to the assembly line."

"How much does being the chip pay?"

"Nine-twenty-five an hour. And if you make it to the assembly line, you'll go up to nine-fifty."

"I'll take it," Lena said. Money was money.

"We'll call you," the manager said.

Burrito Town was 10 minutes away from her mother's house. The neighborhood was gentrifying. Office buildings, the historic old supermarket being turned into a canoe-and-worthless-nice-looking-leather-object store, and a log cabin placed on top of a high-rise. It was supposedly used as an Airbnb. Urban camping was apparently a thing. As Lena drove four blocks down, the barbecue restaurants and bookstores—new and old—were transformed into scorched and crumpling buildings. A group of white kids with video cameras and microphones were breaking into a Victorian home that had once been painted an incredible grape-soda-purple color. It was now patchy with brown spots, almost lavender from the sun.

Down the block was a park where kids she went to high school with spent their days, their skin already fading, their eyes dulling. At least three of them had already overdosed since graduation. Although, Lena knew, this was more of a statewide problem than just the city's. The kids from Tanya's rich-kid school were also starting to die. Open lots of land that were becoming meadow, some that were gardens. Lena drove past sudden stretches of a liquor store, a Church's, apartments, the street with a legendary pothole that could swallow a whole tire, though that could be any street now that it was April.

It was the first no-coat-at-all day of the year and people were walking slow. Despite the interview, the warmth and how alive everything was made her heart rise with its spring joy. On her block there were buds on the trees. Kids on bikes. All the neighborhood aunties sipping decaf with their Bibles on their laps while gossiping. There was an empty chair at the table now, and it was somehow only nice to see that they still left space for Miss Toni, as if she was running late as usual.

Home was the only house on the block with no windows open, curtains drawn. Lena paused in her driveway to take a picture of the large oak tree in the front yard. She sent the picture to Kelly. They rarely texted in words but were having a conversation that darted between day-to-day pictures, selfies, and weird images from the internet. The last thing he had sent her was a GIF of a squirrel waterskiing.

Inside, Lena stepped immediately in what she hoped was spilled soup. She flipped on the lights. Yes, soup. Egg noodles and carrots and diced onions. Vomit was in the hallway between Lena's bedroom and the bathroom. The smell was especially awful, a mixture of canned soup and illness. She ignored it and went on to her mother's room.

Deziree was curled on the bed, a sleep mask over her eyes, one hand resting on her forehead. Her mother was shaking a little. Lena sighed, weighed whether or not to wake her.

Once a doctor had claimed that Deziree's problems were psychological. Something terrible had happened to her, he speculated, and her body was working out the trauma. Therapy, some Lexapro, some exercise, she'll be a new woman in six months. Another had said she just wanted attention. They had gone to a specialist, a woman who had to be booked eight months in advance, who was willing to acknowledge that she didn't understand all the parts of Deziree's illness, but that didn't mean nothing was wrong. To make life easier, we have to agree there is no such thing as normal, the doctor had said while typing on her laptop. If you think too much about how things should be, you forget how they are.

"That's great," Miss Toni had said, "but again, how much is this medicine you're prescribing her?"

"Mom," Lena whispered.

Deziree stirred. She said an opossum as large as a dog had been in the kitchen. It kept moaning and wailing. Somehow, she understood that the sounds meant "Give me a slice of cheese." Her voice was slurred, but it sounded more like sleep, Lena thought, than an emergency. The opossum left after he ate his cheese and said that all the Johnsons were good people.

Her mother, curled on the bed, took a breath, moved quickly, and threw up over the side.

"Migraine?" Lena made her voice as small as possible. It was April, one of Deziree's worst months for them. The air pressure, the pollen puffing out, days that could yo-yo between 20 degrees to 60 and back. It had cost at least $80,000 to find out Deziree's migraines, which were treatable, were a trigger for her "episodes," which were "a mystery."

"Yes," Deziree said.

She allowed Lena to help her up. Lena walked her mom first to the bathroom, hooking an arm around her waist when she realized one of her mother's legs was mostly limp today. In the bathroom, she helped Deziree onto the toilet, then grabbed her washcloth and dabbed away all the mess from her face and neck. Thankfully, none had gotten on her sleep mask.

"Shower?"

"No."

Lena got her mother set up in her bedroom. All her sheets were still back in her dorm room, and she draped her robe over her mother's feet to keep them warm.

"Lena?"

"Water?"

"Yes. But also: I love you. Thank you."

Lena cleaned all three messes, worrying as she did it that the Lemongrass and bleach smell of the cleaning products would make Deziree feel extra-miserable. She went to the store and got Gatorade, a bottle of water with electrolytes in it, and some saltines. Tomorrow was a scheduled day for Miss Shaunté, and she texted back and forth with her until she agreed to stop by tonight just to make sure everything was okay. Then Lena drove the hour back to school. It was only until she was back in her dorm room that she realized there was a little bit of her mom's sick on her sleeves.

Instead of reading the 50 pages she needed to do for class next day, Lena dabbed at her pantsuit with a Tide detergent pen while watching TV. Then she took Tanya's expensive all-natural cleaning kit off her desk and cleaned their dorm room, throwing almost everything out of the mini refrigerator, scrubbing the floor-length mirror, wiping down the seat of Tanya's desk chair. Near the end of it, Tanya returned.

"I could smell you cleaning from down the hall."

Lena smiled, but continued sweeping.

"Do you need to talk or keep cleaning?" Tanya's voice was gentle.

Lena turned away, knew if she saw a sympathetic smile, a gaze that neared compassion or kindness, she would start crying. "Cleaning. Maybe talk tomorrow."

Tanya nodded, gathered more books and notecards, and left.

Hours later, Lena got into her bed—the sheets still dryer warm—desperate for sleep. A worry tapped her on her left shoulder: Should you sell the house? Another pulled her hair: Was it possible for Deziree to somehow live with you next semester? A third asked about homework: You need to keep your GPA at a 3.5 to keep your scholarship, Lena! Another jumped on her stomach and asked her what more could you be doing? You can sleep when everything is settled. Lena sat up, pulled out her phone, and searched for the closest place to sell her plasma. Researched what she would have to do to sell her eggs. Every website agreed on one thing: There was not much of a demand for African-American eggs.

4

On the day before her last exam, Lena's phone rang. Blocked Caller. "You're invited," said a man who introduced himself as a representative of The Great Lakes Shipping Company, "to do further testing for possible inclusion in the Lakewood Project." The pre-screening would last five days. When they hung up, Lena dropped her phone. She was a mosaic of happiness, relief, and the immediate sharp anxiety of getting everything in order in less than two days.

Once she had thought up a good lie, Lena called her mom.

"Mom, I got a short-term job house-sitting for one of my professors."

"Plants?"

"House-sitting."

"I mean, if he has good plants, you'll take pictures and send them to me."

"He doesn't seem like a plant person to me," Lena said.

"I'll figure it out with Miss Shaunté and the neighborhood ladies. Just focus on your exams."

Lena's grandmother would have asked so many more questions—the professor's name, address, landline, how this had been arranged. She would have listened to Lena's explanations, the sound of her voice, searching for a hint of anything untoward. Deziree was always filled with enthusiastic confidence in Lena's abilities. "You have your grandma's brains and my sense of humor. You'll be fine."

Tanya was lying on the floor, oblivious to everything. She was listening to her headphones and muttering in Japanese to herself. Flash cards with kanji written on them were spread around her. When she noticed Lena looking at her, she pulled off the headphones and said, "I'm going to fail this exam."

"You're going to do great."

"Those fuckers didn't use enough vocabulary in discussion. All they ever say they do is video games. And if not video games, they say boku wa anime o mite. Anime o mite. Fuck."

"Have you slept?"

Tanya shook her head and turned away from Lena as if she might start crying. Lena knew if Tanya wasn't so stressed out, she would have noticed how relieved Lena looked. She probably also would have asked a bunch of questions, picked and pulled at Lena's story.

"Let's have dinner," Lena offered. "I'll speak in English and you can only respond to me in Japanese."

"Fine. But you have to speak to me like I'm a very dumb second grader, okay?"

"If you do a good job, maybe you can have some ice cream."

Orientation was at a facility 40 miles west of the college. In her car, Lena searched the address on her phone's GPS app, but all it found was a home address a mile down the road. The street view showed a pasture that housed what looked like yaks, their fur brown and shaggy, all permanently bent over to eat long blades of grass. She shrugged. There was nothing to do now but trust they hadn't given her the wrong address.

She turned off the interstate onto a long gravel road. There were no houses for miles. Horses grazing. What would be cornfields in only a few months' time. She rolled down her window despite the morning chill and listened. Gravel spit off her car's chassis, some cows and birds called greetings to one another. Please let everything go well today, Lena wished upon each animal call. She rolled up her window again when the air became manure-rank.

At the address they'd given Lena was a place she could have driven past easily and assumed that it was an unusually placed high school. It was a large, brick building with three levels. A high wooden fence surrounded it. Parts near the building's entrance looked as if they could use some care. Across the street was a gravel parking lot, part of it still a big puddle from yesterday's rain. All five cars were black, and parked meticulously with the same distance, about two feet, between them. Lena's heart was beating fast. She told herself it was because she'd had too much coffee. When she pulled her suitcase behind her, its wheels kicked up some mud onto the back of her pants. Lena sighed, picked it up, and lugged it across the street.

An animal cried, raucous like a dropped violin.

As Lena pushed open the front door, she made sure to smile, assuming someone would be waiting for her. No people, just a coatrack and two signs. The first one asked her to please leave her suitcase, cell phone, and coat here. The other was a sign that read ORIENTATION with an arrow pointing left. Her loafers were wet, which felt like another sign that everything was going to go poorly. Other than some mud from her shoes, the entrance floor looked freshly waxed, the walls smudge-free and bright white. Lena texted her mom one last time, promised to call her tonight, then slipped her phone in her coat pocket. She left everything as they requested and walked down the hall.

Her shoes squeaked, each step sounded like a surprise fart. It was embarrassing and funny. Lena told herself what she always did in these situations: you hate it now, but in a few weeks, you'll find it hilarious when you're telling Tanya or Deziree. She paused. There was no one she could tell about this without lying.

A whiteboard with WELCOME TO ORIENTATION! written in bubble letters was next to the only open door.

Inside, there were two white men and a white woman sitting at a long table. The woman made eye contact, smiled, and mouthed, "Welcome." Lena squared her shoulders and went in. She scanned the room and noticed a sign with her full name—LENA ANTONIA JOHNSON—by a small round table in front. She said Hi and put her bag on the table. No one responded. There were no spots for other participants. Next to the door was a table with a box of bagels and a stack of small paper plates. She couldn't tell if they were purposefully ignoring her or if her voice had come out too small. A video projector was sticking out of the ceiling. A cup of coffee was waiting at the table marked for her.

"Oh, hi," one of the men said. He stood up from the table and walked over. "I'm Tim, and we are just so, so excited to meet you."

His hand was large and moist, and it clasped hers as if he thought handshakes were a competition.

"Nice to meet you," she said. It came out like a question.

"You've gotta be starving. Eat. Eat." Tim waved her over

to the table. She wasn't hungry but took a bagel anyway. Her back was to the people at the table, who were silent. It felt as if they were all staring. Lena resisted the impulse to turn and see if they were. She grabbed a container of cream cheese, some jam. This was fine. On the way back to her seat, they were all looking at papers in front of them. But all three of their motions were exaggerated: The man who hadn't spoken yet made a deep, attention-grabbing hmmmm, the woman rifled through hers as if looking for a specific line, and Tim stared at his own papers as if he was trying to solve a puzzle.

Lena sat down and took a big bite of the bagel. As she chewed, the woman came over and tapped her shoulder.

"Did you turn in your cell phone?"

Lena covered her mouth. "Yes."

"I'm sorry, but I still need to do this. Please stand."

The woman patted Lena down. She was saying things about confidentiality and safety, but Lena couldn't focus on the woman's words. She was thinking about the woman's fingers, the palms of her hands, and why she thought that Lena would stow her phone in her butt, in her hair, in her vagina. The men didn't look away when Lena made eye contact with them. The woman pressed in on Lena's stomach and between her breasts.

"You're all set." The woman gave the men a thumbs-up.

The one who hadn't spoken moved his hand away from his lapel and put it back on the table. Then he cleared his throat and stood up. He said that the things you would do here would benefit countless others. It was a service to her country, to the world. The United States is a symbol of goodwill, of innovation, of joy to the rest of the world. When we succeed, everyone succeeds. The studies we do here put our scientists and officials on the forefront. The man smiled at Lena. She nodded.

He put up a PowerPoint presentation with white text on a black background. Disease Eradication. Economic Prosperity. Global Leadership. Innovative Solutions. You.

"That was great," Tim said as the man sat down.

Lena sipped her cold coffee. Then the woman stood up and began her presentation. Her speech was essentially the same as the man's before her. As she spoke, she looked around the room, smiling at times, as if she were making eye contact with several participants. It was like going to one of those restaurants that was an entertainment zone and play place for children. The woman reminded Lena of an animatronic mouse built to entertain. As she listened, Lena continued nodding and drinking the cold coffee.

Now it was Tim's turn. Like the others, he kept saying the same words: "innovation," "excitement," "prosperity," and "solutions." It reminded Lena of when Tanya was doing her summer internship at a marketing firm and kept saying things like "pollinators" and "heat." Tim kept beginning sentences with the phrase "You give of yourself."

"It's the culture there," Tanya had said. "You use the language to show that you want to fit in."

At the time, Lena had thought, oh yeah, it was a marketing thing. It was a job whose whole point was to get people to talk about something in hopefully the same positive way. Why wouldn't it filter down to the way everyone spoke to each other? But listening to the three people at the table, Lena thought that maybe this was just how people in this country were starting to speak to each other now. Even when they weren't online, people spoke as if they were bots designed to get clicks. Phrases repeated to get a person's attention, with nothing substantial beneath them. Jokes that meant we have seen the same image on the internet. Lena's grandmother used to say she was part of the last generation that could go for as long as 15 minutes without talking nonsense.

Tim paused and the door swung open. Another white woman, this one wearing a white lab coat, strolled in holding two bags. She placed them on Lena's table, almost knocking over the nearly empty coffee cup.

"I'm Dr. Maggie." She put a thermometer in Lena's ear. Involuntarily, Lena winced. "Your ears are very small for an adult." Dr. Maggie's hair was luxurious: thick, curly, brown, but with shine. It made her look twice as alive as every other person in the room. "Temperature good. Arm, please."

Lena held out her left arm and rolled up the sleeve.

"Are you nervous or is your blood pressure always this high?"

Lena nodded.

"Which one?"

"Nervous."

Dr. Maggie scribbled some things in her notepad, turned, and gave the group at the table a thumbs-up.

Tim stood up again. He spoke about how wonderful it was to give so much of yourself, to let go of fear in the beauty of service. The national anthem came on, a boisterous marching-band version that Lena couldn't tell where it was coming from. Everyone else stood, the man and the woman saluting. Lena put her hand over her heart and stood. She tried not to shuffle or fidget. When it was over, the three at the table filed out, leaving Lena alone with Dr. Maggie.

"It's okay to feel a little overwhelmed," the doctor said, her voice now friendlier. She handed Lena a bag filled with gray clothes. "I'll take you to your room and you can get changed into your uniform. The clothes are a little ugly, but they are comfortable."

"These are still better than the uniform for the job I just interviewed for. If I get it, I'll be dressing as a very feminine blue corn chip."

"What an honor."

Dr. Maggie led Lena down the hall. Every door was identical: old, wooden, with a brass doorknob and a frosted-glass window at the top that only someone over six feet tall could easily peer through. At the end of the hallway was a large staircase.

"Did this use to be a school?"

"No. But I see why you would ask that. We're going to go all the way up to three."

The third floor was in much worse shape than the first. The floors were covered in a brown carpet that seemed hastily applied, with bumps and areas that didn't quite meet the hallway's walls. The walls were the same gray as the clothes Lena was carrying. It smelled of sawdust and mildew. There were no windows and one of the long overhead fluorescent lights kept flickering. Dr. Maggie pulled out a key and unlocked the third door on the right.

"Welcome home." The doctor handed Lena the key, told her someone would be by in about 20 minutes to take her to the first session. Dr. Maggie paused in the doorway. "No exploring, okay?"

The bed was navy. There were three skinny windows approximately the length and width of Lena's arms. A small desk made from brown wood was beneath the windows. It was attractive simply because it was not gray or navy. A thin notepad and an old-school boombox were on top of it. A small dresser was at the foot of the bed. Lena pulled the drawers open to reveal navy towels and washcloths, additional gray clothes, and a pair of gray slippers. Lena found a few CDs that were burned by someone who seemed to have an okay sense of humor. One was titled "Now That's What I Call Mozart!"

She flipped on the overhead light. It did little to fight the dimness of the room. Lena wanted to take a picture of it and send it to Tanya with a caption: "If Depression was an interior designer." Instead, she changed into her gray clothes. They were comfortable. Lena stretched, trying to feel every bit of herself, from her tendons and muscles and bones. She wanted to listen to her body and ignore her brain, which kept thinking over Tim's words: "You give of yourself to make your country a better place. You give of yourself to keep us safe."

5

The first session was with a blonde woman who introduced herself as Dr. Lisa. She was the type of tall, muscular woman who, despite looking close to 50, people still probably asked if she played volleyball or basketball. They started the session by going into the small garden behind her office and walking together as the day slowly warmed, frost melting on the grass.

"How often do you read the news?"

"Not much. Between school and work and family, I always feel behind. Although, I guess, maybe that's a good thing right now."

"Still, how much do you think the news you read influences the ways you see the world?" A small burst of cloud puffed out of Dr. Lisa's mouth with each word.

Embarrassed, Lena's voice cracked as she said she didn't think she could truly answer the question. She looked down at the daffodils, so bright compared to anything inside the doctor's office. The sunlight made the doctor's hair look more white than blonde.

"Do you believe in a higher power?"

"I want to."

The wind gusted, pushed the daffodils around, trailed its fingers through the grass and tree branches.

"What are your views on how America treats women?"

"Can you repeat the question?"

"What," Dr. Lisa said very slowly, "are your views on how America treats women?"

"I don't think that's a fair question."

Dr. Lisa stopped walking. For the first time, her eyes were directly on Lena's face, not on the clipboard she was carrying or on a bird's progress.

"Tell me why."

"It forces me to make an assessment about all women. I am a thousand percent sure there are plenty of white women who think America is great to them. But America is only routinely good to women, especially black women, when it wants something from them."

"How is that different from men?" Some birds bickered on a tree branch, then flew off into the bright blue sky.

"I think men can be absolutely useless and a lot of people will find a way to say something nice about them. Especially white men. But a woman has to be something. If she's not, you know, considered hot or the right amount of smart or good at cooking, people don't see her. And if she's too much of something, then many people hate her."

"Isn't that a little cynical? Demoralizing?"

Lena shrugged. The tip of her nose felt cold, as if it would start running soon if they stayed out in the chill air for much longer. "Sometimes. But most of the time, because it's the way things are, I don't think about it consciously. I just deal with it."

"I think I understand what you're saying," Dr. Lisa said, her voice slow and thoughtful. She scribbled something.

Lena brought her hands up to her mouth and blew on them. Clapped a few times.

"I think you're ready. Let's go inside."

Once Lena was settled into the large wing chair across from Dr. Lisa's desk, the next question came: "How comfortable are you when people of other races attempt to talk to you about racism?"

Lena raised her eyebrows.

"That's a good enough answer. How much do you care about other people's opinions?"

Lena crossed her ankles. She explained that if it was family or Tanya, she cared a lot. But she didn't have the bandwidth to care too much about what other people think. "I'm already tired a lot of the time." Lena coughed. The small fountain on Dr. Lisa's desk burbled water. Its motor rattled. "I lost my train of thought."

Next, it was on to hypotheticals.

"Let's say there was a car with its brakes out heading toward a crowd of people. If it hit the crowd, it would kill maybe five people. You have the option to divert it, only killing the driver. What would you do?"

She paused. "I guess, if I had to, kill the driver."

"A person is plotting an attack against other people at your school. You have the option to stop them, but the way you do it will result in their death. Can you do it?"

"Why do you want to know if I could kill someone?"

"I'm just getting to know you. Now, what if a person was standing in your living room at night, pointing a gun at you? Or at your mom?" Dr. Lisa's white teeth looked freshly painted. "What if a man was sexually assaulting you? How far can you go?"

Out the window was a patch of Queen Anne's lace. A bee

buzzed over it. Didn't they hibernate? Lena had no idea if she could ask to take a break.

Dr. Lisa leaned back in her seat and adjusted the blinds. "Do you need me to repeat the question?"

"Thanks. The light was making my eyes hurt." Lena's lying voice always came out an octave higher.

"Lena, it's important that you answer every question as honestly as you possibly can."

"I guess, deep down, I think I could do a lot to make sure other people survived. But I think everyone wants to think of themselves as a potential hero. And I think I'm avoiding answering the questions because the idea of being in a situation where I have to hurt someone else makes me feel mostly sick." Lena looked down at her hands. There was a patch of dry skin near her left thumb.

"Thank you." The doctor took a sip of water. Another. Then she cleared her throat. "Let's say you found out that aliens are real during these studies. But you've given your word and signed a binding contract. What do you think could get you to break that promise?"

"I guess, I don't know. Maybe if the aliens are going to kill us all. I'd rather be alive in prison than dead by an alien's tentacles."

Dr. Lisa underlined something. Lena rubbed her nose and pushed some of her hair back.

"Do you trust white people?"

Lena took a long sip of water before answering the question.

In the next doctor's office, the furniture was the exact color of the walls. There were no windows. He was a shorter white man with a loud voice and a trendy haircut. He didn't introduce himself. A tattoo was on his arm that made the limb look as if it was trapped beneath a long trail of ivy. Lena decided that if he didn't introduce himself, she would start calling him Vines.

"It's easier if I demonstrate what we're doing rather than trying to explain it to you," the doctor said. He pressed a button on his laptop and played what sounded like a whirring espresso machine. "Now tell me, what does that sound make you immediately feel?"

"Annoyed."

"Anything else?"

"Anxious."

"Great. For all the next ones, you'll just write things down."

The teakettle's scream made her feel thirsty. And if that wasn't an emotion, she guessed it made her feel content. Or maybe about to be content. Cricket-song: happiness. Frogs croaking: disgust.

"Now we're going to get weirder. I want you to tell me what you think these things would taste like."

He played harp music. Lena wrote *Cinnamon Toast Crunch*. A glass shattering. Lena thought that would taste like black pepper. She wanted to ask him if it was weird that this was more fun and less stressful than the previous session, but he was focused on his computer. Now, draw whatever you might see while listening to music. Oh, that pen's out of ink? Here's another. It can help to keep your eyes closed. A bird chirping only prompted another drawn bird. An ugly robin. Music that sounded like default video-game fighting music prompted a ghost and a sword.

They went into a much smaller room. It was so small that there were only a few inches of clearance on either side for the large armchair it held. Waiting on the chair were two pens and a sketchbook. Lena thought it must have been a nightmare to get that chair into this small space. A small speaker was installed directly over the chair.

"There's someone else in the room next to yours. You'll both hear the same loud, clear tone. While you're listening, you're going to make your mind as blank as possible. Clear it out. Take deep breaths. No to-do lists. No worries. The other person hearing the tone is going to be shown an image and they are going to try to 'think' it at you."

"How can you think something at someone?"

"You've never looked at someone else and briefly known exactly what they were thinking?"

"Sure."

"Well, you're going to draw or write whatever image they think at you."

"Feels like a party game."

He frowned. "You need to be focused."

"Okay."

He told her again to write or draw what she sees. "It'll be between 90-second and 3-minute intervals, depending on the image's complexity. Don't worry if the images you draw are ugly. I doubt Picasso could do something good that quickly. Actually, you'll go over to Box 2. Stay relaxed. Loose." He studied Lena for a long moment, then left, closing the door firmly shut.

A noise, low and long, like a whistle.

Lena automatically drew a tree blowing in the wind, tipping to one side, some leaves on the ground. The chair smelled a bit of "scentless" cleaning spray.

Another sound, long enough that she wanted to hum along with it, reminded Lena of a ringtone. A man's face, long beard, oversized clear glasses, stubble. Round eyes. It was like a police sketch. The man as she saw him was completely colorless.

Tone three: A gong.

Lena wrote a sentence: Sometimes, the seeds grow in the morning light.

"Well, how's your day been so far?" Dr. Maggie asked. She laughed before Lena could respond. "That's how most people feel."

Lena was weighed, took an allergy test, ran on a treadmill, and then took an eye exam where she had to look at golden orange-and-black asterisks and have air puffed into her eyes. Then a blood, urine, sweat, and stool sample.

"I'm so sorry about this," Lena said, handing the bags over.

"This is my job."

Lena felt as if she was about to tip over, the soft parts of her face about to crack and fall onto the floor.

"Sit here and eat this." Dr. Maggie pulled out a large cookie wrapped in plastic. It was exceptionally sweet. There was an aftertaste, like medicine, but every bite made Lena feel a little better, so she didn't stop eating or mention it. It appeared the doctor was taking notes about how quickly Lena ate the cookie. When Lena was done and had two glasses of water, they discussed diet, exercise, how long and often Lena menstruated, and any previous or present injuries. There were long pauses after each of Lena's answers, and extended eye contact as if each word Lena spoke was being weighed for the truth.

"Change into this gown."

When Lena returned, she hopped onto the table and put her feet in the stirrups. On the ceiling were several posters of a golden retriever puppy and a duckling. She guessed their fuzzy proximity was supposed to imply best friendship.

"This is going to be cold," Dr. Maggie said.

Another poster showed a lightning bolt hitting a tree, with INSPIRATION! written beneath the image. Lena wanted to know who in the history of the world had ever gotten a great idea while receiving a pap smear. If she had chosen the posters, there would have been one that read, TURNING YOURSELF INTO AN ABSENT VOID. Or maybe PATIENCE, with a picture of an egg and a timer.

Then booster shots. While Dr. Maggie stuck in needle after needle, she asked Lena questions. What are your views on organ donation? Poke. What's your definition of excellent health? Sharper poke. And what are your feelings about aging? What do you think people mean when they say, "You've gotta take good care of yourself"?

The questions were asked lightly. The doctor wrote nothing down, just kept injecting Lena. When it was done and everything was put away, Lena realized she should've asked what exactly they were "boosting" and what additional vaccinations they thought she needed.

"Let's go have some fun," Dr. Maggie said, handing Lena workout clothes. Another outfit change, and they walked into a room filled with exercise equipment. Lena's arms ached. She shook them out, tried to stretch. Dr. Maggie put a CD in a boombox that looked exactly like the one in Lena's room. The music that came on was some kind of off-brand jock jams, a voice saying "Whoo" and "Yeah" mixed in with a bass beat and applause. Lena hopped on the nearest treadmill. As she ran, her brain emptied itself out—every thought blasted away by the pleasure of being in motion after hours spent hunched in chairs. She ran until there was sweat dripping off her forehead and the back of her tank top had turned charcoal with sweat.

"I know you probably want to shower, but I think you should eat again first," Dr. Maggie said.

She took Lena down to the first floor. The door closest to

the staircase led to a dining room. Inside were two small tables with two wooden chairs next to each one. A bowl of salad was waiting at one, a plate with chicken and vegetables and rice next to it. A large counter was built into the wall farthest from the door, holding water bottles, pop, a coffeemaker, and an open brown box filled with tea packets. The floor was old wood. What looked like a small drain was installed in the middle of the floor. The chicken smelled too good for Lena to go investigate it. She picked up the largest chunk of broccoli and popped it into her mouth. As she chewed it, Lena went through the salad, picking all the red onions out, making a pile on one of the napkins.

"Lena?"

She jumped a little in her seat. Standing in front of her was a man who looked almost identical to the one she had tried to draw earlier. He was Korean, though, and had more hair than she remembered.

"Hi."

He told her to look at his face. Memorize it. His eyes were large, the irises so dark brown that they made his pupils look unusually big. He had thin lips and a wide mouth. A small brown birthmark was on the left side of his neck, near his Adam's apple.

"Got it," she said.

He nodded and walked out. As he left, Lena noted that he was probably around average height for a man and when he walked, he moved his right arm much more than his left.

"They're testing my memory," Lena said to herself, then absorbed herself back in eating. There was a green in the salad Lena had never tasted before. It tasted peppery in a good way, but it made her mouth feel extra-juicy. Maybe she was allergic to it, but she couldn't stop eating. Everything that had happened during the day had placed a kind of spell on Lena because she had thought so much, talked so much about her body, it no longer felt like hers. It was closer to a piece of fine jewelry she was having assessed for sale: here's the gold, here are the gems, let's peer closely at their condition. Being alone, eating this thing that made her hyperaware of the spit rising along the ridges of her teeth and the plateau of her tongue, made Lena feel a little more herself. She rubbed her face and took another bite.

6

In the morning, Lena felt the braids she had hastily put into her hair. She had missed a clump of hair and it angled against her neck. Her calves ached from running yesterday, her voice was hoarse from talking so much. Closing her eyes, she heard the pleasing sound of heat pumped through a vent. A knock at the door.

"This is your ten-minute warning. We'll be back to take you to Session 1."

Lena changed quickly, spending most of her time rebraiding her hair, working out the tangle on her neck as best she could with her fingers. After being walked downstairs by a bored woman in a navy dress who responded to all attempts of chitchat with variations of "Yeah," she was taken to Dr. Lisa's office. She was settled back into the chair and poured a glass of water. The doctor fiddled with the settings of her fountain.

The first question: "How did you sleep?"

"Like I was dead."

Then an awkward first date style barrage.

"Do you prefer dogs or cats?"

"Dogs."

"What is your favorite color?"

"Neon-pink or maybe neon-blue. Neons are underrated."

"I can turn the fountain off if the sound is too annoying. What's your favorite thing to eat?"

"This is cheesy, but I think it's anything that someone who really loves me has made for me."

"What is the most unattractive thing a person can do?"

"Pick their nose in public. Or maybe be one of those people who tries too hard to be smart on social media." Lena relaxed, slouched a little in the chair.

"What do you want to do with your life?"

"Something with art, hopefully."

The room smelled like orange peel today.

"Do you think you could give your life for anyone?"

"Dr. Lisa, are you going to kill me?"

The doctor didn't laugh.

Lena cleared her throat and sat up straighter, with considerably less enthusiasm. "For my mom, definitely. Maybe for someone I didn't know if the situation was right."

"What do you mean, the right situation?"

"Like everything you asked me earlier yesterday."

The other woman smiled. The fountain started to whirr again as if the motor was dying.

"The questions are a little repetitive."

"Why are they so murdery?"

The doctor shrugged. She reached into her desk and pulled out a folder.

"Let's get more specific."

"Okay."

"In your school files, it says when you were in fifth grade you were suspended. You picked up your Social Studies textbook and hit a boy in the face."

"Yes, that did happen." Lena leaned forward, trying to catch a glimpse of the papers.

Dr. Lisa pulled them closer to her. "Why did you do that?"

"That was around the time my mom was really sick. She needed to regularly use a wheelchair. She had a seizure in the grocery store. Some of the kids at school saw it. So, they started calling her the 'R' word. Or started asking me questions like 'Why aren't you an "R" like your mom?' Gross shit like that." It was more than a decade ago, but Lena's fists tightened.

"What do you mean, the 'R' word?"

"Come on."

It was the first time Lena's voice was at its usual register, lower. Every time she had spoken so far—Lena realized only when she had stopped doing it—her voice was slightly higher than usual, a tone meant to please.

Dr. Lisa paused. "Oh. Why do you call it that?"

"Because it's rude and hurtful." All of Lena's willpower went into not rolling her eyes as she spoke.

"Back to your story."

"One day, we had a substitute teacher. We were watching a movie and that boy turned around and said, 'My dad said if he had a kid who was "R," he would kill them.' And then he said something worse that I can't remember because the first thing he said broke my brain. I just picked up my book and slapped him with it."

"Why your textbook?"

"I don't know. I was mad." Lena crossed her arms. She looked down at her gray slippers. "I'm sorry that I hurt someone. I feel gross over it. But it's complicated because I'm also glad I did it. Most of the other kids called me Psycho for the rest of the year, but they stopped talking about my mom."

Dr. Lisa scribbled on her notepad. Lena shut her eyes.

"Is it possible for me to talk to my mom while I'm here?"

"No. We're texting her for you."

Lena nodded. "But you would tell me if there was an emergency?"

"Probably. Have you had other violent reactions?"

That's a really melodramatic way of putting it, Lena thought. She adjusted her posture, sat up straight, shoulders back. "I poured a drink on a boy who grabbed my ass at a party."

"Did you pretend it was an accident?"

"No. I turned around and poured it on his sneakers. But I was drunk. I'm sure I would've tried to reason it away if I had been sober."

The doctor nodded. "What makes you angry?"

"Entitled people. That song about happiness. Whenever someone is being treated unfairly for reasons beyond their control—race, gender, sexuality. You know. Sometimes I get deeply pissed off on crowded buses for no reason. The bus can be quiet and no one is sitting next to me, but I just get mad. I think it's like an animal instinct. When white people use the words 'fly' or 'fresh.' Sometimes when I hear the word 'cancer.' When people make an of-course face when they find out I've never met my dad." She took a breath.

"You could probably do this for another ten minutes, huh?"

"Yeah. I haven't touched internet hates. Or food."

"You can stop here," the doctor said, still writing. "One more question. When I say the word Mom, who do you automatically think of?"

"Grandma."

Dr. Maggie started the next session by handing Lena two pills. In her hand, they were shiny and black as night. Held up to the light, they were forest green. She washed both down with a full glass of water. They tasted like nothing.

"Your mouth might feel a little curdled around an hour after taking these."

"That sounds disgusting."

"It's really the best word for it."

Lena rubbed her forehead. Yawned. She could use another cup or two of coffee.

"And if you get a headache, you have to tell me immediately."

The doctor handed her a list to memorize: golden caviar, dead lipstick, broken space station, chocolate loveseat.

"What does it mean if I have a headache?"

"Do you?" Dr. Maggie's eyebrows raised, her mouth parted.

"No. I'm fine."

What Lena hadn't anticipated was how annoying it was to not know what was going on. She wanted to make this work out, to get into whatever the Lakewood Project was. It didn't matter that Dr. Lisa's questions were mostly about killing. They were just questions. Lena decided she would care when the doctor handed her a gun and said, "You have to shoot one of us." Dr. Maggie made her feel unexpectedly closer to her mother. It was probably a small taste of what it was like to be her, trying to sort out her health. Here's a doctor throwing a bunch of tests at you and telling you nothing substantial. You're expected to trust them, but they haven't given you a single reason to believe that they care about you. It's like a word search to them, while to you it's everything.

Dr. Maggie handed her a book. "We need to wait an hour now before doing anything else."

The book was about a woman traveling the world on her

45th birthday. She wanted to understand something new about life. The main character had just got divorced, and traveling was a thing she said that people did after divorces. They did something their spouse would have hated, like a train trip across the country. They went to The Great Wall of China and thought about how it could be seen from space. And how they would never be seen from space and that was sad, but somehow life-affirming. The book was boring, but it made Lena want to get a divorce. The time afterward seemed wild and glamorous.

When the hour was up, Lena repeated the parts of the list she remembered: caviar, dead, broken space station, chocolate.

Dr. Maggie checked her blood pressure, the inside of her mouth, and asked if her eyes or vagina felt painfully dry.

"Thankfully, no," Lena replied.

"Then we can go on to part 2." She pulled out a large needle and injected a clear fluid into Lena's arm. "Make a fist five times really fast."

The doctor watched her as she did it. Lena yawned. The doctor kept staring. Lena's left arm itched. She checked it for a rash, hives. Then, heat. Burning. A wildfire spread from the middle of her left arm to her fingers, up her shoulder. Lena's mouth was saying a blur of "Oh my God, Help, Fuck, and What?" and sounds that in her pain she hoped she wouldn't remember making.

She was on the floor in a ball.

The doctor was writing notes, pen moving fast. Her mouth was moving.

Lena sweated from the pain.

It was in her throat, claws out, scuttling quickly to her face. I'm going to die, she thought, and for the first time in her life she wasn't being dramatic when she thought it.

A spasm in her lower back. Her mouth and face were wet

from drool and tears. It was over. Lena's vagina ached. She was relieved when she felt down there that she hadn't peed.

"Now, tell me," Dr. Maggie said, eyes still on her sheet, "which of those phrases do you remember?"

"What was that?"

"I said, 'What do you remember?'"

"Caviar. Couch. Dead. Broken. Golden caviar."

And then her feet were moving. She was in the hallway. If Lena could have sprinted, she would have. Her fingers were pressing against the wall, leaving sweaty prints. There was loud air coming through vents and a noise Lena realized was the sound of her breathing. A woman was standing in the middle of the hallway wearing gray workout clothes identical to Lena's.

"Mom?" Lena asked. Her mother's skin was gleaming as if it were freshly lotioned. Her hair in fresh braids. "I don't feel well."

Lena vomited. Looked up, shook her head.

It wasn't her mother.

The woman was significantly taller, at least 10 years younger. She took another long look at Lena and sprinted away. She went to one of the doors and slammed it behind her. Lena followed, tried the door, but it was locked.

"Please, I'm sick," Lena said.

If someone had asked her, she could not have said why it was so important to get this woman to acknowledge her. Maybe it was to think about anything other than what had just happened. Or how much her body still hurt. She knocked again on the door. In the instructional material they had talked about the need for isolation. From beneath the door came the sounds of what could have been a documentary or maybe a podcast. A man's voice talking about recycling and plastic bottles that would be on the Earth for longer than anyone could ever possibly live. She leaned against the door, shut her eyes.

When Lena opened her eyes, she was being shaken awaken in her bed. Two people she didn't recognize were looking down at her. Their faces were hard to see in the dark—only their white teeth and the shine of their eyes were visible at first.

"Don't be scared," a woman's voice said. It was soft and kind, as if she were speaking to a child she loved. Lena coughed. She sat up, rubbed her eyes.

"It's time to do some work," a man's voice said.

They led Lena to a room on the second floor that reminded her of a TV police station. She stood yawning and blinking while looking through what she assumed was a one-way glass. I am not afraid, Lena told herself. This is the place where I want to be. I'm okay. The man was checking his watch, as if he had somewhere important to go. Lena yawned again, her jaw popping a little with its force. Five men of East Asian descent walked into the glassed-in area. They faced forward. The lights in the area got brighter.

"Do you recognize any of these men?

Lena stared at each man carefully, understanding they were asking her about the man she had seen the first day, the one who had asked her to remember his face. Two of the men had unshaved necks, but none had the birthmark she had noticed earlier.

"No," she said.

They thanked her and took her back to her room. In bed, she tried to figure out what day it was. She remembered talking to a man about how to make your brain louder than usual, how to force it to talk at someone. And Lena had been confused. "That sounds like comic book shit," she had started to say before correcting the word to *stuff*. He had laughed and said, "No—

like when your best friend has something stuck in her teeth and you look at her face and suddenly she understands something is wrong with her face." But when was that? And when had they given her the injection? And had that happened once or twice?

The light softened with the beginning of another day. Lena went to the desk and wrote Dear Tanya on the open page.

She flipped to the beginning.

Dear Tanya, read her handwriting, I had grilled shrimp for lunch today. They were overcooked but Shrimp Is My Pizza. Always good.

Dear Tanya, another injection day. I woke up and my grandmother was here in this room. She was humming to herself and reading a magazine. Told me that a celebrity couple was breaking up, and if those cute white people couldn't hold it together, who could, anymore? She flipped the page, looked up at me, and said, "Are you sure this is the right thing for you?" And then she was gone. I woke up. I'm glad you'll never read this. We would have to talk about it for hours. Sometimes, dreams are not omens. They're just your brain stitching things together.

Lena's fingers trembled. She kept reading. Sometimes her handwriting was as it always was, upright, straight, easy to read. But there were times where it was clear she had written while still in pain, fingers cramped, palm trembling.

Dear Tanya, today we talked about grieving. I thought about my grandma's voice, her laugh. The way she said the word "raccoon," the emphasis on the oon, the way she said "vase" as if it didn't rhyme with the word face. How she was the one I always wanted to show my grades to, to talk about the future, who knew exactly what I was thinking. At her funeral, I didn't really have the time to cry. I had to take care of everything and everyone else. I hoped that talking about her, especially to someone whose emotions I didn't care about, would make it all burst open, all big and embarrassing, body curving in on itself, sobbing. But my voice stayed still.

Tanya, I am making three thousand dollars this week. It would have taken me probably all summer to do that as Ms. Blue Corn Chip.

Last night, Tanya, they woke me up at what felt like three in the morning. And they made me run until I felt nauseated. My heart was in my ears and I swore I heard an explosion, whoosh, bang. I realized it was my heart and I had heard myself dying. I closed my eyes and when I opened them, I was drinking a large glass of orange juice and it tasted so good. I used a white towel to wipe off all the sweat on my face. It was the softest towel I've used in my entire life. One of the doctors' fingers was on my wrist. There was a mark on my hand. A new bruise that looked like Pac-Man. After I told her everything I felt, after I repeated the phrases again, I talked to my mother on the phone. They watched as I did it. I told her things were very quiet here at the professor's house. She told me that she really liked the picture of the plant I had sent her. He's got great taste in foliage. We both laughed at what she said.

Deziree told me she also had been dreaming of my grandma. They had baked a pie together. Inside was apple and old telephone cords. In the dream, my grandma said we were going to need extra luck this year. Said to do that, she needed to paint at least one room in the house green. I told her not to do it. Paint smell was a known headache trigger for her. And she was just getting over a migraine she described as like a tsunami. You sound tired, she kept saying. And when I was off the phone, the doctors told me I was a natural.

More and more pages. Sometimes her handwriting was an

illegible scrawl. Another page where she had written the word blood in large capital letters. And two paragraphs down: If I don't get an ice cream sundae soon, I will throw myself out a window!

How could I, Lena thought, only have been here a week?

Dear Tanya, I sat in a dark room for an entire hour. I had a blindfold on. I was asked to write down all the sounds I heard. When they took the fabric off my eyes, a man wearing a top hat and gray lipstick was sitting in the chair across from me. Talk to me about sex. Do you like it? Are you scared of it? A person came in wearing one of those terrible unicorn masks and asked me about risk-taking. How often was I scared? Would I ever go bungee jumping? What were my rational fears? Then everything was twisting and I saw colors on the walls—lavender, orange, fruit-punch red. My spine was sparking with pain. All I wanted was to lie on a hardwood floor. Stay still until it all floated away.

Lena covered her eyes.

Déjà vu spread across her like sunlight pushing through a set of blinds. How many times had she done this, looked at memories written by herself, felt this same mix of confusion and annoyance and fear? Did she think every time this was worth it as long as I'm taking care of my mom?

She hoped so.

7

Lena knew it was the last day when, at breakfast, she was given her phone, her luggage, and a check for three thousand dollars with "Thinking of you during this difficult time" scribbled in the memo line. The money was coming from an account that belonged to an R.M. Johnson. Lena was sure that person did not exist. And really, it didn't matter. It would have taken her all summer at her work-study job or Burrito Town to make this much.

She took another bite of her fruit salad. Dipped a piece of cantaloupe into strawberry yogurt.

"Knock, knock." It was Tim from orientation. He was dressed as if he was working in the electronics section of his local Target: pleated khakis, a red polo, and a cell phone in a holder strapped to his brown belt. "Do you remember me?"

"Yeah, of course." Lena wiped her mouth with the back of her hand in case any yogurt was lingering around the corners.

"So, we've been thrilled with your results. You have a wonderful memory, an incredible tolerance," he said, smiling. She could tell he was very pleased. "We would love to officially invite you to be a part of Lakewood."

"Lakewood?" Lena asked as if she hadn't heard the name before, as if it hadn't been hinted at all the time.

Tim poured them both coffee. "You would be working more with Dr. Lisa. The two of you seem to have connected." His smile widened. Lena gripped her knees beneath the table. His tone, the expressions on his face made her wary. Why did he feel the need to sell her on this? They had to know she was desperate for money. Whatever they wanted her to do would have to be much worse than the things that had happened this week.

Slowly, Lena said that while Dr. Lisa was great, she cared much more about what she would be doing in this project.

"That's a great question."

"It wasn't a question."

"We like what a straight shooter you are."

And that was another lie. Here she had made an effort to be soft. It hadn't been conscious most of the time, but she had been eager to make a good impression on everyone.

Lakewood was the name of a small town about two and a half hours north of Lena and Deziree's home. Tim explained they were building an "undercover site" there. "We'll have what looks like a regular job set up for you, but you'll be doing research studies most of the time. You'll get a free place to stay, generous health insurance for you and your mom, and we pay very, very well."

He handed Lena a contract, flipped to the page with the amount of money she would be paid.

"It's not a typo. And of course, complete health coverage for your entire family. Nothing paid out of pocket."

On the money line was an amount so big that it embarrassed Lena. Below that were the terms of a new nondisclosure agreement. Potential jail time. Up to a million dollars in damages as decided by a federal judge's ruling. A section detailing the amount of money she—or her designated beneficiaries—would receive depending on what happened to her. If she died, $100,000. For sustained brain damage or neurocognitive issues, $75,000. Smaller amounts for blindness, irreversible changes to her appearance. If she lost a foot, $15,000.

"How could I lose a foot?"

"Oh, our lawyers have to think of every possibility, you know, liabilities. You got to be one hundred percent protected in this business."

"I see."

It was the healthcare. Her mom could start getting Botox again for her migraines, go to the recommended physical therapist. She could always afford her medication and being hospitalized again. A new wheelchair or cane for when she was having episodes. No more negotiating with Miss Shaunté about when she was getting paid. Lena could give her mom something her grandma couldn't: a stable life. Routine. If Tim wasn't staring directly at Lena, she would have teared up with relief. Still, a big sigh of relief puffed out of her mouth.

"Right?" Tim said. "I know, it can be overwhelming. But this is life changing." He started talking about how much better the country would be if everyone could have access to health insurance. And wasn't it a shame that the true health insurance was being nice to people online and hoping something so dramatic and interesting happened people would buy into the story and get invested enough to give you money? He was talking and talking, but it felt to Lena like he was doing a magic trick.

Pay attention to the things my mouth is saying, how wetly I'm talking; don't watch my hands, don't ask where the quarter came from, don't look closely to see whether it's real.

Lena flipped the page and signed.

Back at home, Lena's mom was in the kitchen looking at paint samples she had taped to the walls. Mint, Cash, Mid-Spring Leaf, Toxic Waste, Palm Tree Leaf, Bottle.

"What feels the luckiest to you?" Deziree asked.

"All of these say the longest weekend of our lives. Painting, taping, cleaning."

Deziree turned, about to say something, then paused. Her eyes widened. "Are you okay? You look exhausted."

"I think I'm coming down with something."

"You look like you've lived a million years."

"Thanks, Mom."

Her mom made chicken soup. They sat side by side in Lena's bed, watching TV. Lena rested her head against Deziree's shoulder. On the phone, someone pretending to be Lena had said, "I love you, Mom," every day. That person had conversations with Lena's friends, sent them pictures and weird GIFs. No one had realized it wasn't her. Deziree's hair smelled like coconut, her skin: roses. It could be like this all the time soon.

On the phone, Dr. Lisa explained Lena's cover position would be working for a trucking and warehouse company, Great Lakes Shipping Company. It would be a brand-new business in Lakewood. Floor 1 would look like a regular truck dispatch space with offices and cubicles and a warehouse. The second floor would have conference rooms and areas set up for the studies. The third floor and basement were off-limits.

"So, I have to learn how to be a dispatch operator?"

"No. Well, you'll learn enough about it to have conversations. And every day, we'll give you a card with what happened during your workday to use when you speak with friends and family."

Deziree walked by, knocked on the door, and said, "Dinner in ten."

All her coworkers, the ones in the office and the warehouse, would be in the experiments with her. Truck drivers would be dropping off and picking things up, but most of them would not be affiliated. Lena would have to be vigilant about how her actions appeared to others.

"Why have real truck drivers near this?"

"We've thought of everything, don't worry about it." The doctor cleared her throat. "The town is small, and people like to talk. We wish it could be simpler, but no one will believe you just moved to Lakewood."

"What should I wear?"

"The town is small, and people like to talk," Dr. Lisa repeated. "So dress like you're going to church. Like you're trying to impress someone's mom. Ugh. As long as you don't dress like you're going to a club."

Lena couldn't tell if the doctor was stressed out or if she had sized her up and was having second thoughts about her maturity or her age—or maybe someone had forced her to make the hire. Everything she could think of to reassure Dr. Lisa seemed like it would only make the doctor certain Lena was a bad decision.

"Got it."

"Here are your phrases for tomorrow. Silent butter. Corkscrew

Idaho. Careless Regulations. Violet. The order is important this time."

Lena repeated the phrases back once, twice.

"Great."

"I need to be there by nine tomorrow, right?"

There was silence on the other end of the line. Lakewood had patchy service. Lena waited, but the call was over. She still hadn't finished packing. The clothes on the floor were pinching at her hands, the unmade bed and makeup scattered around were flicking at her eyelashes.

"Steaks," Deziree yelled.

Dinner looked great—steaks, baked sweet potatoes, a big salad, a bottle of cheap champagne resting in a bowl filled with ice cubes.

"I'll get the silverware," Lena offered. In the kitchen, taped to the front of the refrigerator was a Don't Forget list with Lena's new address and a description of the job she'd be working. When her mother's back was turned, Lena scribbled on the sides: I love you. Call me anytime. Make all bill collectors contact me. I can come home. I love you. Don't paint the whole house without talking to me. She drew hearts around all the things that looked harsh, hoped it softened them. On the refrigerator Lena taped a note to Miss Shaunté with all the essentials and a small bonus check.

When Lena returned with the silverware, Deziree patted her hands and arms as if she were going away for years. She kept repeating the name Lakewood. At first, she said the word as if it was an unknown or an unexpected ingredient. Snails? Are you sure? Snails? Lakewood.

"It's fine, Mom, everything's on the fridge."

"Lakewood, Lakewood, Lakewood, Lakewood, Lakewood, Lakewood," Deziree said, clawing at her own face, her voice getting higher with each iteration.

Lena grabbed her hands, held them firmly but gently. "Let's eat."

"I'm fine. I'm fine."

Halfway through the meal, Deziree spat out a piece of steak. It landed on the table, narrowly missing Lena's arm. Deziree stood up.

"Mom?"

"The spirit loves raw potatoes." Her eyes were focused on the wall behind Lena. Deziree waved her hands as if a cloud of mites was swarming around her head.

The refrigerator hummed. Lena wasn't sure whether to keep eating, wait for it to pass, or to do what her grandmother would sometimes do: describe exactly what was happening and try to ground the moment's details. We're just having a nice dinner, Deziree. The steak is medium-rare. The sparkling wine is very dry. It's 7:38 at night. Your sweet potatoes are incredible with the chili sauce you made. Our life is about to change, but we'll both be great.

Deziree sat down in her seat quickly.

"Mom?"

"I'm fine. Just tired."

"Mom."

"Will you please just accept this lie, so we can have a nice dinner?" Deziree's voice came out clear.

Lena nodded.

They ate quietly for a few moments. Deziree's hand shook a little as she cut her meat. Lena wondered if it would ever be possible to be relaxed while her mother struggled, to live fully in the idea that her mother would ask her for help when she wanted or needed it. There was a difference between helping someone you loved for their sake versus helping them because it made you feel good. But it was hard to be measured and thoughtful in the moment.

Her mother put her knife and fork down. "I understand that you have to do this. But you have to promise me you'll go back to school when everything is settled."

Lena nodded. "I swear, if it means I'm one of those ninety-year-olds that they put on the news."

Deziree smiled, but her eyes were sad.

"My great-great-grandson Demetrius only got a B minus on the final. This old bag of bones"—Lena pointed at her chest—"A plus."

If she were in a better mood, Deziree would have joined in. Asked about the grandkid's name. Did her own old-woman voice. Or maybe pretended to be the teacher on the news talking about how it was great to see that learning could happen at any age. Instead, she pushed around the sweet potatoes on her plate for a few moments. Then she excused herself and said she probably was going to sleep until morning.

Lena scrubbed the stove, washed the dishes. Going to her bedroom, she went through her phone. There was a photo message from Kelly: a calico cat with its tongue sticking out as if it was trying to catch a snowflake. She sent back a picture of the desk wedged into her bedroom. The room was the size of a generous walk-in closet. Enough room for a twin bed, a very small desk, and a skinny wardrobe one of the men at her grandma's church had custom-made for her. Any hint of mess was overwhelming in the space.

Then she called Tanya. Talked her ear off about how it might only take a year or two to make everything back in order and get them safe again. The word "safe" surprised Lena as it left her mouth. She had meant to say "steady." Tanya was obviously thinking about something else, since she kept saying variations of "That sounds cool." And though Tanya was home, Lena pictured her sitting at the desk in their dorm room, online shopping for boots or practicing her kanji while her mother talked at her on the phone.

When things were bad, Thinking Lena tied Feeling Lena up, led her into a deep labyrinth, and then ran out and got to work. It was necessary. Feeling Lena would distort and confuse and slow things down and want to talk and cry. Thinking Lena needed to get things done, not completely see the full situation, but focus on the easiest route to the other side. "Safe," Lena said again. And it made her think of how bad she would feel if Lakewood hadn't come around.

Tanya told her she was also doing a research study this summer. Lena's fingers tightened around her phone. Relaxed as Tanya explained, lowering her voice, that it was a female orgasm study. She would get a hundred dollars per session and an expensive vibrator for doing it.

"I'm telling my parents it's a massage study."

"I mean, it kind of is."

Tanya cackled. She told Lena that after agreeing to do it, she had gone into a weird spiral. She thought about backing out, then it was like there would be no other time in her life where she was going to get paid to just—*you know*. But then she read about research studies on the internet.

"Have you ever read about government-run research studies? Did you know there was one in the sixties for people who swore they had alien encounters?"

"I haven't." Lena touched her desk, glad Tanya couldn't see her face. She suddenly understood the thought experiments better based on this feeling: the uncanniness of someone you love being able to abruptly articulate a secret feeling. Friendship, family, and romance breed a telepathy that comes from kinship. She tried to think of something to say, felt the danger in the moment. As a child she had drawn a large cartoon hand on her desk. Her grandma had tried to get rid of it with salt and soap, but it remained. The fingers were so long they seemed sinister.

"I need to clean my desk," Lena said.

"What?"

"Yeah?"

Tanya sighed. "I can't believe you're dropping out."

Lena coughed. "Not forever."

"Can't you just do like an online fundraiser?"

Lena pretended the suggestion was a joke and laughed.

"Well. Fine. Sorry. But what about being patient? Or finding something closer to your mom?"

"Please don't bring my mom into this. You know this is about you."

Tanya hung up.

"Rude," Lena said into her phone, but knew she was talking about the both of them.

Lena reached up, stroked the ends of her hair, rubbed and lightly scratched her scalp. When she was a child and upset or unable to sleep, her grandmother would lightly scratch her scalp until everything in the world was gone. It helped a little.

She turned back to her phone. Searched government experiments for the third time since she got the job offer. So many forums and web pages devoted to discussing declassified experiments. The San Quentin prison experiments, Tuskegee, Operation Sea-Spray, Project Artichoke. How could all these things that sounded like well-meaning after-school programs for kids be so awful? Lena read again about the rumors that in different countries—all ones she noted that coincidentally had bad relationships with the United States—people were being taken against their will and experimented upon. A beach sprayed with a substance that made all the jellyfish spawn and all the kids who rolled around in the sand have severe sinus infections. There was no way that was a simple accident.

Another forum where people posted about a part of the FBI whose focus is ESP testing. They incorporate questions into ordinary things. Standardized testing in the schools, SATs, driving tests, customer satisfaction surveys. They read college applications that ask about the future and see what people say. If someone's answers hit a threshold in an algorithm, they're investigated. All social media is consistently monitored for this, one post read. They (the US government) are rounding all these people up because of the war on fucking terror.

Lena laughed a little at that line, unable to repress the part of her brain that liked to make dumb dad jokes: What would it be like to fuck terror? There are psychics living beneath the White House and being deployed to military zones. *Ones that will not corporate are being killed.*

A text message from Tanya appeared at the top of her screen: I'm sorry. I know you're going through a lot. Lena ignored it.

She reread the line she had just been reading. *Corporate?* Oh, cooperate. When they die, their brains are taken for study. Sometime soon, our DNA will be modified to make this the next step of human evolution.

A little grain of this must be true. The psychic stuff had to have been why the man had been testing. Maybe, Lena supposed, it could all be true. I'm lucky enough to be absolutely terrible at mind reading. Right now, I could be packing my things and getting ready to live beneath the White House. My summer spent telling the president who hates him and when the next big earthquake will hit.

She lowered the brightness on her phone's screen. There was something about conspiracy theories that she'd always liked.

How a person's brain could find the smallest threads to reaffirm a creative, false truth about the world. Most of her favorites were about celebrities. A child beauty queen who everyone thought was murdered had been kidnapped, brainwashed, and turned into a very religious pop star. Secret romances between teen drama stars who were now hiding their secret babies. Some of this stuff couldn't be considered conspiracy theories, though. There were people on these boards who believed that all people had to do to stop climate change was to learn how to speak to the weather respectfully and just explain the situation.

Lena typed back to Tanya: I wish you could just support me. She deleted it.

She typed: I wish everything didn't have to be about you. Deleted.

You're the only person in the world I feel like I can be completely honest with and I'm sorry, but things have to be different right now. Deleted.

Sent: Everything sucks, but I have to do this.

A different website. White text on a black background: TV shows us the lies we want to distract us from what's real.

You need to take care of yourself too, Tanya replied.

Lena put her phone down. Everything on it was upsetting her. Instead, she focused on her room.

Everything she took would be the foundation of her new adult life. The problem wasn't the being an adult part. She looked at the textbooks, the nail polishes, the art supplies, the clothes—it was figuring out what kind of adult she wanted to become. Lena texted Tanya three red hearts. Then packed her most be-patterned, brightest clothes to wear on the weekends. Gathered all her favorite pictures of her family. A painting Tanya gave her for Christmas.

Then she tried to sleep. Couldn't.

Lena went into the living room. There was nothing to clean. She touched the doorknob to her grandmother's bedroom. Brushed aside the urge to knock, to ask if she was still awake. She pushed open the door, shut it softly behind her so Deziree wouldn't hear. Lena got into her grandmother's bed. The pillow still smelled of roses. Rolling onto her side, she pressed her nose into it, allowing herself to do this until her nose got used to the smell, until there was nothing. Lena pulled the silk pillowcase off the pillow, went to her grandmother's vanity, took out the rose hip oil. Sprinkled it on the cloth and didn't care about the greasy blot of it. Now she had everything she needed.

8

At five a.m. there was no one but Lena on the road. The air was chilly, the weather refusing to admit that in six weeks it would be summer. Lena was tired enough to feel dulled, but that was good. It gave her enough brain space to focus on driving safely and sipping the extra-strong coffee Deziree made for her. No tears, no anticipation of what was to come.

After the first hour of driving, it was all country highways. The sun rose as she passed the beginnings of rows of cornfields. Houses grew farther and farther away from each other—the only clusters popping up when Lena drove through villages. These were named either for parts of the landscape or Native American tribes, which deserved better than being immortalized as a place with one stoplight, a bar, a gas station, and some squat white ranch houses. Deer scampered across the cracked and potholed highway. No wonder she had never heard of Lakewood. There were more animals here than people.

She made a turn, another. The dirt in the roads changed from dull brown to tinged with red. Houses popped up again. Lakewood had a downtown: a small courthouse, a bar, some restaurants, a surprisingly big library, two different donut shops. An old man on a bench alternating between puffs of his cigarette and bites of a pastry. Cars were on the roads, people were walking dogs. Seeing people was reassuring. Lena drove on, following the main drag to a chain supermarket, a gas station, following the curve that narrowed into a long gravel road that became a driveway.

And then she was there.

The black security gate was open, no guard at the post. A large blue-and-white sign was next to the building, clean except for a small smear of grayish bird poop: GREAT LAKES SHIPPING COMPANY.

The conference room was small and packed with people. Dr. Lisa was standing at the head of the table, her skin freshly tanned, a watch tan line on her left wrist. The man next to Lena was chewing on a bagel in a loud, enthusiastic way. She was sure she could hear every drip of spit being produced in his mouth, the pull, the tear, the tooth grind of every bite. The woman to her left had a tattoo of the moon's phases on her forearm. Her hair was thick and black, her skin brown in a way that made Lena assume wherever this woman went, some white person asked her, "What are you?"

"These first two weeks we're going to be baselining you again," Dr. Lisa said. "You'll also learn some of the skills—if you don't have them—of your cover jobs here, so you can talk convincingly about them." Dr. Lisa's eyes were focused more on the people standing around the table, all of them wearing gray hospital scrubs. "There will be several observers watching you while you're here. Please don't try to be friendly with them. The crew is trained not to get attached."

Almost all the people—"the observers"—were white. All the study participants, Lena noted, except for an older white woman, were black or Indian or Latinx. She kept her face neutral, filed that fact away to process later. The doctor's voice sounded as if she was getting over a cold. As she spoke, she kept alternating between calling them "the crew" and "the observers." Lena preferred crew. It made her think of terrible dance movies where friendships could only be salvaged by coming together for one last pop-and-lock. It was hard to focus. She was hyperaware of everyone's hands. Someone smelled like grapefruit-scented cleaning products. Someone was clicking a pen in two-four time.

"We highly encourage you to be moderate in your drinking when you're not here. And in general, you should all be avoiding situations that can impair your judgment. Create a distance between you and people who can get you to confide in them. No drugs." She made direct eye contact with Lena.

Dr. Lisa gave all six office members a tour of the facilities. They walked back through the cubicle farm and down the first-floor hallway. She pushed open the large double doors. The warehouse was lit with fluorescent lights that made them all look as if they were recovering from the flu. There were rows of high shelving that contained several cardboard boxes. It smelled like vinegar, dirt, gasoline. She said Floor 1 would be for Great Lakes Shipping Company work and low-risk studies that could be performed at their desks. She led them back out, down the hallway, and to a room that contained cubicles, adjoining long tables, and a receptionist's desk. She pointed out the break room, the conference room they had already been in, and the small supply closet.

"Remember, on Floor 1 you can come and go anywhere. You should only be on Floor 2 when asked to see me or if you've been assigned there for a study. Floor 3 and the basement are invitation only."

They all claimed desks and were encouraged to decorate their spaces, then were handed folders. The first piece of paper in Lena's folder listed her job responsibilities. The second was a piece of paper that read Day 1: Lena at the top. Below it was the following: You attended orientation where you met your coworkers, Charlie (the branch manager), Bethany (the receptionist), Ian (dispatch operator and inventory clerk), Tom (IT), and Mariah (HR). You learned that you were going to take classes to get certified in Microsoft Excel. You are very happy about that. You don't like the headset you have to use at work. It pinches. The next sheet was a reminder about confidentiality. After that, contact info. Another sheet with Lena's address and a key taped to it.

Dr. Lisa assigned each staff member to a trainer who was responsible for walking them through their job details. Lena's trainer was a short white woman with large eyebrows that moved three times more than the average person's. When the woman was listening to Lena's questions about call logs and spreadsheets, her face fell into an expression Lena decided was best called why-are-we-people-not-meteors-or-dirt?

Then it was morning break. All the office workers went into the break room, where a large box of donuts was waiting for them. A younger guy, the only other black person Lena had seen since coming to Lakewood, introduced himself as Charlie, the supervisor. His voice sounded so Michigan—he pronounced Charlie with a long, nasal "A."

He was born in Lakewood, lived there his entire life. He had hazel eyes, and Lena knew that, at least based on looks, Tanya would have called him an absolute yes. As Charlie reached to shake her hand, he knocked over a cup of pens. While picking up the pens, his cell phone fell out of his pocket. Tanya wouldn't have cared that he was clumsy. She liked men—clumsy men, or with a slightly weird voice, or who were shorter than her—who might have to work a little harder.

When Charlie was standing again, and everything was where it should be, Lena told him she had never lived somewhere so small. Charlie lowered his voice and leaned close enough that she could smell his coffee breath. "Not everyone is as redneck as they might seem."

She laughed, hoped it didn't sound as painfully high pitched and uncomfortable to him as it did to her. Lena took a donut and looked around the room, then realized Charlie had probably said some variation on that to everyone in the room except Bethany.

In the afternoon, Dr. Lisa made the group watch a video of a computer-animated man doing a comedy routine. Sitting on opposite sides of the room were two white men wearing khakis and polo shirts and watching the group watching the video. When they flicked the lights on, everyone filled out surveys about how comfortable they felt about the computer man's appearance. Did his voice synch with his face? Did they think their responses were at all shaded by how other people in the room seemed to be feeling?

Next, everyone returned to their desks and were given similar videos to watch while wearing headphones. One of the performers looked more like a reptile than a person. He told jokes about air travel that should have been tired, but the idea of a half-chameleon, half-man having the same boring complaints as everyone else about aisle seats made her laugh. She watched videos and filled out surveys for the rest of the day.

Lena's apartment was fully furnished, and less than 10 minutes away from work. There were pots and pans in the cupboards, a bag of towels with tags attached in the bathroom. A brand-new dishwasher. Hardwood floors in the kitchen, dining room, and bedroom. It looked like a place where someone would want to live. She wanted to post a picture of it on social media, but that felt like a bad idea. Instead of unpacking—because the apartment felt so clean, so new—Lena took a drive through town.

She liked seeing large, white wildflowers poking up out of the ditches along the highway. The air alternated between smelling like sewer and the sweet joy of corn growing under sunshine. Unexpected graveyards surrounded by fields told Lena that Lakewood had been around for hundreds of years. She didn't feel ready to stop in any of the small diners or restaurants. Maybe people would leave her alone, but she was worried about drawing too much attention—"It's a small town and people like to talk"—or worse, feeling trapped. Every time she had been in a place like this in the past, at least a few white people would stare at her or do double takes. It would be hard to stay under the radar if she said to someone, "Yes, black people are real."

Lena passed a field with green stems rising out of the dirt. Wooden signs announced it as home to premium Michigan sunflowers. She was used to a Michigan that was cities, vacant lots, and boarded-up houses. Cute university towns, billboards that reminded you to brush your teeth for four minutes a day, looking across the river toward Canada. Here she felt like an explorer. There were roads where she saw no one, only dull-red barns and green fields.

When she started to get hungry, Lena turned back toward Lakewood. As she drove past one of the downtown parks, in her rearview mirror she saw six teenage boys fighting. The right word might be a brawl. They were punching and kicking and slapping at one another, but through her open car windows, Lena could hear no yelling. One boy was wearing a white shirt and there was a solid line of blood leading from his nose to his shirt bottom.

As Lena circled the block, she saw another car pull up and park. Three teenage girls got out and ran to the boys. One of them kicked off her flip-flops so she could run faster. A second girl was wearing a lemon-print dress. It was full skirted, and her red hair was in ringlets.

When the girl in the lemon dress reached the boys, she jumped onto the one closest to her and wrapped her arms around his neck, pushing him forward with her momentum. Her curls bounced around. She pulled his hair, kept yanking at it, and all the other boys paused. Still he thrashed. She slapped the top of his head as if she were playing a bongo drum. Still no one yelled. The boy stood straight, and the girl allowed herself to be dropped off his back. They started to make out while all the others—and an older man sitting on a bench—watched.

9

That night, a storm kept Lena awake. Hail rattled against her windows, the wind argued with itself, and she could hear a dog in the apartment next door whining after each thunder clap. The rain, a sound that usually made her sleep deeply, sounded as if it was clawing and scratching its way through the building's bricks.

Around six a.m., Lena turned her alarm off, and realized she didn't own a coffeemaker. She ate her breakfast, washed the dishes, changed. Every motion took effort. She yawned twice, three times. In the parking lot there were five lawn chairs—red and white gingham—where she almost tripped over a tree branch. Her windshield was shattered over the driver's seat. Glass decorated the car's insides. The offending branch's leaves wet on the wheel and on the seat.

"Shit," Lena said. "Triple shit."

The air was silver. No one else was around; there weren't any lights or televisions on in the apartments facing the driveway. Lena went back to her apartment, dug a jacket out of one of her boxes, and then called the number Dr. Lisa had given her. A person on the line said they would take care of her car for her, and then connected her with Charlie, who lived two blocks over.

He showed up with two cups of coffee and they drank it while looking over her smashed windshield.

"Well, welcome to Lakewood," Charlie said.

On the way to work in his car, they stopped at a small brick house. "Be back in two."

He removed fallen branches from the sidewalk and pushed the tipped-over garbage and recycling bins inside the garage. Next to the mailbox was a tipped-over tomato cage that Charlie righted, though nothing seemed to be growing yet. When he got back in the car there was dark soil underneath his fingernails. He didn't seem to mind.

"Sorry about that."

"Is that your house?" Lena leaned forward in her seat.

"It's Mrs. Thompson's. My second-grade teacher. My parents said I was in love with her when I was eight. So, they think it's really funny to make jokes now that I help her out. When she's away I take care of the garden. In winter I shovel the walks." He put on his sunglasses and drove with his knees. "My mom's favorite joke is 'My daughter-in-law and I can share a room in the retirement home.'"

"Sounds annoying."

"It can be a little funny sometimes." Charlie yawned. "She was a good teacher. And her husband's been sick a long time."

Lena liked how kind his voice sounded while he talked about his mom and teacher.

"Can I ask you an awkward question?"

"You just did."

Lena sipped her coffee. She didn't know Charlie well enough to know if he was teasing her or if he thought she was being annoying. He was taking the back roads, passing old houses.

Long, spindly plants that looked like asparagus were growing alongside the road.

"Sorry. Ask your question."

"Why do you think they're doing these experiments? What do you think they're trying to learn?"

"I don't think we're supposed to ask that question." He drummed a little on the steering wheel.

"That's why I'm asking you."

"I can't figure it out. I think it's something about memory." Charlie made a noncommittal noise.

He pointed to a store on the right called Family Home and told Lena when he was a kid, all his friends had refused to go inside. They said it was built on an Indian burial ground and the ghosts of the people buried there haunted the entire store. The ghosts were especially interested in little white kids. They wanted to punish the ancestors of those who had wronged them. It was a weird mix, he said, of racism and historical self-awareness.

He kept talking in an obvious let's-change-the-subject way, pointing out the Wendy's and a chain mattress store he pretended were Lakewood originals. The Wendy's family has lived here for seven generations, perfecting their hamburger recipe. One day, they'll be world famous.

"I read online that people in other countries were disappearing and being forced into studies like these."

"Lena." Charlie's voice was easy and smooth. "Don't ruin this for yourself. You have to have a good reason for being here."

"I do. I need money for school," she said, surprising herself with the lie. She opened her bag and made herself busy rummaging around for sunglasses, pulling out mint gum. "Thanks again for the coffee."

⌘

In the office, the observers handed out their Day 2 slips. Lena's read Day 2: Lena. You accidentally deleted a bunch of files. You were too scared to tell Charlie (the manager). Tom (IT) helped restore the files. You forgot your lunch and split a pizza with him and Mariah (HR). Your earpiece still hurts.

Then they were given their morning assignments. Charlie and Ian were taken upstairs. Lena and Bethany were given handbooks about their jobs. They practiced taking phone calls and read theoretical situations. Lena's book asked her what she would do if a driver was late bringing an extra-large shipment of pickles. After reading the handbook, she watched some tutorials about how to build a database.

Halfway through the day, Bethany knocked on Lena's cubicle. "Hello, Neighbor. I'm Bethany and I live over there." She pointed to the receptionist's desk. They shook hands and made small talk about how annoying learning all these computer programs was and oh, wow, what a storm that was last night. Bethany was wearing a lot of blush, with her hair up in a high ponytail that looked painful.

"You see him?" Bethany nodded at the man with a large beard, Indian. The IT guy.

"Tom?"

Tom was wearing a navy polo shirt and khakis. He was sitting at a long table, taking notes, and wearing headphones. He looked as if he was on the verge of tears.

"I heard from Ian." Bethany pointed at a desk. "That Tom is doing a solo experiment to explore the grieving process. He's listening to audio recordings of his dead wife's voice."

"That's—" Lena couldn't choose whether to say awful, terrible, or sad.

"Romantic, right?" Bethany turned and went back to her desk.

After another hour of tutorials, an observer came over and told Lena it was her turn upstairs. Lena got excited as she took the stairs. Maybe there was a cool thing—some incredible new technology, aliens, a cool health breakthrough—she was going to get to see. The observer led her to a small room that looked like a doctor's examination room. A sink, a counter, framed drawings of potted plants behind the examination table. Dr. Lisa was sitting on a low stool, holding a clipboard and writing something.

She took Lena's blood pressure, her temperature. "Healthy."

"Great," Lena said.

The doctor had Lena hand over her cell phone. A man wearing a navy shirt stood in the doorway. "He's going to take you to your experiment."

Lena got in the front seat of the man's sedan. It smelled of rental car, a scent pumped in to make the car feel new.

The man tapped the window. "Sorry, you have to get in the back." His voice was hoarse as he asked her to lie down. "It's policy, to help protect all of our privacy."

He started the car. It was older, and every part of it was loud. The windows rattled on the dirt roads. Something squeaked in alarm every time the car made a left turn.

Lena could feel they were going up a hill. "It's a nice day," she said. The observer didn't acknowledge what she said. He was older than the other ones; most of them seemed to be in their late twenties, early thirties.

"Do you know why the dirt here is so red?"

Another dip in the road. She could feel every pothole. Bumps and rattles. It sounded like they had gone off road.

"The air is so clean here," she tried.

When the man parked and she was allowed to sit up, Lena could see they were in a forest, light dappling between green leaves. The observer got out of the car and opened the back door for her. He walked as if he knew the path, gesturing at a high root.

"Has it already started?"

The man turned. He looked as if he was almost on the verge of laughing. "Sorry, my throat." His voice came out high and thin. "I thought you could hear me in the car."

"Oh. Feel better," Lena said.

They walked on, passing white mushrooms and dead leaves. A blister was forming on each of Lena's big toes. Sweat dripped along her hairline and down her back. "You all could have told me to wear sneakers today," she said.

The man gave a short laugh, which turned into a cough.

The woods were a dream. Birds chattering so loud that they sounded as if they were inside every tree trunk and below the ground. In the distance, a deer with its head and neck bent low. After about 10 minutes, where Lena almost walked into a patch of poison ivy, they came upon a small cabin.

Some cigarette butts and crushed beer cans were scattered around it; they made Lena feel as if they had scared off a bunch of partying teens. All the windows were nailed and boarded shut. The observer opened the cabin's door and turned on his phone's flashlight. On the ground were shotgun shells. Empty plastic bottles. She cleared her throat. He didn't take the hint.

There was a small pile of empty water bottles all crushed in the middle. A beach chair Lena kicked lightly, making it wobble, confirming that one emphatic plop would force it to collapse into a heap of rust, metal, plastic.

"So?" Lena asked. "What are we doing here?" Grass poked through the floor slats. It was a place where you would see zip ties, blood, knives, plastic, shovel. A woman's voice asking for help. The floorboards creaked beneath Lena's feet.

"You're going to stay here. You won't be able to leave the cabin." His voice was so hoarse, he sounded as if he had been struck by lightning. "I'm going to tell you a secret."

In the dark, Lena rolled her eyes. Never in her life had she felt so simultaneously scared and annoyed.

He told her when he was a boy, a woman who was so good-looking it made him nervous to even look at her lived next door to him. She was good and kind and liked to bake cookies for his family because his mom was always busy. Her husband was terrible. They could hear screaming and the sounds of an argument at all hours of the night. Lena took a breath. No matter where this story went, it would not be pleasant. One night, when he couldn't sleep, he looked out his kitchen window. His flashlight wobbled as he spoke, illuminated different parts of the dirty cabin floor. Their kitchen windows faced one another. Sometimes, the moms would wave to each other as they cooked. You know, real neighborly. He saw the wife and husband arguing. The husband slapped her once, twice. Lena's hand crept to her mouth. She felt that in daylight, with people around, this story might mean very little to her, just more proof of how horrible people can be to one another. Blood coming out of his neighbor's nose. So much blood, he said. It was coming out of her mouth. Then she reached into the drawer, pulled out a knife, and stabbed her husband. "I was only a little boy, 7 years old. But I thought, good. Good."

Lena turned toward him. She let out the breath she had been holding.

"Don't tell this to anyone."

"I understand," Lena said. She sneezed. The air stunk of rain and mold. "Did she get in trouble?"

"I don't remember," he said. She could tell that was a lie. He pointed the flashlight over to a box. "Food, water. Be measured."

She stepped toward the box to look through the supplies. The door creaked, opened, then slammed shut.

"Well, bye," Lena said. Once her eyes adjusted, it was easier to find the sources of light. A small chip off the cabin's door, parts of the roof in need of repair. She practiced walking, arms spread wide. A scuttling was coming from above. It sounded like an animal on the roof. At least it wasn't inside.

A person with a clipboard was crouched in the darkest corner. They were bent over, but Lena could feel their eyes on her. Her hands curled up into fists. Especially if the person was a man, she felt completely unsafe being alone in a small cabin with him.

"Hello?" She tensed up and took a few steps toward the person. No reaction. She moved closer until, even in the dark, she could see what she had mistaken for a person was a second chair.

"I almost gave myself a fucking heart attack," she whispered. Leaning against the wall, she let her heart reset to a normal rhythm. Relaxed and stretched out her fingers.

It had to be almost dinnertime now. If Deziree was feeling well, she would be eating a salad, probably out on the small porch. If she wasn't, Miss Shaunté and Deziree were probably splitting takeout. They would talk about men or gardening or yoga. Her mom would have all the medicine she needed today. Tomorrow was her first physical therapy appointment. If they were trying to scare Lena, they were doing a bad job. She could live in this cabin alone, using the corner as a bathroom. Stay long enough to lose her sight, if it meant not having to do the mental calculations of what was better: paying the water bill or asking her mother to be miserable.

She sank down to the floor to give her feet a break. Something brushed her hand, but she ignored it. Better not to know. Lena wished she hadn't drunk that last cup of coffee. She got up and walked slowly over to the box of supplies. Felt through and squinted at parts of it. Jerky, tinned fish, dried fruit, water, granola bars, a small first-aid kit. She took out some Band-Aids and removed her work shoes. A rumble of thunder. The wind picked up. Rain dripped through the roof and down onto Lena's head.

The cabin shook throughout the night. There were patches and gulps of calm, then the storm would start again. The air smelled of mold and urine; Lena would get used to the smell, fall asleep, and then startle awake and get annoyed by the scent again. After waking up another time, she felt restless. Lena tried daydreaming: a vacation to Tokyo, eating ramen on a small stool, and buying a bunch of cool, small things she didn't need. When that became hard to focus on, she tried screaming for a while. Not out of fear, but because it was fun being able not to care. There were times she was sure she saw things—the shape of a bat flying in a circle, a man's shadow—when the cabin was illuminated by close lightning. Lena spread out on the floor and fell asleep.

Awakened by the cold, she stretched. Her back felt good. She did a few yoga poses. Her face and teeth felt gritty. As she ate, Lena thought about her mother. For the first time in a long time, she considered what kind of person her father might have been. Deziree never spoke about him. All Lena ever knew about him were the differences between her and her mother: Lena liked doing math; her ears were very small while her mother's and grandmother's were big; she had always been a little distant from religion; the ugly second toe on her left foot; her stubby eyelashes; her looser curls. She couldn't imagine what she would do now if she met her dad. The idea of it no longer made her feel emotional, only curious. The time in her life when it might have mattered to have a second parent was over.

When Lena got bored thinking about him or all the possible types of people he could be, she did multiplication tables. More yoga. Wondered what was the point of this? Was it a test to see how much isolation it would take to make her feel moderately nuts? Was it something about survival? And how were they watching her? She went to the four corners of the cabin but couldn't see or feel anything that wasn't wood. A nap. More multiplication. A small meal of a granola bar. There were 24 in the box, but she wanted to be measured even though her stomach wanted her to be reckless. The night was windy, but she slept through most of it.

In the morning, there was a tablet next to her and more bottles of water in the box. Lena used the smallest amount she could in an attempt to wash her face, but she knew whatever she did had made it worse. She tried to ignore the tablet as long as possible. There was no possible way it could be a part of something positive—they weren't going to let her watch a fun movie or scroll through fashion blogs. Lena drank some more water.

She picked it up. The screen was so bright that Lena closed her eyes, but still saw bright white spots across her vision. There was a survey for her to fill out: On a scale of 1–10, with 1 being negative and 10 being excellent mental health, how do you feel? Using the same guidelines, how do you feel physically, with 10 being the best fitness of your life? On a scale of 1–10, with 10 being the utmost level of trust a person can feel, how do you feel about Great Lakes Shipping Company? The next screen asked her if, for an undisclosed monetary reward, she would reveal the secret she was told. It felt as if this was all a test of her ability to be discreet. The choice was easy: Lena selected no. The screen faded to black.

A video played. It had no sound, the footage in gray scale. She watched herself sit at a long desk. A man with his back to the camera was speaking to her. On-screen Lena nodded at something he said. Then the man leaned across and slapped her. It didn't seem hard. Her reaction on camera was more stunned than angry or in pain. He slapped her a second time, a third, again, again. More force with each slap. On-screen Lena did not fight back. The footage was too grainy to see if part of her nose or the eye closest to where he was slapping was swollen. She noticed her fingers were gripping the table as if to steady herself. The man paused. He said something to On-screen Lena. She said something back. There were a few moments where nothing much happened. She continued to grip the table, but her shoulders and her neck relaxed. It gave her an uncomfortable pleasure to see that whenever this was recorded she had refused to cry. Then the man lunged. Grabbed her by the throat. Lena dropped the tablet. Her mouth was dry. She watched as he choked her and she kicked and pushed and scratched. The video faded away to another questionnaire.

Do you remember the events of this video, yes or no?

Lena's hands shook as she picked no.

Do you recognize the man in this video, yes or no?

No.

Does this video make you doubt your commitment to Lakewood?

When her grandmother had started talking to her about sex, Lena had expected it would come with Not until you are 30, Not until you are married, It is a sin. She expected the vehemence that so many of her friends were getting from their mothers. Deziree's role was almost always Good Cop. She would be the one who later, after grandma had scared her, would come in and be reasonable. She would talk about condoms and safety and emotions and being ready. But her grandmother had surprised her. She had spoken about saving yourself, not for marriage—although that would be great and really what Jesus preferred—but for someone who respected your body as much as you did. Her grandmother had said it was better to love your body as much as possible before letting someone else have access to it. That they could permanently damage in unexpected ways how you saw yourself. Lena could still remember exactly how her grandma sounded because it sounded as if she was telling a secret. Her grandmother didn't apply the idea of respect only to sex, but to other situations: what she ate, how she dressed, even something as small as crossing the street.

Lena couldn't remember the man's hands on her throat or the fear she must have felt.

Does this video make you doubt your commitment to Lakewood?

Lena pressed no.

10

⬱

Another day passed. The tablet disappeared while she slept. Lena made a mental list of all the things she would eat when this was over, repeating it every time she started to feel hopeless or wild: macaroni and cheese, chocolate donut, a salad to feel responsible, a pizza with green olives, a whole pound of really fresh red grapes, a chicken, another chicken, a tequila shot for every day I was in this nightmare. She kept dreaming about white chocolate mochas, though she didn't like sugary coffee drinks. Drinking them, bathing in them, peeing them— between dreams of someone punching her in the face. Lena visualized a storm or a fire or a band of rogue beavers looking for wood to destroy this cabin and set her free. They could not penalize her for acts of nature.

Another morning, this one rainy. The sound of it on the roof made it easier to be alone. She was pacing back and forth trying to focus on her feet, her hands, pushing away all thoughts when the door to the cabin swung open.

"You can come out."

She rubbed her eyes, let them adjust to the light coming in

before stepping outside. Waiting for her was a man Lena didn't recognize. She stepped out, slipped a little on the wet ground. He tried to grab her and hit Lena on the shoulder.

Later, she would consider what happened and realize he was trying to keep her from falling. That she had been more affected by being alone, by the video, than she understood. But in the moment, his hand ignited a flight instinct. Lena turned, ran. Darted between trees, ducked under branches. There were still leaves on the ground from the previous fall, white flowers and long blades of grass poking up, all slick. She fell. It took a moment to realize how she was suddenly on the ground, another painful half-second to register her right wrist had connected with a large root. And had there been a snap? Her throat and face were hot. Lena thought no, I won't cry, but her eyes were already leaking.

She stood up. Her wrist stayed at an angle that made it look like something from a nightmare. Lena took a few steps. Every part of her wrist was keening, telling her to stop moving. She stood still.

The man approached her, taking large, slow steps. He was young, white, dressed more like he was going to a dive bar—hooded sweatshirt, expensive-looking boots—than like he was part of Lakewood. Lena considered whether he was a part of it; maybe he was just a local who had come across the cabin while hiking. Then she noticed the clipboard he had squeezed under his armpit. Her forehead was wet. Lena reached up with her good hand and felt it. Blood on her fingertips. The man's eyes were dark beneath his glasses. He was saying, "Easy, easy, easy."

Lena woke up in a hospital bed. At her bedside was Dr. Lisa in a rocking chair. She was reading a book, a pink blanket wrapped around her shoulders.

"Good morning," Dr. Lisa said. She set her book down on a small table next to the chair. *Murder in the Tropics*. An old woman holding a large black cat and wearing a very big sun hat was on the cover. "How are you feeling?"

Lena's wrist was in a plain white cast. She felt fuzzy, probably from painkillers and maybe too much sleep at once. It could have been an hour, or three days, later. There was an IV hooked into her arm. Her mouth still felt crusted over with dirt and bacteria.

"If it helps, I told them you weren't ready for this one." Dr. Lisa's voice was wry—she was speaking like they were friends who could laugh about anything.

"Do you remember the words I told you? On the phone before you came here."

Lena shrugged.

Dr. Lisa fished out a pen from a bag at her feet, flipped to the back of her book, wrote something on the last page.

"I broke my wrist?"

"A bad sprain. If I offered you a thousand dollars, would you tell me the secret?"

Lena coughed. Forced herself to speak lightly, as if she was joking. "Ten thousand."

The doctor scribbled some more. "How would you describe how you felt in the cabin? If you were afraid, on a scale of one to ten, with ten being I thought I was going to die there, what would you give it?"

"Are you fucking kidding me?"

The wall above Dr. Lisa's head was so white, it almost glowed. There was dirt beneath the fingernails of Lena's left hand. When she sat up, the IV pulled a little. She slouched and leaned her head against the pillows.

Dr. Lisa pulled the rocking chair she was sitting in closer to the bed, then sat back in it. She picked up her book, opened it for a moment as if she was going to read a passage to Lena to help her get back to sleep. Folded a corner of the page, closed the book. "It's normal to be pissed. Healthy, even." Her voice was low.

"What was the point of that?"

The painkillers took over. Lena rambled about quitting, about pain, and fear, and what it was like to get fucking slapped, and how did she know the bone wasn't broken. How was it legal to treat people like this. It wasn't. It wasn't. They couldn't do this. Dr. Lisa poured Lena some more water, then took the blanket off her lap and put it on Lena. A bin behind her chair was filled with blankets, another pillow. She pulled out the pillow, helped Lena prop up her wrist, putting pressure on the cast. That hurts, Lena thought. The doctor leaned over, still holding onto her cast. She whispered into Lena's ear, "Before you talk like that to any of us again, think about your mother."

11

When Lena returned to the office a folder was waiting on her desk. Inside were her Day sheets. Day 3: You helped Ian (Inventory and Dispatch) begin inventorying the warehouse. You saw a bat roosting in the corner and called animal control. Day 4: A large shipment of cereal was delivered. You began taking an online course to build your spreadsheet knowledge. You and Bethany (receptionist) had lunch together. Day 5: Charlie (manager) organized a pizza party on Friday for the group. You continued inventorying the warehouse. Day 6: You hurt your wrist over the weekend. Mariah (HR) organized a card for everyone to sign. You thought that was very nice. You continued taking your online course about spreadsheets.

There were six different observers in the office today, all wearing gray polo shirts and slacks. Lena tried to guess which one wrote their days for them—maybe the tall, thin man with clear plastic glasses. Or the brunette woman, the one who parted her hair directly down the middle.

No one asked Lena how she got the cast. The expected Feel Better! card was handed over to her by a smiling Mariah, who was called quickly away for another experiment. The pain-killers smoothed away the edges of any emotions, so the day felt blurred. Bethany talked earnestly about how she was going to convert this office to using only eco-friendly cleaning products. She made Lena look at the new poster she had put next to her desk. It was a white poster that was mostly an illustration of a pineapple upside-down cake. Underneath it was the slogan STRESSED IS JUST DESSERTS SPELLED BACKWARD!

Spreadsheets. An experiment where she watched another stand-up comedy video: A sofa talked about rolling up to the club but having too much junk in the trunk for ladies to want to get down with him. Staring at her phone. She read long text conversations with her mother performed by someone pretend-ing to be her. Ignored texts from Tanya, Kelly, and Stacy. Sitting in the break room and eating a bag of chips, she felt someone was watching her. It was Dr. Lisa, standing next to the coffeemaker, arms crossed. "Hi," she mouthed, smiling as if she was pleased to see Lena.

"Hi," Lena mouthed back, pretending to be happy to see her too.

Around lunchtime, Tanya texted Lena again to see when she could come visit, and what was her address so she could send letters. Lena ignored the address request, knowing in an impulsive mood, Tanya would just show up at her apartment despite the long drive. She took a selfie of herself with her cast, stopped herself from sending it to Tanya. That would mean a visit, fussing, concern, questions about how it had happened.

When Lena's grandma died, Tanya had put together an elaborate care package. A bottle of nice bourbon, different beauty supplies, Lena's favorite cookies. The gesture had been nice, but Lena didn't want to touch anything in the package except the three-dollar cookies. Everything else felt too special-occasion.

Why couldn't Tanya have just bought the cookies and said Let's watch a dumb movie? It was always too much: trying to pay for the Saturday-night dinners when their dorm's cafeteria was closed, movie tickets, supplying top-shelf liquor in their dorm room that she claimed had been given to her as gifts. As if people approached Tanya on the streets and said, "A woman who looks like you deserves high-quality liquor," and pressed the unopened bottle into her hands, then vanished.

Lena tried not to care too much; she never complained, tried as much as possible to act like it was normal. The few times they had talked about it, Tanya was supremely relaxed. She was frank about her admiration for Lena having a work-study job, going home to help her mom and grandma almost every week, and still holding her GPA high enough to keep her scholarship. "You deserve to be the one taken care of, sometimes." Lena couldn't imagine how far Tanya would go over a wrist injury, plus living in a place with no friends.

Instead, Lena texted the selfie to Stacy. He immediately texted back: Ouch. Then: You look very pretty today. It was the first time in weeks he had used words, not a picture. She smiled, happy no one was looking at her face and noticing how dumb she probably looked. He probably didn't mean anything by it. Lena knew if she texted back right away it might be opening another door. More flirting, conversations. She put her phone down.

"You okay?" Charlie asked.

She started. This was the first she had seen him all day. Lena shook her head. His eyes went to her wrist. She looked away from the kindness in them. Then to the observer who was heating up what smelled like chicken curry in the microwave. "I'm in outer space."

"What?"

"Painkillers. I'm high. Sorry, I feel like I'm being really weird right now."

Near the end of the workday, Lena received another text from Tanya: Are you mad at me? Why don't you want me to visit?

Lena started typing. My life is already completely different, she began. Lena described the cabin, the scrutiny, her wrist, Dr. Lisa mentioning Deziree. How much depended on keeping secrets. And she had already gotten hurt. Already she was pushing away the thought that she had made a huge mistake. But what else could she do? And if Tanya came to Lakewood, it would be too hard. I have to make space between my old life, Lena typed. She saw the echo of Dr. Lisa's orientation speech. She looked at the long text and deleted it.

"Sorry," Tanya texted the next morning.

The key to surviving Lakewood, Lena decided, was making some real friends she could talk to. She started eating lunch with Mariah and Charlie and made plans to go see a movie with them. She accepted an invitation to have dinner at Tom's house with Ian and Bethany after work on Day 11. The most awkward part of that night was when Tom's teenage son approached Lena in the kitchen. "You're not that much older than me," he said. "I'm a senior. We can be friends." She tilted her head, reached past him, and opened the refrigerator. Lena took a can of pop, closed the refrigerator, and went out to dinner. She was not lonely enough to start hanging out with high-schoolers. Tom gave them each a bag of zucchinis, large and curved, that he had grown in his basement garden.

That night, no longer on a heavy dose of painkillers, Lena couldn't fall asleep. In the dark, every shadow was a man she didn't know. She would drift toward sleep, only to feel fingers wrapped around her throat, pain in her face. She turned the lights on. Still, sleep only arrived in short bursts. She kept waking up stroking the silk pillowcase, turning to look at the lamp on her nightstand. When she bought the owl lamp it looked cute, but now its stern white face was less than reassuring.

Lena wanted to text Tanya.

She was up late every night; Tanya would be thrilled if Lena called and asked if she wanted to watch a movie at the same time. Tanya coped with her insomnia by making things—art, desserts—and would have been happy to send Lena pictures of whatever project she was working on.

The next morning, Lena woke up at 9:30. She threw on a pair of leggings, started to pull on a dress, and got her bad wrist stuck in an arm hole. Tears welled up. She had to yank her arm hard to get it out. When Lena looked in the mirror, she hated how she looked but didn't have time to change.

On the way to work, Lena fantasized about all the bad behavior she wanted to indulge in. Childish ideas like taking scissors off Dr. Lisa's desk and cutting some of the doctor's hair when her back was turned. Or stealing something small off her desk like a nice pen or a photo or the large geode, and then throwing it into the woods behind Great Lakes Shipping Company. Or she could tell the observers all the terrible nicknames she had for them: Crooked Nose, Haircut, Dad Jeans, Pancake Butt, Einstein Eyebrows. In the office, everyone was gathered in the conference room. Lena slipped into the room, stood at the back. Mariah was the only one who noticed her. She mouthed something that looked like You good? Lena nodded.

"Part 2 of this project is to see if intimacy increases thought receptivity," Dr. Lisa said. She paused, as if she was fighting the urge to make a hand motion or some sort of joke. She took a deep breath and said there was a theory that sometimes, when you were bonded too closely with someone, you couldn't truly hear or see them. Your impression of who they were and who you thought they should be was permanently in the way once intimacy was established. You see the people you don't know well the clearest.

Dr. Lisa began pairing people off. "Lena and Charlie." She handed them a sheet of paper with questions to ask each other. They were encouraged to go somewhere and talk without observation.

Charlie drove them to the meadow near the lake. They small-talked about her car, how the observers had her windshield fixed for her. He couldn't stop glancing at her wrist.

"You should make sure to come here in August," Charlie said as he parked. "It's one of the prettiest places in Lakewood then. There are these tiny flowers. Purple and red. And you can eat them."

"How do they taste?"

"Like flowers."

They walked through the tall grass until they could see Long Lake and the woods bordering it. Although it was May, Lena could see some patches of purple flowers where the grass was shorter. Two squirrels were chasing each other through the meadow, up a large tree, back down, around the brown city-provided recycling bin. Chattering at each other in a way Lena thought could only mean If I get my paws on you, I'm going to waste you.

Lena and Charlie sat down and looked at the sheet. There were at least 50 bullet-pointed questions, the text small and close together.

"This is like speed-dating." Lena ran her finger along the

question WHAT THREE ITEMS WOULD YOU BRING TO A DESERT ISLAND?

Charlie tore some grass out, rubbed it between his fingers, let it flutter down to rest on his knees. "Miss Lena Johnson, if you could have a famous singer sing to you, who would you choose? Why?"

"I hate the idea of someone singing to me," Lena said. "Just thinking about it gives me a somebody-stepped-on-my-grave feeling."

"Isn't there a special word for that feeling?"

"Probably not in English. English has no special words."

"Why does singing make you think about death?"

"Someone looking in my eyes while singing doesn't make me feel like dying. It makes me feel so embarrassed that I long for death."

They paused. Charlie stared out in the distance. Lena looked again at the sheet. "These questions are stupid."

"Maybe they're stupid on purpose. I read once that army training officers are real assholes to give their cadets a common enemy. People do things better, like each other better, when they have something to fight against."

"I doubt they want us united against them."

Sunlight peeked out between white clouds passing overhead. Every negative feeling Lena felt over the past few days festered. It might make her feel better to vent about the cabin, her wrist, to tell someone about the video. Or how it pissed her off that her mother could text for hours with someone else and not notice it wasn't Lena. Her mother was the one person in the world who was supposed to notice. But Lena didn't know if she could trust Charlie. And besides, they probably weren't alone.

"What was it like to grow up here?"

"Do you mean in general? Or." Charlie gestured at himself.

In the distance, she could hear what sounded like a speedboat. Birds. Wind. Lena was still used to her neighborhood at home, and school, where it was rare not to feel like you were in a constant cloud of conversations. Sounds of people walking around, half-heard televisions.

Charlie said it was weird sometimes. People were always asking him "No, where are you really from?" They wanted to hear him say Detroit or Chicago or out East; they didn't believe he could be born in Lakewood. Or sometimes they said, "Oh. No wonder you talk so white." "And that was the, you know"—he made his fingers into quotation marks—"the not racist people." As he spoke, Lena considered apologizing to him. She hadn't thought he would interpret the question as "What do you, fellow black person, feel about this mostly white place?" She had been more interested in what it was like to realize your childhood hometown hosted a secret government operation. But as he continued talking about how his family in Chicago couldn't resist saying how light he was, how mixed, how he was basically white, how one uncle kept saying it was better for him in the long run to look that way, Lena could hear the relief in his voice. As Charlie spoke, his eyes focused on Long Lake. He ignored all her attempts at trying to make eye contact. She could tell it was maybe the first time he had ever spoken about this.

"In high school," Lena said, "people were always teasing me about how I talked. This group of kids would call me Your Majesty, the Queen."

Lena's grandma used to say the difference between us and them is they try as hard as possible to never think about us, and we have to think about them all the time. Tanya said the way to build strength in knowing who you are is to understand and acknowledge all parts of yourself. When Lena was feeling petty, she thought it was easy for Tanya to say that because she had rich lawyer parents who, yeah, were black. But she got to go home to a big house, secure they would always have nice things. It sounded like something she had read on social media. In a big-box store it would be reduced to a sign that read CHERISH YOU!

"Like the Queen of England?" Charlie asked.

Deziree said there were good and bad people of all races. And really, maybe you shouldn't trust anybody completely until they proved they were going to treat you right.

"Yeah. At first, I thought they were flattering me in a weird way. Then I realized it was because they thought I talked and acted like an old white lady."

"What does the queen sound like?"

Lena ran her hand along the grass. The clouds were gathering, darkening. Rain was coming. "Like Harry Potter, I guess. Prissy."

He laughed. "Harry Potter is not prissy."

"He talks like he pours champagne on his cereal."

Charlie laughed harder. When he stopped, he finally made eye contact. "Am I being weird?"

The only places in Lakewood where Lena regularly saw people who weren't white was at work and when she went to the one Chinese restaurant in town. In the grocery store filled with people, it was sometimes uncomfortable to look around and realize no one at all looked like her. How had Charlie done this his entire life?

"No." She told him one thing she noticed is how obsessed with control most people are. Like those kids at her school. They wanted to think their way of being black was better than her way of being black. While that's not racist, she thought it was tied into it. As long as we can be thought of as static, Lena said, as all the same, we're never going to be just people.

Lena took a long look over at Charlie. He seemed relaxed, thoughtful. "Charlie," she said softly, making sure her voice didn't carry, "don't you think it's really fucking weird all the observers are white?"

He opened his mouth, shut it. Charlie turned and looked around. She knew as he did it that whatever he was going to say would be dishonest. Charlie sat up straight. "Does that cloud over there look like an octopus to you?" He pointed. She looked toward the cloud. Beneath it was a solitary woman standing by the lake.

"Only if I squint. It looks more like one of those big cactuses to me."

Charlie told her one of the most interesting things about Lakewood: It's one of the few rural areas in the state that has a legacy of black land ownership. He spoke to her in a teacher's slow, easy rhythm while keeping his eyes on the woman. His dad was related to one of those families. He came to visit, met Charlie's mom, and ended up building a life here.

The wind was picking up. Lena didn't like being aware of it and its different moods. She missed city sounds, the bass leaking out of some bro's car, sirens at night, dogs barking at each other as they passed on the sidewalk, wheels on the road. Lena plucked out a long blade of grass and twirled it between her thumb and forefinger.

"We should head back."

When they returned to the office, they were separated. Dr. Lisa told everyone to write down a description of an object and put it in a sealed envelope. They had two minutes to describe a location. Then 20 seconds to write down a color. In a completely skeptical voice, Dr. Lisa told them to inhabit a double consciousness.

Keep your brain as open as possible to the other person. Let your thoughts find a mutual place, like tuning in to the same radio station. Don't overthink it. When you're tuned in, listen to the static of your own thoughts, but also the bursts you might be receiving from your conversation partner.

Lena kept turning to look at Charlie from across the room, as if it might help them to synch. His hair was cropped short and it emphasized how small his ears were for such a big head. A grass stain was on the right shoulder of his white dress shirt. No thoughts came to her that seemed obviously from someone else. She imagined instead that Dr. Lisa was going to show every-one their answers. Everyone else, including Charlie, would have read each other's minds perfectly, somehow connected.

Maybe the government was creating a vast psychic network they would use to monitor the globe. And they were doing it by using a questionnaire that seemed better suited to a Find Your Good Christian Spouse website.

Dr. Lisa handed Charlie's envelopes to Lena. She said the envelopes were not to be opened, but Lena could hold them and respond to what Charlie had written. "Write down how you think he responded." For the first, she wrote Bacon cheese-burger, good bun, no tomatoes, extra fries at the bottom of the bag. Lena pushed her fingers against the second envelope. Looked again at Charlie. His ears might be smaller than hers, despite him being so much bigger than her. She scrawled This dumb office. Scratched out dumb, scribbled over the scratches to make it impossible to read. For the last one, Lena wrote Coral (pink-orange, not pink-red).

When the exercise was complete and Dr. Lisa had read everyone's responses, Lena expected her to make some grand announcement: Some of you have achieved perfect sync. But in-stead she gathered her clipboards, the envelopes, her laptop, and slid them into her tote. She kept checking her cell phone as if she had somewhere important to be. She took off the pullover she was wearing to reveal a T-shirt covered in a print of pink and yellow ponies galloping. Tied her hair back and told them all to have a good night. She looked like a cool mom. Lena imagined her sitting across the dinner table from two kids, asking them, in the exact same tone she used while doing hypotheticals: "On a scale of one to ten, with ten being the best school day and one being a disaster, how was your day?"

12

That night, sitting alone again in her apartment, Lena started a new list, titled it "You're an Adult." She wanted to learn how to cook more, take better care of her car to save money, better understand the insurance paperwork she was getting sent about her mother's care.

She showed it to Charlie the next morning, Day 14, in the break room. He went through the list and starred all the things he could help her learn. They worked on that instead of the six-month job performance plan they were given in their folders. That night, he went to her apartment and showed her how to change the tires on her car. It was impossible for her to do it wearing her cast, but she wrote down all the steps.

As he worked on the tires, Charlie told her which people he knew in town were super-racist, as if she would go up to people and get their first and last names before they said or did something awful. He thought the best thing to do when around those people was to smile, be on your most polite behavior, and never make direct eye contact. Lena knew all that already, but it was kind of Charlie to try to give her advice.

There was dirt under his fingernails from changing the tire, sweat on his forehead.

She didn't tell him these were things she'd known her entire life. Or, just on the being-a-woman level, Lena made sure to almost always wear headphones when she was alone in public. Almost every time she walked or ran, a car or pickup truck would drive by with a Confederate flag bumper sticker or front plate. She would force herself to smile as if her favorite song was playing, and nothing they could do or yell would make her unhappy. Or how she kept the music loud enough so when people did try to yell slurs or sex stuff out their car windows, it was all distant. Charlie wiped his hands on a rag. Lena could tell he didn't mean to be condescending—he wanted to feel like family.

The next morning, Bethany walked into the office clutching her chin and massaging her cheeks. Her face was swollen. She said nothing, which didn't seem like her. Bethany loved to chitchat. She never slipped in and went directly to her desk; she liked to act like the mayor of the office. Going back and forth, greeting everyone as if it hadn't been only less than a day since they'd last seen each other. Charlie and Lena exchanged looks. Mouthed at each other a conversation about whether they should, or could, ask if she was okay. Instead of logging into her computer, Bethany sat at her desk. She stared at her STRESSED IS JUST DESSERTS SPELLED BACKWARD! poster as if there was something deep and wonderful that she could learn from the motto or the cake illustration.

Day 15: You are told by Charlie (the manager) that you will be doing online leadership courses given by corporate. Someone is stealing Bethany's (the receptionist) yogurt and she is fed up. The water continues to taste weird and everyone is annoyed that Bethany has forgotten to order a water cooler. Lena showed Charlie her sheet and whispered, "Maybe she's really into the idea of being fed up that someone ate her yogurt."

"Maybe," Charlie replied. "She's probably getting divorced. That seems like a my-romantic-life-is-a-mess face, not a someone-ate-my-fucking-yogurt face."

They both turned to Mariah as if she were a real human resources person and might say something. She was watching a video of cats knocking things off desks and muttering to herself, "Nice one."

Lena went back to her desk. She tried to psych herself up to ask Bethany what was wrong. Bethany was visibly crying now. She opened her mouth. Her tongue was black as if she had swallowed printer ink. She reached in and pulled out a tooth. Whole and bloody with what looked like a vein still attached. The moment pushed Lena briefly out of her body and away from her emotions. She felt she could see everything in high definition. Bethany's blood-smeared chin. The drops of blood on the neck of the light-pink blouse she was wearing. Dark red on her fingertips. The off-white tooth. Bethany's black tongue, the vein in the center a graphite-gray. Then Lena returned to her body, sure she was going to faint. She focused on her keyboard, the gray stain on the letter "I." She took a gulp of water. Her neck and ears felt sweaty.

Charlie stood behind her. He put his hands over his eyes.

One of the observers, whom Lena thought of as Haircut, scribbled a note but didn't say anything.

Lena dug in her purse, pulled out a bottle of pain pills she was prescribed for her wrist and her tiny first-aid kit. She placed them on Bethany's desk without looking directly at her bloody chin and mouth. "Bethany, maybe you should go home."

Bethany opened her mouth and another tooth fell out. It was pointed, probably a canine.

Ian walked back in holding a bag of potato chips from the vending machine. His eyes traveled from Bethany's bloody mouth to the tooth on the ground to the tooth she was still clutching in her hand. He sat down in the closest chair. Dropped his chips. They scattered on the floor.

Charlie's voice was firm. "Please go to the hospital, Bethany." The observers, all of them, were looking at Bethany or looking at their notepads as they scribbled down everything that was happening, their mouths a thin line. One murmured, "Interesting." The sound of their pens scratching on the paper sped up as Bethany moaned in pain.

"Good data," one said, pointing at another's sheet.

"I'm fine," Bethany said, her voice muffled.

Lena wondered how Bethany could talk. The pain must have been incredible.

Tom put his head between his knees and was taking deep breaths. Lena clicked around on her screen, pretended she was working. Disgust was pressing its lips against her ears, her mouth, her neck. The tangy smell of blood and bad breath was in the air. Lena's face was hot. She refused to give in, to vomit or faint. Lena covered her mouth and nose with her hand, breathed in the hand sanitizer smell.

Bethany held seven teeth in her hand, rattled them. She stood up and walked over to Lena's desk and touched Lena's shoulder. Her fingertips were wet, and Lena shut her eyes for a moment. Bethany touched a front tooth with a finger. Pulled. It slid out. Lena smelled blood again and stale coffee. Bethany held the tooth close to Lena's face. "I never thought teeth could be warm. They feel so cool in my mouth."

Lena turned and threw up in the recycling bin near her desk.

She didn't bother to wipe her chin. "This is a fucking nightmare."

Another observer came out into the work area and walked down the aisle between the cubicles. He was pale in a way that people probably couldn't resist commenting on. His hair looked as if he had just pulled off a winter hat. It was the observer from the morning after the cabin. The hair on Lena's arms stood up. Her mouth opened, and she shut it quickly. Maybe his job was to deal with study subjects whenever they were about to have a meltdown. Taking Lena to get treated, he had spoken to her the entire time so she wouldn't think about the pain. Lena couldn't remember now what he had said, only the sound of his voice: calm, low, smooth. He brushed past her, didn't seem to notice her, and took Bethany's arm. "Let's see if we can make you feel a little better."

Dr. Lisa let everyone go home for the rest of the day. Ian celebrated a little. "Yes, long weekend," he said to himself, not noticing everyone else's uncomfortable looks.

As they pushed open the doors to the parking lot, Dr. Lisa touched Lena's shoulder and whispered, "Holy shit, that was the grossest thing I have ever seen."

Before Lena could figure out how to respond, Dr. Lisa was already in her car, swinging the door shut.

13

Lena drove to Larson & Sons, the locally owned grocery store. She had what she tried to call a case of the Sunday Nights, too anxious about the work week ahead to enjoy her time off. What if they did something to make her lose all her teeth? What if they sent her back to the cabin? She cleaned her apartment, but it was only 6:30. Texted a little with Tanya. Her 8 p.m. video-chat date with Deziree only lasted 10 minutes; she'd had unexpected dinner plans with some of the ladies on the block. Had to get back over to Miss Cassandra's for dessert and cards.

To take her mind off of everything, Lena puttered around the store, picking up containers of things like cookie butter and looking at them for a long time. Was it butter flavored like cookies? Cookies that had somehow been turned into a paste?

From the corner of her eye, she saw a man wearing a white T-shirt, a baggy jean jacket, and a backward blue baseball cap. He wasn't pretending to look at the soups at the aisle's end. Face and body were turned toward her. He was sizing her up, carefully watching her hands. He had a blond mustache, no beard, eyes that were maybe blue. His face was red, as if he had been rubbing it in frustration, or maybe as if he'd been drinking before coming to the grocery store.

Lena turned away and left the aisle. She grabbed a basket and went to the produce aisle. Tomatoes, olives from the salad bar, fresh parsley. The misting system came on and she resisted the impulse to put her hand beneath, catch some droplets. When she turned, the man was at the strawberries, his arms folded. Again, he didn't pretend not to be watching her.

Tomorrow would be her third week in Lakewood, and Lena was starting to get used to someone watching her. But here she was aware, if he wanted to, he could easily pick her up. No one knew where she was. Her car was parked at the back of the grocery store parking lot. beneath the flickering light, probably out of the range of the security cameras. Every time she engaged with the news, there seemed to be another story about a black person getting murdered in a public place by an angry white man or a scared white man or a high-on-drugs white man. She pulled out her phone to call someone, then put it back in her pocket. It was better to be aware. And besides, what was she going to say—I have a weird feeling? And PS, I'm currently in a well-lit space, with people around.

She grabbed chicken thighs, milk, cereal, yogurt. He followed. Lena went to the aisle devoted to tampons, pads, adult diapers. He stared at the diaper display and her profile as she read the back of a tampon box. In the checkout lane, she feigned interest in the magazines—some famous people were breaking up, someone was cheating, you could be thin if you just ate soup for three weeks. The cashier was a teenaged girl; she looked mixed race, black and white.

When she was at the front of the line, Lena took a deep breath. She wanted to describe the man to the girl, ask her if he was still watching her. Instead she said, "I like your hair."

"Thank you." The cashier paused and smiled as if no one had ever said that to her before.

As Lena bagged her own groceries, she scanned the area. He was gone. As she walked to her car in the dark, Lena visualized what she would have to do if he jumped out at her or was waiting for her in her backseat. If he jumped out, she would hit him with her grocery bags, run inside the store, and call 911. If he was somehow in the backseat, she would take a picture of him, then go inside.

The car was empty. She put the groceries in the backseat and drove home in a slow, roundabout way filled with unnecessary turns in case he was following her.

Monday morning, Day 16. You jammed the printer and spent most of the morning trying to figure out how to fix it, until you gave up shortly before lunch and told Tom (IT). Spreadsheet class continues.

No one gave Lena any assignments, so she spent the morning reading about apartment design on the internet, sending herself links to DIY projects that could fill her weekends. She looked around and realized no one had been given assignments. Only two observers were around. Dr. Lisa hadn't shown up at all. Neither had Bethany. The bloodstains and teeth were gone.

Around 11:30, Lena followed Charlie into the break room to see if he knew what was going on.

He crunched on his apple. "Just because I'm 'the manager' doesn't mean I know what's going on around here."

One of the observers, Pancake Butt, came in. Coffee and what looked like purple paint was spilled on her gray shirt. She went to the sink and started dabbing at the stains.

"My weekend," Charlie said, spitting out some rogue pieces of apple as he spoke, "was super-relaxing. Yours?"

"I'm still tired." Lena opened the refrigerator, pulling out one of Bethany's cherry yogurts and tearing off the red foil. The mix of dark red and cream reminded her too much of the tooth, the vein. She stood, fixated on a cherry, getting more and more nauseated, as the observer dabbed dish soap on her shirt.

"So, you're the yogurt thief," Pancake Butt said while blotting herself with paper towels. "I'll have to put that in your file."

Lena pretended it was a funny joke.

On Day 17: You spent the day watching videos about workplace safety skills—Charlie and Mariah were out of the office. Lena spent the morning reading about TV shows and blogs about how the pros get truly good at blackjack. She tried to ignore Bethany's desk.

At one point the receptionist's desk phone rang. Lena pretended not to hear. It kept ringing. She turned around. Ian and Tom were saying to each other, "You get it."

After another ring, Lena stood up, walked over, and answered the phone. "Hello, Great Lakes Shipping Company."

She could hear the faintest sound of a voice on the other end, the sound of movement and wind, as if they were trying to talk via speakerphone while driving. On Bethany's keyboard, there was a dried drop of blood on the "G" key.

"I can't hear you," Lena said. "Can you please call back when you have better reception?"

The voice spoke again. There was a sound like someone said Lena, but it could have been "Let me." Some thunks. Then the line went dead. Lena hung up. She went to the supply closet to get cleaning spray, some paper towels. Someone tapped her on the shoulder, and she turned.

"Dr. Lisa wants to see you," said Einstein Eyebrows.

Lena climbed the stairs, holding the railing. She paused before entering the second floor. Felt her hair, made sure every curl was behaving as it should. Took a deep breath and willed her face into neutral. Dr. Lisa's door was open, and she was adding raisins to what smelled like a mug of oatmeal when Lena entered.

While stirring her oatmeal, the doctor asked, "How many teeth did Bethany lose?"

"I think nine."

"Are you sure?"

"How could I forget?" Lena scratched her hand. "It was the grossest thing I've ever seen."

The doctor handed her a survey: On a scale of 0–10, how disgusted did you feel when Subject B lost her teeth? How frightened—on a scale of 0–10—were you when this happened? On a scale of 1–10, how much did it make you want to leave the studies? If this same thing happened to you, would you leave Lakewood, yes or no? Have you lost trust in these studies, yes or no? Lena was glad they did this one on paper—it was easier to lie. Of course, she hadn't thought at all about leaving. No way did she distrust them!

"How is Bethany?" Lena asked after returning the survey.

Dr. Lisa ate a spoonful of her oatmeal. "You should get back downstairs."

On her way home from work, Lena called Deziree. Her mother was in a wonderful mood. She talked about how well she felt: going to yoga twice a week, no migraines, she hadn't called off work in two weeks. "I've even gained some weight," Deziree said.

"That's great." When her mother was very sick, it was hard to keep her eating, keep her hydrated. She was so thin sometimes people who didn't know her stopped and said, "I'll pray for your health."

"Lena, I went to a mall." The music, the smells of perfume and fast food and cleaning products, the dry air, kids having tantrums were all proven migraine triggers. Going to a mall for her mother had once been as unlikely as her going to the moon. Her mother's voice was light, happy. She needed her cane occasionally still but hadn't had any days where she needed to be in her chair.

"And maybe this is heading toward bragging, but I can concentrate better now."

There was an ugliness in Lena that made her angry when she heard this. All her life she had wanted a healthy mom, one like all her friends'. Someone who didn't need her to take care of things or to be extra-quiet or to be comfortable making dinners, getting a job as soon as she could to help pay the bills, to clean. And now, when she no longer needed a mother, when she was no longer there to experience her, Deziree was the person she had wanted for so long. And the only way it could continue was for Lena to be hours away, to keep risking herself. She was so emotional that she pulled over into a gas station.

"Lena, I—" Her mom swallowed. "Thank you. The health insurance is."

All the ugly feelings evaporated, replaced with embarrassment for feeling that way and a small, uncomfortable joy at being able to give her mother something she needed.

"Mom, I love you. I would do anything for you. You know that, right?"

"Get me some of that Disarono water," a woman yelled. "My water tastes bad."

A young man was pumping his gas with an unlit cigarette tucked between his lips. His dog was watching. Its eager expression, the way it wagged its tail, seemed as if he was encouraging the man to light it. The dog wanted to watch the gas station burn, film the carnage. Lena understood maybe she was just projecting and the dog was just being a dog.

"Mom? Are you there?"

After a few more moments of silence, Lena hung up. She leaned back in the driver's seat, tilted her head up. The fabric on her car's ceiling was puffy and shredded from age and humidity.

The next morning, Charlie gave Lena a ride to work. His eyes were glassy. As Lena got into the car she automatically offered to drive.

"No, I'm good," he said.

"Where were you yesterday?" Lena asked.

He turned on the radio.

"Did you do anything cool?"

He turned the radio up a little louder. The song was a country song about dreaming each other's dreams, holding each other's heart, big sky, cute dogs, our little farm. She asked him one more time. He turned up the radio a notch louder. She opened her window. The day was warm and the air felt nice. If they drove around like this for another hour or two, Lena thought she could learn to like country music.

When they reached the office, Charlie got out of the car quickly and walked five paces in front of her. On the back of his arms were five bruises. Perfect circles about an inch apart.

Day 18: You find that someone has left the microwave filthy, but you don't say anything. You leave it and eat your cold lunch. You accept some deliveries and help do inventory with Ian.

At 10, Lena sent Charlie an email that said only "I'm sorry." She didn't mean it and it annoyed her to give in, but she couldn't handle the silent treatment any longer. Five minutes later, Charlie came over and offered to buy her a snack out of the vending machine.

In the hallway, he pointed to the drawing of a lamp smoking a cigarette on her cast. "Who did that? It's weird."

"I think it's more weird that they gave me a cast."

"Isn't it weirder? Not more weird."

If they hadn't just made up, Lena would've rolled her eyes.

Charlie jingled the quarters in his palm. "I hate that lamp."

"For your information, I plan on getting it as a tattoo. Across my entire back. Huge. Full fuckin' color."

"Sure." Charlie closed his eyes, as if the overhead lights were too bright. He rubbed his forehead.

"Headache?"

"A little."

His eyes were on her cast again. She had drawn a bunch of anthropomorphic grapes on it eating smaller, non-anthropomorphic grapes. "You have a future at *The New Yorker*," Ian had said when he noticed Lena drawing it. "Just caption it something like 'Working hard or hardly working.'" Some of her coworkers had signed it or written customary Get Well Soons. She asked a few of the observers if they wanted to sign. One laughed and said, "Oh, Lena."

"Charlie?"

He turned to the vending machine and bought pretzels without asking Lena what she wanted.

"Is everything okay?"

Charlie handed her the pretzels. He hunched his shoulders. His eyes were bloodshot. "I was visiting my grandparents."

"What?" Lena checked around, sure there was an observer she had missed.

"My grandparents are getting older and they missed me. You know how it is." He leaned forward and whispered, "Stop trying to get me in trouble."

"I'm not. I just thought."

"Come on, Lena."

She rubbed her forehead. Couldn't think of what to say that would de-escalate the situation.

"I don't know where I was," Charlie said. "I was at my grandparents' house, but I know I was also somewhere else at the same time."

"I don't understand what's going on here," Lena said.

Ian and Dr. Lisa walked into the hallway.

Dr. Lisa was saying, "My favorite queen is the one who sometimes dresses like a combination of a sexy-cat Halloween costume and an anime character."

"I didn't realize you were so campy," Ian said. They laughed.

Charlie shook his head at Lena and headed back to his desk.

14

Day 25+: You were asked to work overtime on a Saturday to coordinate a delayed shipment.

Lena put in eye drops that burned and smelled like rubbing alcohol and old plastic. Haircut set a timer and told Lena she had to keep her eyes shut for five minutes. When the alarm went off, Lena opened her eyes. Winced against the light. The observer held out a mirror, smiling. Lena's eyes were blue.

"I look supernatural."

"Well, write that down," Haircut said, passing her the sheet.

On a scale of 0–10, 0 being not at all and 10 being excruciating, how much do your eyes hurt? Are you experiencing any burning or stinging? How do you think you look? Be specific. With 10 being most attractive, how would you rate your appearance on an average day? Looking in the mirror now—same 1–10 scale—how do you rate your attractiveness? After looking at the mirror for an additional five minutes, how would you rate your appearance now?

"Are my eyes going to be like this forever?" Lena asked while giving her comfort level a 6.

"Put it on the page."

As she stared more and more, Lena liked how the blue looked so bright against her brown skin. She looked like someone who would be in a magazine, maybe, wearing a big gown, looking a thousand feet tall, incredible shoes on her feet. When she returned the form, Haircut drove her to a bar in the city 40 minutes away.

As she sat alone at the bar, sipping a Dark & Stormy, people couldn't resist talking to her. A black man who looked slightly older than Deziree started calling her Miss Twilight. He told her that he used to be an artist, liked to paint girls like her when he was a young man, before his wife. You, Miss Twilight. He shook his head. A drunk Korean woman did a double take when she noticed Lena's eyes and said loud enough for everyone to hear, "Toni Morrison would be ashamed of you."

Two white guys close to her age kept offering her drinks and asking when her friends were coming. Their frat was having a party. Flip cup, beer pong, shots. They said it as if there weren't a million parties happening in the world that night with those same events. Someone sent her a drink, but she only pretended to sip it once. She was wearing jeans and a T-shirt, grubby sneakers. Some people, once they saw her face in good lighting, acted as if she were dressed in stilettos and a tight Hello-I'm-here dress. Haircut, sitting farther down the bar, was sipping a beer and filling a notebook. There were other black women in the bar, but they were clearly ignoring Lena; she was not used to that. Although, to be fair, she was not used to any of the attention.

She ordered another drink. The bar was set up so that pool blue and golden lights shone on all the top-shelf bottles. A bottle of Grey Goose was illuminated in such a way that it looked as if God was about to speak to her through it, give her some commandments to live by in this modern age. She stared at the display while contemplating how malleable her body was. A body is like outer space: The more you actively think about it, the smaller you feel, the more detached you feel from the business of living. Lena's body was constantly doing things her brain wasn't actively aware of: shedding skin, releasing eggs, waking up to inexplicable aches, pains, bruises. Blinking. She tipped her head toward Haircut. Here was a person she had given—without completely understanding what she was agreeing to—the power to make her body more unknowable. What would she do if her eyes were blue for the rest of her life?

Lena finished her drink in one big gulp, and then went to the bathroom. As she washed her hands, one of the black women was at the sink next to her. "I love your shoes," Lena said. The woman's sandals were bright red, adorned with an oversized bow that looked like it was made out of leather.

"Thanks." The woman's voice came out tight. She stayed focused on her fingers, the sink. As Lena dried her hands, the woman turned to her. "You know, you don't have to look white to look good. You should get rid of those contacts."

Before Lena could say anything, the woman wiped her hands on her jeans and walked out. It was one of those moments Lena knew she would return to over and over again, finding the right response. A return insult? A way to say this wasn't her choice without violating her NDA? Something personal and melting that would make the other woman say something like "Oh, I'm so sorry, I shouldn't have judged you. I had no idea what you were going through."

"You are going to have to work twice as hard to get the life your white friends will be able to get," her grandmother had told Lena when she was 16 and said without thinking that maybe someday she would like to be an artist. She was in an art club at school and the advisor had told her a few days ago, "I see real promise in you."

You should become a lawyer or a doctor, you're smart," her grandmother continued, "And when you're older and you have money, a house, then you can go back to art."

"Mom, that's not true," Deziree had said. They were in the living room. Lena's homework was spread on the coffee table. Deziree had been lying on the couch, a hot washcloth over her eyes. Miss Toni had been in her chair, flipping through the newspaper.

"How am I lying?"

Deziree sat up, the washcloth falling into her lap. "Just because you work hard doesn't mean anything will work out for you. There are people busting their asses at all kind of jobs just to make minimum wage."

Miss Toni had lifted her eyebrows the way she did every time Deziree swore. Lena knew before her mother was sick, there was a strict None-of-that-ugly-talk-in-my-house policy. "You know that's not what I mean."

"And if Lena works twice as hard and goes to a top law program, she might not get hired at any good law firms because she's black. Or she might get hired somewhere, but she can't do her job the way she wants because all people see is their own racism, not her."

"So, it sounds like you're saying she shouldn't try at all."

Miss Toni shook her head. Deziree crossed her arms. If either of them had been paying attention to Lena, they might have laughed. Lena was looking back and forth between them, head swerving. They rarely disagreed on the right way to raise Lena. She would do her homework, babysit for the neighbors, go to church, volunteer in church-sponsored community service. She would not date until she was 16, she would go to college, she would learn at least one other language, she would speak proper English, be courteous to her elders, would not relax her hair until she was 18, because her hair was perfect as it was, and because a doctor had seriously cautioned them all against what the exposure to chemicals like that could do to all of them.

Deziree was clearly getting angry but trying not to show it. "I'm just saying she might as well pursue a passion. If Lena loved the idea of being a doctor, I would tell her to do it. You'll always feel better if you at least like what you're doing. Lena, do you want to be a doctor?"

They turned to her. She looked down at her homework. "I don't like blood."

She didn't understand why they laughed.

Lena left the bathroom, went back into the bar, and took out her phone. She ordered another drink and snapped a picture of it. Sent it to Kelly.

When she returned to Lakewood, Lena was given another survey: How much do your eyes hurt on a scale of 0–10, with 10 being you need medical attention? Do you feel more or less attractive? Describe how you feel about your body—be specific. Do you think people found you more or less attractive with blue eyes? If you had the option, would you change your eye color to blue permanently? Do you think you have friends who would spend money to have their eye color changed? And if so, what race are the friends you're thinking of? Did you feel more or less African American with your eye color changed?

"My eyes will be brown tomorrow, right?" Lena asked while filling out the sheet.

"Don't worry, if they're still blue, you'll get a bonus."

"I would prefer to look like me."

Haircut snorted. "Yeah, over $20,000. Sure. For $20,000, I would have an operation that turned me black."

Lena's face fought between a What-the-hell? expression and an Oh-no-that-can't-be-possible expression and an I-am-too-emotionally-exhausted-to-have-a-real-conversation-with-you expression. "Okay."

When she returned home, Lena felt hyper-observant. She stared at the dishes in her sink, the cereal crusted to the red bowl. She kept looking at her reflection, catching a glimpse of the blue eyes. Tried to look at them objectively, but the more she looked, all Lena felt was distance from herself. She looked at her bank account. For the first time, she had money in savings—already almost $10,000. All her bills and her mother's bills were on autopay.

In the morning, her eyes were brown again, extra-watery. She put on sunglasses, took a walk around her neighborhood. People were walking their dogs, some were parking their cars on the way to church, others walking with a box of their Sunday donuts. Teenagers were vaping on benches and reading books with titles like *Demons and Rebellions*. Every person she saw had a look on their face as if they were trying not to laugh at an inside joke that only Lena didn't know.

Day 26: You ask Charlie (the manager) for a new headset. He says he'll have to think about it. You take an online diversity seminar administered by Mariah (HR).

Tanya texted Lena later in the day to say she was going on a date with a guy she met in a coffee shop. Lena responded with exclamation points and all the best party emojis. She waited for Tanya to tell her more: the guy's name, where they were going, what was she going to wear or buy to wear. The bubble with three dots popped up, lingered, disappeared.

Day 27–30: You're attending an event: creating your five-year path with Great Lakes Shipping Company. You meet some people in your position from other branches.

Dr. Lisa walked around the office carrying a cardboard box. She handed Lena a clear plastic bag containing bags filled with differently colored pellets: bubblegum pink, cream, sky blue. They were heavy. Lena prodded a pellet through the packaging; it felt gummier than it looked. Each bag was also labeled with a meal: breakfast, lunch, dinner. A sheet explained that she could take a maximum of five pellets per meal during the study. She was not allowed to eat any other foods unless authorized by Dr. Lisa.

During her break, Lena called Deziree to check in. Her mother was making a smoothie that a woman in her yoga class said would boost her muscle health.

"I like saying the word turmeric more than I like tasting it," Deziree said. "It's relaxing, though. I feel mellow after I have some."

Lena shifted her phone to her other ear. "You're still taking your medicine though, right?"

A blender whirred. A long pause. "Sometimes, you forget that I'm your mom."

Lena counted to 10 in her head. She cleared her throat and said, "I'll call you later. I have to go back to work."

She went to the vending machines, felt like she deserved a candy bar after that conversation. The vending machines were empty. Crooked Nose tapped her on the shoulder. "Remember, no outside food."

Lena nodded. He wrote down: "Subject LJ craved outside food after only two hours."

At her desk, she looked at the bags of pellets again. They would probably make her super-high or shed all her body hair or lose her teeth. Tinge her skin purple. Make her vagina smell like gasoline for the rest of her life. Could she go the next four days without eating? Lena pulled out one of the cream lunch pellets, worried it between her fingers. Smelled it. Like baby powder. She threw it in the trash, tossed some napkins over it so no one would notice.

At noon, Dr. Lisa told them to take a group lunch. They all grabbed a bag of cream pellets and went to the break room. Mariah's stomach complained. Lena hated hearing other people's stomachs. It made her think about intestines and stomach acid and the word duodenum, which made her think of butts dying and seeing unexpected vomit on a city sidewalk.

They sat at the long lunch table, everyone looking at their pellets. By the way they were all quiet, looking at the pellets, it was clear how much things had changed, how much they had all seen, and experienced. Week one, Lena would have popped a pellet in her mouth, no big deal.

"On the count of five," Charlie said. "Five."

Mariah shrugged. They all reached into their bags and pulled out a pellet. They counted down together. Lena winced as she popped it into her mouth. It tasted like burnt toast.

"Dirty spinach?" Charlie said, eating another.

"Kale?" Ian said.

Crooked Nose made an interested noise.

Lena rolled her three remaining pellets around in her hand. "What are you going to do if these make you pull a Bethany?"

"I guess get dentures." Charlie opened his mouth. "Everything look good?"

His tongue was coated light white, but there was no blood. All his teeth were present. A large silver filling in one of his back molars. Lena nodded.

"How much money do you think they gave Bethany as a bonus for that?" Mariah asked. She had eaten only half a pellet and was still holding the other half between her thumb and forefinger.

"I bet $2,000 per tooth," Ian said.

"It has to be higher," Lena said. "Your teeth are so important."

"I'm going to guess $50,000," Tom said. He had already eaten three out of his five pellets. "Does anyone else taste tomato?"

"For that much money, I would gladly lose my teeth," Ian said. "I meant total, not per tooth."

As the rest started talking about how much money would make losing their teeth worth it and what they would do with the money—pay off loans and credit card bills and buy their mothers houses—Lena put another pellet in her mouth. She rolled it over her tongue. This one tasted like dirt. If Crooked Nose hadn't been sitting there, Lena would have said, "I think having my teeth for as long as possible is more valuable than money."

That night, she wrote Tanya a letter describing the pellets. The dinner ones had tasted like olive oil, pepper. But she was so hungry now she couldn't sleep. Lena wrote about what it was like to change her eye color. Put the letter in an envelope and addressed it, as if she might send it. Then tucked it between her box spring and the frame.

The next morning, Dr. Lisa called Lena to her office. 8 A.M.–6 P.M. was written on the whiteboard. Beneath each hour were five hot-pink sticky notes with small cursive notes on them that were too far away for Lena to read. A line graph with six different colors was secured with magnets. Dr. Lisa handed Lena a survey about the pellets, questions about how satisfied she felt within an hour, two, three, of eating the pellets. Their taste. Did she have any cravings?

Dr. Lisa started talking about her sister, how she had been in assisted living for years. Their parents had died unexpectedly within three months of each other. She stopped talking and rubbed her forehead. The sunlight coming in through the window showed that there were freckles on her cheeks, peeking through the light concealer she was wearing. The doctor was slumped over, as if her personal life was pushing her shoulders forward.

Lena looked up from the sheet. Her natural, immediate inclination was to talk about her own mom, the last month of her grandmother's illness. Form a connection. Here was someone who—as long as she wasn't lying—seemed like she understood what it was like to always have to think about someone else. Down the hall, it sounded like someone was playing a movie that featured children—the sound of laughter, screams. Lena leaned back and shut the door. She thought about how Dr. Lisa's fingers felt on her wrist. The way she had spoken about her mother, her interest not in Lena as a person, but as data: from sympathy to frustration to anger to sympathy. She forced her face blank before the doctor could look up.

"Sorry, I'm being inappropriate." Dr. Lisa cleared her throat. She sat up straight and became the person Lena knew.

After work, Lena sat alone on a bench reading a book. She was so hungry she had to get out of the house. There was an apple she had thrown in the trash, coffee grounds with some dirty paper towels over it, but it would still be so easy to get it clean. Her neck and shoulders were stiff and painful; she couldn't tell if it was from the office chairs or from repressing emotions, pushing herself away every day from wanting to go home.

A man crossed the park and sat next to her.

"I saw the most incredible thing in the woods near Long Lake," he said, his voice high and excited. "I saw Bigfoot."

Lena kept her eyes on her book as he spoke.

"I don't mean like a big, detached human foot." He spoke so quickly. "Although that would be gross and cool too. I mean Bigfoot. His fur was so clean. Holy shit, so clean."

Lena looked up from her book and asked to see a photo. The man smiled—his teeth were straight, movie-star white. They were shocking next to his dirt-smeared cheeks. Leaves were stuck in his thick, wavy hair. He reached for his pockets, patted down his chest. Stood up, reached in his back pockets.

"No," he said. "Stay here, okay? I'll be right back." He looked around and broke into a sprint.

"Talk to you later," Lena yelled at his back. She picked up her phone and texted Tanya: People are nuts here.

By the end of the experiment, Lena was so hungry it was all she could think about. The pellets tasted like grains with no sugar, a generic nut taste, and seemed to make the hunger go away for only 30 minutes. Then her stomach would start complaining again. She had already lost seven pounds and felt like most of the weight had somehow come off her face.

"What is the point of this?" she asked Charlie, with only four more hours to go.

"To get us all bikini ready."

Lena pulled a stack of yellow sticky notes out of her desk. "I'm so hungry these look delicious."

Charlie laughed. Lena picked up one, stuffed it into her

mouth. It was a pleasure to chew on it, just to feel something different that wasn't water or pellet.

"If you swallow that," Pancake Butt said, "you'll have to start over."

"It was a joke," Lena said, the words hard to understand through the sticky note. She leaned over and spit it out. The sticky adhesive had been the best-tasting thing that had been in her mouth in days.

Day 31: You meet Judy (the receptionist). You accept deliveries throughout the day. Charlie (the manager) is still considering your earpiece request. Someone is still leaving the microwave filthy.

Dr. Lisa took the new receptionist to each person, introduced her as Judy the receptionist. She looked almost exactly like Bethany: older, white, a little thinner and taller, with blonde hair Lena knew was dyed because of the uniformity of the color.

She had brought in a plate of candied ginger scones. "They help with your digestion."

At 11 a.m., Judy stood up from the receptionist's desk. She did lunges, stretched, rolled her neck around, made sounds as if she were doing exerting exercises rather than moving her body.

At 2:15, she did it again. Then she walked over to Lena's desk. "I noticed your face looks a little dry."

"What?"

"Your face." Judy pointed. "That means you need to incorporate more oranges into your diet. Oh, and drink only sparkling water for the minerals. That one is easy because the water here tastes so weird."

Lena said she had to go take care of something. She went to the women's bathroom, sat in a stall, and read on her phone for 20 minutes.

Day 32: Judy (the receptionist) begins a Get Fit! program for the office. The person with the most steps at the end of the month wins a special prize from corporate. You are suspicious that Tom is the person leaving the microwave dirty. A truck driver flirts with you over the phone.

At 11 a.m., Judy again did her stretches, letting out a moan Lena described in her head as Oh-no, my-groin. When she was done, Judy opened her desk drawer and pulled out what looked like a grapefruit. She peeled it, and the smell filled the air. She walked over to Lena's desk, stood over her shoulder, and began talking at her. So, she was dating Charlie, right? No? That was surprising. Young people especially need love or they'll just wilt, she told Lena. And didn't Lena think Tom needed to lose 15 pounds or he was going to need a CPAP machine? You could just tell by how he sounded that he was a snorer. She paused to take a big bite of the grapefruit, gnashing it between her teeth and making a loud, wet noise that made Lena wince.

This time, Lena went to the supply closet, sat on the floor, and just stared at the piles of copy paper and the cleaning supplies.

Day 34. Judy sent everyone an email suggesting they plan a Christmas-in-July office party, though the day she had in mind was over six weeks away. When Charlie replied Sounds fun(!), the bombardment began. Email after email about Christmas dinner ideas, cheap decorations, game ideas, dress codes, playlists, guest lists, who should play Santa because, no offense, Santa should be authentic, so maybe they could all chip in and hire an actor if it was okay with the higher-ups to have an outsider in here.

After the third email with no response from anyone, Judy wandered around the office eating a grapefruit and asking people pointed questions about email etiquette.

"I wish someone would give me a pill that makes me forget

the phrase, 'Christmas in July,'" Charlie whispered as he and Lena went upstairs to the conference room. They were going to do another synching activity.

"She's made me hate Christmas," Lena said. "I hope they Bethany her."

"Whoa, harsh."

"I know. Too far."

Day 36. Lena came back from the weekend ready to engage with Christmas in July. Maybe they could make their own decorations? It could be something fun to do. A blonde woman Lena didn't recognize was putting a poster up over Bethany's old STRESSED IS JUST DESSERTS SPELLED BACKWARD! poster. This one had an illustration of five slices of chocolate cake with a cherry on top over a light-pink background. In the middle, in large red cursive, it bore the same slogan: STRESSED IS JUST DESSERTS SPELLED BACKWARD!

This woman looked like a combination of Judy and Bethany. Small, close-set green eyes. Blonde hair was cut into a long bob.

"Hi, my name is Judy," the woman said. "And you must be Lena. I'm your new neighbor."

"Hi. Did you know our last receptionist was also named Judy? Isn't that."

"No, the last receptionist here was named Bethany. Or at least that's what they said in my interview."

Lena paused. When the other woman didn't laugh or say she was joking, Lena turned to the poster. "I like this. It's cute."

This new Judy's voice was higher. She talked seriously about the poster as if they were at an art museum together: The theme was cheerfulness, perseverance, finding the joy. Her explanation grew more and more condescending, but Lena continued nodding. She imagined herself interrupting this weird lecture on the importance of understanding stress as a manageable state of mind by ripping down both versions of the poster. She took the pieces and burned them in the parking lot. This is what I call desserts, she would yell at Judy. Instead, Lena smiled and said, "Well, I've got some work to do," and went to her desk.

Day 37. Lena woke up at 3 a.m. to a text from Tanya. Are you mad at me? I'm sorry if I was an asshole about something. She continued, writing more in a rambling, misspelled way. She obviously had been drinking while she texted.

Day 39. Lena responded: Work is kicking my ass, I'm sorry.

Day 40. Lena took a walk by herself in the woods behind Great Lakes Shipping Company. Everyone else was doing an office yoga session led by Judy; Lena refused to participate. The woods were quiet, peaceful, and no one there was telling Lena how bad her balance was for someone so young.

Sitting on the path, as if it were a domesticated cat, was a raccoon. It was very clean, with a thick, full tail. The raccoon opened its mouth. "I'm dying here," it said. Its voice sounded familiar, but Lena couldn't place it. "I'm dying here," it said again.

"That's sad," Lena replied. She turned around and kept on walking.

15

L ast night, I had a dream a doctor performed wide-awake surgery on me. He pulled apricot after apricot from my abdomen and throat. When he was done, the scar on my stomach looked like a diamond bracelet. He said I had to come back every time I have an ache there or if I pee more than six times in a day; those would be signs I was growing apricots again. The doctor lifted an apricot up to me. It was perfect and un-blemished. He bit into it and it hurt me so bad. I said, That's a part of me, but he didn't care. He took another bite, juice dripped down his chin."

Dr. Lisa took notes. "What do you think that means?"

"I don't really know." Lena looked up at the ceiling. "Maybe it's insecurities about my body. Or maybe I'm worried about getting sick like my grandma. It doesn't take a genius to leap from a dream about things growing in my body to—" She paused. "Cancer." Lena still hated the word.

Dr. Lisa's hand rested on the desk between them. "I feel like you're really starting to be less guarded in these sessions."

"Thank you?" Lena said. She stopped herself from raising

her eyebrows at the implication that before she had been dishonest.

Dr. Lisa poured Lena a glass of water and set it next to her hand.

"Let's shift over to hypotheticals. Say there's an earthquake or tornado. What happens if one neighborhood is spared? Do they start thinking it was a miracle? Do they try to find the cause or just enjoy their luck?"

"I don't think I could speak for an entire neighborhood." Lena waited for the doctor to prompt her to talk about what she would do. Or to pull out more pictures. Tell me what you see. Another thought experiment. When I say "viper," you say _____. The dim light in the office made Dr. Lisa's pupils and irises indistinguishable.

"What if a friend told you all the mailmen in her neighborhood were spies. They read her mail, including the catalogs. She is sure they're keeping track of her entire life. Would you believe her?"

Lena scratched the side of her face. "Only her? And does she have a theory about why she's so special?"

"Only her."

"Does she have proof?"

"Just her word."

"I—" Lena exhaled, shook her head. "In the scenario, have I been in her neighborhood? Because maybe if I'd been there, and if there was a weird vibe, I might be more likely to believe her. But if I had never been there, I would think about nice but frank ways to talk to her about her mental health and how I wanted her to be okay."

The fingernail on Dr. Lisa's ring finger was unusually long, as if she had forgotten to cut it for over a month. She seemed unimpressed by Lena's answer. "Let's circle back. If a neighborhood has suffered a disaster—maybe a flood, maybe something that makes it much harder for them to live, whatever—how many people do you think find a new faith? And not just in Jesus, but in their government."

"I doubt I would. But I think a lot of people turn to God when things are really bad." The skin beneath Lena's cast itched. She held herself still.

"How do you think people would react if they found out the government purposefully waited to help?"

"Why would they wait? It's their job to take care of their people."

"Is it?"

"Yes." Lena shook her head. Her toes were cold from the air conditioning. "You're talking about total devastation."

"How do you think they will react?" Dr. Lisa picked up her pen and clicked it a few times.

Lena folded up. An ankle tucked beneath her butt, her arms crossed so each hand was resting on the opposite shoulder. Her lips so dry it felt as if they were withering. Dr. Lisa wrote something down. "I think people would lose faith," Lena said finally. "They would be outraged. Well, it depends on the people affected."

"Let's move on."

Lena repositioned herself, uncoiled. Arms at her sides, feet back on the ground.

"How do you think people will react when a small amount of the population can get a shot that extends their life span? You know: keeps them younger longer. Twenty years from now, seventy could be the new thirty-five for the rich. People your age could make money by regularly selling blood to help older people delay their aging."

"I would much rather sell some rich old lady my blood than doing a lot of the stuff we do here."

"Is selling your blood that much different from what you're doing here?" Dr. Lisa's reading glasses slipped down the bridge of her nose. Her pen was on the desk.

An alarm chimed on Dr. Lisa's phone like a kitchen timer going off. It sounded like the one Lena's grandma used to have, shaped like a lemon, that was always falling in the space between the refrigerator and the oven.

"No, not really." Lena cleared her throat. "Wouldn't it be better than what you're doing? You would get to just sit in a chair, probably watch TV, and get your blood drawn. And they would probably give you free sugar cookies. Juice."

Dr. Lisa laughed. She pushed her glasses up. "I think that would be a little too boring for me." She tilted her head. "What do you think we're doing here?"

"I don't know," Lena said. "Sometimes it feels like you're just torturing us." She laughed, but the doctor didn't join in.

"What do you really think?" Dr. Lisa touched Lena's forearm.

Lena jerked away. "Sorry, I'm just jumpy." Lena tried to make her body and face soft.

Dr. Lisa withdrew her hand. Her eyebrows were raised and the left corner of her mouth was turning up. She made eye contact with Lena. "This was a good session."

When Lena left the office the second-floor hallway was empty. Usually there was at least one observer writing on a clipboard. Or someone else was waiting to go into a session with Dr. Lisa. It was like being in a store and finding out you had somehow been locked in for the night.

There were eight rooms off the hallway, but Lena had only been in three: the upstairs conference room, Dr. Lisa's office, and the small room where different medical equipment was rotated in and out. She walked toward the stairwell, paused. The doctor's door was shut. Lena looked around but did not see any video cameras. It would be so easy—risky—to walk past the doors she hadn't been in. Peek inside.

It was so easy that Lena paused and considered whether the situation itself was an experiment. Will you do what we ask when you think we're not looking? On a scale of 1–10, how loyal are you? On a scale of 1–10, how curious have you been about the purpose of all this? How loyal are you now that you know more about us?

"Fuck it," Lena muttered as she walked in the direction she had never gone before. I'm looking for a bathroom, it's an emergency, I'm so sorry, she told herself once, twice, and had it ready to say in case she ran into anyone.

The first door was closed. She hovered for a moment. Inside someone was typing loudly, a person's muffled voice. Walked past the next door. Turning the corner to the right, she heard the sound of kids talking, playing. A door was open and natural light seeped out into the hallway. On the door was a picture of a group of kids, about 10. Below that posters of three different letters dressed to look like people: M wearing a top hat, A with pigtails and holding an umbrella, and a letter Lena didn't recognize, like a combination of a Z and an E.

A few of the kids were speaking English. Some others were speaking a language Lena couldn't guess. She peeked in. On the wall were more posters: a picture of an apple with the word "apple" beneath it in English, and below that, in presumably the language they were speaking. A jumble of letters and symbols. Other pictures of a dog, a violin, a slice of cake.

There were eight small desks. A larger one for an adult, with a few adult-sized chairs placed around the room. And a container filled with Legos that was big enough a kid could get completely covered in them.

A boy was standing alone in a corner, holding a soccer ball and whispering to it, "I hate you, Dad. I hate you, Dad."

Two girls were holding dolls. The dolls and the girls were wearing name tags: Madison F. and Madison T. The girls were whispering to the dolls. The girl on the left with eyes like polished brown stones looked up at Lena. She waved. Made her doll wave too.

16

Charlie turned 26 and threw a party to celebrate. His house was small—even before the party had officially started, it felt filled with the friends who had come to help push furniture against the walls or set up the bar and desserts. Lena was used to college parties: If it started at 10, you got there around 11:30 when everyone was buzzed enough to have fun. Here the party started at 8:30 and people were almost perfectly on time. A small crowd was already formed around Charlie. They were telling jokes and asking him what he was going to do during this 27th year.

A woman with curly red hair pushed through to say, "No wonder you're this way. Cancer." The woman burped and walked away. Charlie looked upset for a moment, then shrugged.

Everyone resumed talking quickly to smooth the moment away. Lena looked from talking mouth to talking mouth. She couldn't believe all these people could pretend something so weird hadn't happened. Lena pulled out her phone to text Tanya, knew Tanya would think everyone's reaction was just as weird as the thing the girl had said. One of the pleasures of going to parties with Tanya was they equally enjoyed people-watching. They could spend hours afterward talking about the way a girl danced using her scarf as a prop, the guy who was trying so hard to be deep, the couple who were obviously fighting but thought they were being convincingly in love. Lena overheard the red-headed woman saying, "Well, it could be worse. He could be a Virgo. Nothing is worse than a Virgo man."

Lena put her phone in her pocket. She didn't want to spend the rest of the night worrying about whether or not Tanya would text her.

The doorbell rang. It was Charlie's parents stopping by with a cake from the grocery store. The royal-blue cake frosting read HBD FROM DINOSAUR LORD!!! A toy raptor wearing armor and a black coat was sitting on the cake next to the message.

"Someone somehow got your cake," Charlie's dad said. He kept looking at Charlie, the cake, his wife, the people gathered around to celebrate. He touched the side of Charlie's head, his shoulder, and said, "I'm so proud of you."

Lena felt emotional watching Charlie's dad's reactions and went to get another drink.

"God, Charlie better hope he ages like his dad," a woman was saying.

"Black don't crack," another white woman said with a pleased look on her face.

Lena spoke a little to Mr. and Mrs. Graham. They were very polite and they, too, said, The longer you're here, the easier it gets. When Lena walked away to get a beer, she overheard some of Charlie's friends talking about how formal his parents were. It's forever middle school with Josie and Andre. They acted like it was a bad thing, but Lena thought it was nice. A woman handed Lena a shot. It tasted like watery coffee and grain alcohol. "We're calling it a Charlie," the woman yelled in Lena's ear.

"Rude," Lena said, but the woman didn't hear her.

Mariah grabbed Lena's arm and told her a person's soul is completely formed by the time they turn 24. She was drinking a cup of tea out of a mug. "I don't mean someone can't change." She blew at the steam. "But all the margins for change are fully formed."

Lena had no idea what that meant. "Cool."

"You have so much soul-growing left. I'm jealous." Mariah showed Lena the long piece of cedar she was going to give Charlie as a birthday gift. A note taped to it had meditation and mindfulness instructions. A reminder that depending on what he wanted the coming year to focus on, he needed to choose between a full moon burning and a new moon burning.

"That's a lovely piece of wood," Lena said, trying to keep the disappointment out of her voice. She owed Charlie $20 now; he had bet Mariah was going to give him something to burn: sage, or a piece of wood, or an unsettling doll. Lena had said it was going to be crystals or some sort of jewelry that incorporated power stones.

Ian and his boyfriend, Mark, looked like they regretted coming, or maybe like they were pretending not to be fighting. They were huddled in a corner, whispering to each other. Ian held a small plate of cornichons and cheese cubes. It seemed like he was refusing to share them. He kept shifting the plate between his hands whenever his boyfriend reached for one. Behind them was Pancake Butt, sipping a beer.

Lena put her drink down, deciding that if an observer was here, it was better to slow down. The cake was served; it was marble, chocolate and yellow. Charlie's parents took photos of their son with his cake, then told them all to make smart choices tonight. When they were out the door, Charlie grabbed two glasses filled with the shots named after him and double-fisted them. "Now it's my birthday."

He beckoned Lena closer. A Chuck Berry song was playing, and two white kids started break-dancing to it. Their movements were so out of sync with the rhythm and mood of the song it made them seem more like they were on the verge of a medical crisis than people enjoying and responding to music.

"Lena, listen to me, your elder." Charlie's breath smelled like cheap liquor and fruit punch. "Dinosaur Lord is a defender of space and time. By day he's a man. By night he's a raptor who beats ass."

"Are you high?"

"Lena, stop ruining my birthday."

A hand touched Charlie's shoulder and he turned around.

"Don't look so nervous," Dr. Lisa said to Lena.

Charlie laughed—he seemed genuinely happy to see the doctor there. Lena looked around the crowd, noticed it wasn't just Pancake Butt. Einstein Eyebrows was handing Mariah a beer. Haircut was eating cheese and seemed to be flirting with the redheaded woman. Crooked Nose was texting someone. And the man from the woods, the man who had taken Bethany away, was sipping from a party cup and treating the dessert table with the utmost seriousness. Dr. Lisa was complimenting Charlie's home, asking if these were the original wood floors, liked the wallpaper a lot in this room.

"Finally, someone I know," Judy said. She talked at Lena about how she should dress her age. "You're only young once." Lena didn't understand how a tank top and jeans weren't age-appropriate. "Don't make that face." Judy pointed at Lena's chest. "I'm just trying to make you live your life to the fullest. Soon you'll look in the mirror." Judy made a face that looked as if she had been electrocuted, put her hands on her throat as if she were being choked. "That's how you'll feel every time you see the sags and lines. Embrace your youth!"

Lena walked away and grabbed another beer, then went out to the backyard. The party was so loud she had to go farther down the sidewalk before calling her mom to do their nightly check-in. Deziree was excited because Miss Shaunté was dating a new man. He seemed nice enough, but Miss Shaunté was unsure of him because he did not open doors for her. Lena said the times were changing; some women thought it was creepy and patronizing when men did that. A new song came on in the party and someone yelled, "Oh, hell yeah."

"People get mad about the dumbest shit now because they're too lazy to engage with the stuff that matters," Deziree said.

"I guess," Lena said in her best I-don't-feel-like-arguing tone.

"So, I'm going to go on a double date with Miss Shaunté and her new man."

"What?"

"You heard me."

"How do you feel?"

"Do you want me to talk to you like I'm your mom or your friend?"

Lena paused. If Deziree had dated anyone since Lena's child-hood, she hadn't heard about it. "Whatever you need."

"I'm scared shitless," Deziree said. "But I'm also—I don't know—part of me thought I might never have room for some-thing like this in my life. I guess I'm excited. It'll probably be awful, but still."

"I miss you."

"Is everything okay with you?"

"I wish I lived closer." Lena tipped her face up to the stars. Although the party was technically in the city, the stars were so clear.

"This morning, I realized I didn't think about her at all yesterday," Deziree said.

"Is that good or bad?"

"Both."

When her mother hung up, Lena sighed. Homesickness encouraged her to get into the car and drive home. She finished her drink. Pulled her phone out and used its camera to attempt to fix her hair and makeup. What if her mother fell in love? What if she got married? Lena wished her grandma was around for this; she was the only person who could be trusted to know whether a man was good in the right way.

Back in the party, Charlie was smoking a cigar.

"Since when do you smoke?"

"It's a present."

"Did you open the one from me?" Lena fished her box off the pile. Charlie clenched the cigar between his teeth as he pulled the wrapping paper off, trying to be careful not to rip it. It was a mug that read WORLD'S GREATEST BOSS. "Now will you get me a new headset?"

Charlie laughed and held the mug up in the air. One of his friends grabbed it from him, almost dropped it. He steadied it, then poured cheap tequila in it. "Birthday toast for the birthday boss."

"I would like to thank you all for being the best employees in the world," Charlie said. He puffed on the cigar. It smelled like an expensive recliner. Across the party, one of his friends smiled at Lena and mouthed, "Do you want to dance?" Charlie turned and said something to Lena, but she didn't hear it because she was too busy mouthing "Yes."

Sweaty and stinking of cheap beer, Lena stumbled out into the backyard. Music and laughter and conversation at just the right distance to make her feel good and not overwhelmed. She liked being able to go back and forth between the loud and the near loud, to watch the sky and touch the cooling-off grass.

"Hey," a man said.

Lena smiled automatically, then turned and saw who it was, which snapped her into sobriety.

The man from the woods pointed at her wrist. "I just wanted to say I was—I mean I am—sorry. If I said the wrong thing or if I scared you too much."

Lena dropped her beer, picked it up quickly, but it left a stain at the bottom of her jeans.

"I'm sorry again."

"It's okay. This was a buzzed spill, not a scared spill."

He shuffled his feet, looked back toward the party. Took a long drink.

"What's your name?"

He hesitated. "Call me Smith." The way he said Smith made it sound like it was something he had thought up on the spot.

"Do you want to sign my cast?"

He pulled a pen out of his pocket. Held her arm steady. He smelled like black tea. Under other circumstances, she might have thought he was flirting with her. Smith drew seven stars, a quarter moon, a speech bubble coming from the moon: "Get well, soon?"

"Why the question mark?"

"Because I've been drinking."

There was a pause. He was still standing a little too close. Lena sipped her beer and made her voice sound more drunk than she was. "What happened with Bethany was nuts."

He took a step back. His face was shadowed. He pulled at the label on his beer bottle. "I don't know who or what you're talking about."

"The older white woman. She lost a bunch of teeth. Blonde. Didn't want to leave the office, when you were leading her away. It was a fucking nightmare. Bethany."

Smith finished his drink and put the bottle on the ground. He pulled out a cigarette, lit it, and walked away.

17

Day 46. Charlie (the manager) has agreed to buy you a new Bluetooth headset. You are excited to begin corporate leadership training. Ian (Inventory) is revealed to be the person leaving the microwave disgusting. You find another bat in the warehouse.

In the conference room, Dr. Lisa read all the participants a statement about the potential risks and consequences of the experimental medication they were going to begin taking on Day 47. Permanently damaged short-term memory. Periods of confusion including times when you might struggle to differentiate between what has happened, what is happening, and dreams. Headaches, including migraines. Depression. Paranoia. Anxiety. Hearing voices. Increased sensitivity to colors.

"What does that last one mean?" Lena asked.

"Bright colors might be painful to your eyes, but some subjects appear to have greater ability to differentiate between colors."

Dr. Lisa paused and then continued. This was the fifth version of the drug and the odds of permanent health issues were lower than ever before. She attempted to joke about taking up sudoku, integrating more fish into people's diets, but it turned into more of a ramble. Some of the symptoms were similar to Deziree's: lying in bed every spring in pain, wading through migraine after migraine, getting lost in the grocery store aisles, believing for two days that Lena was a child who looked exactly like Lena, but was not her. They had never done this before: read out any possible side effects. Here, take this. Do that. And now, how are you feeling?

"That all describes me already," Judy said.

Lena kept her eyes on the table while everyone laughed. When her grandmother was diagnosed, one of the first things she did was take Lena to a lawyer, getting everything set up so Lena could make medical decisions for her and for Deziree. They talked—though Lena wanted to be doing anything else—about all the things Lena might have to do, what both of them wanted to do. Her grandmother did not want to be in a coma longer than three days, Lena was to respect her when she said she didn't want extraordinary measures taken. It was hard to know this when you were young, or if you lived a life where you weren't regularly in pain, but she would rather die in two years than live terribly for five more.

Who, Lena wondered, would take care of her, would take care of Deziree, if all these things happened?

After work, Lena went to the library. She looked up the forms for universal power of medical attorney, printed them off the internet, and filled them out for herself so Tanya could make decisions for her if the worst happened. She puttered around for a few moments. Went to look at a display of *Star Trek* serializations. Flipped through some issues of *The Lakewood Gazette*. A local family designed a corn maze to welcome aliens. An unidentified body had been discovered in the woods. An older man gathered his things from one of the computer stations and left without logging off. Lena sat down quickly at his station and searched "pellets that taste like other food." That only brought up a blog post about someone's attempts to create long-lasting jawbreakers using food oils. Apparently, it was hard to find roast-beef-flavored oils. Searching "changing eye color" brought up color contacts. It was like giving in and scratching your mosquito bites to search the internet on a probably unmonitored computer.

"How do you break an NDA and not get fined?" she typed. The definitive answer was that it's complicated and the instances would have to be extraordinary to avoid it.

Lena's favorite professor from last semester had spoken frequently about his favorite sculptor. The sculptor's partner had been very jealous, once breaking a bottle over another man's head for flirting with the sculptor. The partner would monitor the sculptor's phone, go through his letters, and rummage through his coat pockets looking for proof of other men. Why did the sculptor stay with him? Because sometimes people confuse attention with love. So, the sculptor created secret caches in all his works. He would leave notes in the unsold pieces, authorized the gallery to let his lovers touch and press gently on his sculptures' feet or stomachs. The sculptor donated a statue to a park on the other side of his town. He would walk there and leave gifts and love letters in the hollowed-out leg.

Lena remembered this because it was romantic and titillating, and because it was one of the few times when college felt the way it was supposed to feel: aspirational. People rarely wore leggings to class. No one was on their phones. The professor was clearly enjoying getting to spend part of his day talking about art and the different ways to write and think about it. Now Lena wondered how she could find a way to hide something in plain sight. To have a way to share the truth, spread it like a cold.

The weird kid in her dorm had told Lena there was a whole forum devoted to figuring out if there was a secret mercenary and assassins organization operating freely in the United States. At the library computer she searched for it, muttering an apology under her breath to the old man, who was probably going to get on a government watchlist for this one. The people on the forum believed the organization distributed all their kill commands into a website's coding via key extraneous words. Pink cupcake meant "poison the target's food." Sharp stick meant "make it look like a mugging." Some people said it was all just part of an augmented reality mini game designed to hype up the third installment in the *Killing Is My Business* video game series.

Then—her fingers twice mistyping it before it was clear—Lena typed the words US government human experimentation.

A recent news article—with the word "US" crossed out in the search—was about a recently deceased dictator's palace that housed the cremated remains of at least 25 people beneath the structure. It appeared he and his staff had been putting the ash in kale smoothies. Lena found a long quasi-medical argument about the potential nutrients in the ash. There were claims it increased longevity, reduced joint pain, and helped reduce hair loss in men.

Several nations, including the US, were being investigated for utilizing human augmentation strategies on their soldiers and world-class athletes. A new kind of amphetamine that made people engage in risky behaviors, but made them stronger, faster. New, untraceable steroids. A nanotechnology program designed to curb aging. Limb lengthening.

The US government refuted these claims. They had not engaged in unauthorized human subject experimentation since the late 1960s. And in fact, as a response to all these troubling claims, the National Institutes of Health was doing a necessary audit of all government-based programs and experiments that utilized human test subjects, to make sure they were behaving ethically, following proper procedure, and the United Nations' human rights code. Many human rights organizations refuted this claim, citing cases happening in different prison systems as examples.

Lena took out her phone. She searched the web browser for How do research studies on people work? Her phone couldn't connect to any pages. She searched cute dog video, and suddenly her phone worked again. All the world's cute dog videos were at her fingertips.

On the library computer she typed How do research studies on people work? There were so many hits—about informed consent, the proper ways to collect data, how no data could be compelled or forced. She tried one more time on her phone, checking to see if she had too many browser tabs open, but every time it went to a plain white screen.

Lena cleared the search history on the library computer, then on her phone. She went home. It had been close to two months in Lakewood now and still most of her things were packed in boxes. The only picture on the walls was the framed photograph of Lena, her mother, and her grandmother from her high school graduation. On the refrigerator was a small wall calendar. Her only big indulgence was an armchair in burnt-sugar brown wood and lagoon-blue velvet. Lena rarely sat in it because it was so nice. Everything else big, like the mattress, was theirs. The room that felt the most like hers was the bathroom because of the floral shower curtain and striped bathmat she had chosen. Her lipstick and face products in the medicine cabinet.

"I could be out of here in less than an hour," she said.

Lena did the math again in her head. If she could last four more months, she could pay off all their debts, have enough money set aside in case her mother got sick again, and have a small buffer while she found another job. If she made it a year, Lena could comfortably go back to school, pay for the last year if she needed to, take care of Deziree, and still have money left in savings. She could buy them both the best health insurance for that year. Lena put the filled-out power of attorney form in an envelope and placed it in the top drawer of her nightstand. She called her mom and asked to hear about her day.

18

Memorize the following words and phrases: pink slip, froideur, sinking. The eyes tell the brain what to devour."
Dr. Lisa cleared her throat. "Seven, wrapping paper, excursion.
In the attic, you can smell the seeds. Do whatever you need to
remember these phrases. Write them down, recite them. We're
going to ask you to repeat them throughout the day." The
doctor repeated the phrases over and over.

Lena wrote them down on the back of her Day 47 form.
In her fake life, she was taking a warehouse safety seminar. On
the long conference-room table were clear containers filled with
small gray pills. Low dosage. Minimal risk. But if you do experience a headache, confusion, disorientation, you need to tell us
as quickly as possible. You will be observed throughout the day.

"No shit," Lena mouthed to Charlie. He grinned.

Dr. Lisa's eyes were on her sheet of paper. She kept looking
up, her eyes drifting from a woman with thick black eyebrows
that made her look pissed off, to Pancake Butt, to Smith. The
paper in her hands fluttered a little; she was shaking. There was
a tension in the air that was not aimed at the study participants.

It felt like being seated at a restaurant near a couple who had obviously fought in the car but refused to take an L on that particular date.

Lena touched the side of Charlie's hand. He turned toward her and she mouthed, "What's going on?"

He shook his head slightly. Mouthed something back that looked like ice cream sandwich.

"Do you have any questions?" Dr. Lisa asked.

"How will you be able to tell the difference between me now and me under the pill's effects?" Judy laughed at her own joke.

Dr. Lisa smiled faintly and asked, "Any real questions?"

"Pink slip, froideur, sinking," Mariah whispered.

"Can I ask a question?" Lena raised her hand.

"You just did," Charlie muttered.

"If I decided to opt out of this study halfway through, what would happen?"

"You can't opt out."

Lena kept her face measured, nodded. "I have another question."

Dr. Lisa raised her eyebrows. "Shoot."

"What is froideur?"

"A word. It's not important."

"It can be used to describe a falling-out between people." Lena turned. Smith's eyes were on his clipboard. "It's like a frostiness. Being reserved. I think."

"Sure. Whatever." Dr. Lisa scratched her neck. "It's time to get started."

Lena picked up her pill, put it in her mouth, and kept it beneath her tongue. It tasted like the stuff dentists used to numb the mouth when filling a cavity. "Seven, wrapping paper, exercise."

"Excursion," Tom corrected. "Wait, no. Exercise."

"Excursion?" Ian rubbed his head.

The pill was starting to dissolve in Lena's mouth. She took her water bottle and went to the break room. Lena turned on the sink faucet and put her mouth to it. She let the water run on her cheek, opened her mouth wide. The water, like most water in Lakewood, had a tang to it. The partially dissolved pill dropped out of her mouth into the sink. The water's force pushed it down into the drain.

When she came back with a full water bottle, Lena said to Judy, "My mouth feels like it's wearing a raincoat."

"My tongue tastes like metals." Judy took the bottle from Lena's hands. Squeezed some into her mouth. It dropped onto her chin, down onto her blouse.

Ian was going through his desk drawers over and over as if he was looking for something. Charlie was flipping between a spreadsheet and what looked like his research for Fantasy Football. Mariah was singing the phrase "In the attic, you can smell the seeds" over and over in a flat tone while watching a video of someone meditating.

Lena sat down. She took all the pens out of the cup on her desk. Arranged them to look like a square, a house, an "L."

The woman Lena called Angry Eyebrows tapped her on the shoulder. "Dr. Lisa would like to see you."

The two of them walked up the stairs. Lena's sandals slapping, and asking for attention with each step. Dr. Lisa was adjusting her air-conditioning unit. "I can't get it to stop blowing directly on my face."

"Crank it to the left," said Angry Eyebrows.

"No, right," Lena said.

There were piles of folders and notebooks strewn across the doctor's desk. A photo of Dr. Lisa with kids peeked out of one. A little boy was holding a soccer ball. He was smiling and missing a front tooth. He looked so much happier here, not as if he was about to clutch the ball closer and start whispering, "I hate you, Dad."

Dr. Lisa sat down. "I used to teach kindergarten." She touched her hair as if checking to see if anything was out of place.

Lena made eye contact. "What was your favorite part of that?"

"So, I gave you some things to memorize."

"Sinking, froideur, pink slip. One of my best friends is going to be a teacher. What made you choose kindergarten over middle school?"

Dr. Lisa checked a box. Wrote a note. "And the other set?"

"Headache. Wrapping paper. Swamp."

"Do you have a headache?"

"Nope."

Dr. Lisa handed Lena a form. On a scale of 0 to 10—with 0 being complete apathy and 10 being intense focus—how much effort have you put into memorizing the words? Lena wrote 5. She peeked at Dr. Lisa. The other woman was staring into the distance, chewing on the end of her pen. Which word did you find easiest to memorize? What did you have for breakfast? Were you experiencing mouth pain? How easy was it to focus? The doctor was looking at Angry Eyebrows. What did you have for breakfast?

"Are you okay?" Lena asked while writing down the word "toast." She crossed it out and wrote cereal.

"What?"

"Never mind." Lena wrote on the form Of course, I showered.

"Sometimes I wonder if this is all a box inside a box," Dr. Lisa said.

"Nesting-doll style."

The doctor had a birthmark in her left eye. A dark asteroid orbiting the light iris. She was looking up at the ceiling. Lena followed her gaze.

"I feel the same way," Lena said. "A lot lately. I think it's why this has been so hard." She set the pen down on the table.

"You know, you really remind me so much of my best friend from college. She was tough like you. Hard to connect with. But if she loved you, like, really, really loved you, she would climb a mountain for you."

Lena smiled.

"Lately." Dr. Lisa stopped. She looked at Angry Eyebrows, the ceiling, her door.

A knock at the door. Smith poked his head in. "Is everything okay in here?"

The doctor's eyes watered. "Look over the phrases. And make sure to let me know immediately if you have a headache."

Smith lingered in the doorway, his hand near the light switch.

"We're fine," Dr. Lisa said. She pulled out a pillbox and explained that this is a slightly higher dosage. Everyone would be given different dosages from what they were given this morning. She had Lena say, "pink slip, froideur. The eyes tell the brain what to devour. In the attic, you can smell the seeds." The doctor handed Lena a small paper cup with two pills in it. "This round of pills is chewable," she said.

Lena covered the small cup with her hand. She tried to figure out how to slide one into her hand. Didn't think she could get away with palming one.

"You can't leave until we watch you take them."

She put the first pill up to her lips. It smelled like vitamins. When she chewed, it tasted terrible, as if someone had sprayed lemon-scented cleaning spray directly into her mouth. Both pills left a layer on Lena's tongue. Smith's eyes and the doctor's were on her mouth. Lena chewed with her mouth open, hoped it looked disgusting.

"This tastes like shampoo in my mouth."

Lena was taken downstairs. She sat at her desk, read an email from Judy about how to keep the microwave clean. Tried to think of the words they had told her to remember. The only one she could remember was froideur. There was a slimy feeling, radiating down from her brain to her sinuses to her esophagus. Lena gagged. Took a drink of water. She turned to Judy. "Why did you send that email?"

"You said that three minutes ago."

"Stop messing with me."

"I'm not," Judy said. She scrunched her face up as if she was smelling something disgusting.

"When did I go see Dr. Lisa?"

"That was over an hour ago."

"No, it wasn't." Lena blinked. She touched her hair and it felt like another hour passed as her fingers felt the strands, traced over the "S" and "Z" shapes her curls fell in. Judy was talking, but Lena couldn't understand the words she was saying. What did her scalp look like underneath all her hair? What if she cut it all off? Dark, thick clumps on a shiny white floor. Would it look like blood?

Judy turned back to her computer.

Lena typed an email. She browsed online, looked at her tabs. She had opened the same article about an abandoned amusement park taken over by feral cats seven times. She had replied twice to Judy's email about the microwave with a GIF of a champagne tower. Dr. Lisa said it was boxes inside of boxes. And what if that meant that she, too, was in an experiment? But what did that mean for everyone? She clicked a link to an interesting article about an amusement park.

"Did you know that Charlie has been eating my yogurt?" Judy held an empty container in front of Lena's face.

"No, I've been eating your yogurt."

"You don't like key lime." Judy smiled. It faltered. "Lena, honey. I think your dosage is too high."

"I feel like they gave me the gas. And I want to lean my head on everything." Lena laughed. It came out high and silly. She couldn't stop laughing.

She stood up. Sat down. Tried to stand again, but her legs gave out. She hit her back on the chair's seat. She tried to pull herself up, but her legs flopped and kicked. She moved her arms breaststroke style. People were yelling. Lena tried to tell them that they needed to ask her to smile, to say something complicated, to write something. People didn't just fall. Her mouth refused to do what her brain said. It spoke only in gurgles and moans.

Charlie took her hands. "Are you okay?"

Lena's head felt like someone was pushing it. She slapped at the area above it, but no one was there. Felt tears coming out of her eyes, nose, mouth, and ears. She reached for her face to wipe away the wet, but Charlie grabbed her hands and kept them still.

Dr. Lisa bent over her. Some of the observers were pushing everyone back, some were taking feverish notes.

"I need help," Lena meant to say, but it came out as "wrapping paper."

19

Dr. Lisa and Smith showed Lena a picture. A few other people wearing lab coats watched. Lena stared at the picture: four legs, a bottom, a back. The name was on the tip of her tongue.

"It's something you sit on," Smith prompted.

"Froideur," Lena tried. The word felt important.

Dr. Lisa told her to walk around the room. Lena waved her arms in big circles. "Washing machine, dude."

"That's not right," Smith said.

He asked Lena to tell him something about her childhood. She told a story about one of her childhood best friends, Saturday. She and two other kids in the neighborhood learned how to sign because they liked Saturday and because they could say whatever they wanted. But the neighborhood parents made such a big deal about Lena and her friends being "good kids" that the whole situation became awkward, made them self-conscious about signing. It strained their friendship; it made Saturday think that they did this only to feel good about themselves, not to be friends with her. When her mom found out, she said, If you're doing something good—and you're enjoying it—don't let other people spoil things for you. Try to remember this your entire life, if you can. It still took years to sort out all her feelings about how everything went down.

As Lena spoke earnestly, Dr. Lisa and Smith struggled to keep their expressions neutral. They kept glancing at each other. Lena heard her mouth saying "cheese" and knew she meant something else but couldn't find the word. They seemed to understand the story at least a little, maybe because Smith was nodding as she spoke. Her mouth said, "lipstick." She made a frustrated noise, tried to find the right word again. Her hands shook. Everyone in the room was smiling, but she understood it was because they were trying to reassure her. Lena covered her eyes. Blotted all the people out because they were making her more scared. The man in the lab coat said Lena needed to relax. He gave her a shot.

Lena woke up. Her body smelled sour, the stink rising from her mouth as if something inside her was dying. Her eyes adjusted to the low light. An observer was sitting in the chair next to her.

"You're awake?"

The observer spoke to Lena in a low, patient voice. She explained that she was going to walk Lena around the facility. That the doctors thought it was best that she kept walking and moving. She helped Lena out of the bed.

Lena's arm looped through the other woman's. She kept her face slack. She still felt sleepy, but more like herself. Before, thinking for her felt like trying to read a page that had been scribbled over in black permanent marker.

They walked out into the hallway. The walls and tile flooring were the same white. Lena blinked against the bright. At the end of the hallway, there were two large open doors. Inside one room were two large cages. In one, a cat-sized rat holding a strawberry in its paws. As they got closer, Lena could hear it slurping and enjoying the strawberry, its large mouth smacking in delight. She was sure that she was dreaming or hallucinating.

"Roscoe loves strawberries," the observer said. "I mean, subject R."

They went into the room. Lena went over to the cages to watch the large rat eat. Kept herself still. This was all happening, she told herself. Lena had no idea why this woman had her here. Her impulse was to find a way to disappear, to keep exploring, to find something to steal, to find a way to take a photo of this whole operation. But it was better to act like she was still sick, still very confused.

Lena turned. In the back of the room there was a zoo-style enclosure. Inside were two oversized fawns eating grass. They looked closer in size to ponies than deer. A cage against the wall was filled with large bats that grossed her out more than the rat.

"Roscoe, you beautiful boy," the observer whispered. She gave him more water, stroked his white head.

Along the walls next to the doors were computers on standing desks and potted plants. Some had leaves that looked as if they were made from pastrami—the new growth light pink and looking especially raw. Another plant was the color and texture of orange cat fur. Lena wanted to touch that plant, see if it felt like it looked.

"How are you feeling?" the observer asked.

Lena stared longer at the plant. The rat squeaked.

"Lena, how are you feeling?"

"Seeds," she said.

"I hope you're not too worried. I can't imagine what it would be like," the observer said in a soft voice. "Let's get you walking some more."

She helped Lena up out of the chair. Walked her to the back

of the room. The fawns were sleeping. They didn't startle as Lena and the observer moved closer.

"That's King Kai, that's Goku."

They walked back to the hallway, went into another room where the walls and ceiling were covered in grass. Thick and lush. Lights were installed in the ceiling, and in those spots the grass around them looked golden. On the floor, corn was growing. Some stalks were too big, like the animals in the next room. Others were slate gray. A woman was bent over photographing the gray corn. She turned.

"Hey, Helena," she said. "What are you doing?"

"I'm helping out T group. One of their subjects got fried again."

The woman with the camera rolled her eyes. "The shit people will do for money."

The observer—Helena—laughed, but it sounded fake.

"I hope you feel better," the woman said, turning back to the plants.

"Sausage," Lena said, making her voice slow and dreamy.

The soil beneath her feet felt warm. Lena thought a room like this would be incredible to have in a house. It was probably so expensive, and you would have to cut all the ceiling grass by hand while standing on a ladder.

"Anyway, I need to make her walk around for a while. I'll be back to help in an hour or two."

"No worries. Almost everyone's at the presentation, so we probably won't do all the cage freshening until late tonight."

Lena and the observer went out to the hallway. Lena let herself go limp, sagged a little in Helena's arms. Here, everything was so white and clean. The dirtiest thing was the soles of her feet.

"You have to keep working," the observer said. "This is the foundation for the rest of your life."

They walked past a large door where three people were showing a man in a lab coat their arms. Growing on them were lines of mushrooms, the exact color of their brown skin. They looked close in shape to the baby bellas Lena liked to use in spaghetti.

"Did it hurt when they sprouted?" the man wearing the lab coat asked. He reached out, gently touched one of the mushrooms. "Slimy," he said in a bored voice.

They walked on, the observer leading Lena to a bathroom. "Can you do this?" she asked Lena.

Lena felt the closest she did to breaking. She did not want to let this woman help her use the bathroom, but if she didn't, the woman would know she was faking it. You want to know more, Lena told herself. She let the woman help her into the largest stall. The woman took Lena's hands and guided her in pulling down the soft pants and underwear she was wearing. Then she turned and looked away while Lena peed. When it was over, the woman guided Lena's hands to the toilet paper. Lena felt nauseated by the experience but told herself it could've been so much worse. The observer helped Lena wash her hands.

"I do hope they're paying you enough for this," the woman muttered to Lena, "because they're definitely not paying me enough." Lena pulled out her phone. "You have to walk for at least ten more minutes."

Lena moaned.

"I know. But if you could remember this, you would thank me."

They went back to the hallway. Lena's feet were cold. It was harder than she expected to keep her face slack, uninterested. She was certain if this woman wasn't so sure that Lena was "fried," she would see what was right in front of her. But this woman was sure she was sick, didn't really see her as a person. She seemed only to care about doing what she had been told to do.

Where were they? It was so quiet.

No street noise, birds, or dogs. No windows. The observer and Lena paused near a room where three women were playing around with what looked like a robotic Bigfoot. One was using her laptop. Another was saying, "Now make him look at Beatrice." The robot didn't move. The third woman, presumably Beatrice, was taking what looked like a cat brush and combing the robot's chest fur. Bigfoot gazed at Lena. Its large eyes were yellow-brown. Its mouth curled down, as if it had just heard some real bummer news. Lena thought no one would believe this Bigfoot was real. He should be filthy, covered with brambles, soaked with mud, not looking like a great throw blanket. Bigfoot gazed up at the ceiling. "I think I messed up a little writing the code," said the woman working on the laptop.

The woman combing Bigfoot's hair glanced at Lena. Her hair was dyed green and she was wearing a black headband with pens clipped to it. "Fried?" she asked the observer.

"Yeah."

"Make sure to have her move her arms, too, after you do the walk."

"I feel like I'm in *Weekend at Bernie's*," the observer said.

"I've never seen that movie."

"Oh, well. It's about these two boys who try to scam."

"We don't need a recap," said the woman on the laptop.

"Oh, right. Sorry. We should keep moving anyway." The observer adjusted herself so that her right arm was around Lena's waist. Then moved Lena's left arm and dipped her head underneath it so that it was resting on Lena's shoulder. "I think this is a little better," the woman said.

They walked on. The woman opened another door and stepped into a room that looked exactly like Great Lakes Shipping Company. The combination of brand-new and terribly outdated computers. Judy's dumb STRESSED IS JUST DESSERTS SPELLED BACKWARD! poster. At what would have been Lena's desk was a copy of the photo she had at her own work desk: she and her mom laughing on their front porch. A bunch of Great Lakes Shipping Company pens in a blue-and-white Cedar Point mug. The dark spot on the ceiling all the study participants said looked suspicious, like black mold, and the observers said was just an old tile that needed to be replaced.

The observer had Lena sit in a chair. She lifted Lena's arms over and over. Took one and made it turn circles. Lena thought it felt good to let someone else gently stretch and massage her arms. She sighed.

"Soon, I promise, you can go back to bed."

The woman spoke at her about neural pathways and movement and the brain's wiring in a way that Lena couldn't really understand. When she was done with both of Lena's arms, she helped her up again.

They walked in a few circles around this replica office. The wall next to the break room was covered in neon notecards. There was a picture of each office worker, and below there appeared to be plotlines. IAN COMES OUT TO THE OFFICE. LENA THINKS ABOUT GOING BACK TO SCHOOL. MARIAH TELLS EVERYONE SHE WANTS TO CHANGE HER NAME TO GEODE. TOM FORGETS TO BACK UP A SERVER. JUDY SAYS SOMETHING RACIALLY CHARGED TO CHARLIE. CHARLIE QUESTIONS HIS FUTURE. There were many more, with big and small details. They must've been meant for their daily sheets, the things they were supposed to tell people when they were asked about work, about their days.

Lena felt distant from her body seeing the next eight months of her life spread out and annotated like that. There were notes for interactions outside of work: barbecues, a trip to the county fair, happy hours. Maybe nothing in Lakewood had been real. Maybe they had planned Charlie's party, smashed her windshield, sent the man to talk to her about Bigfoot. Maybe they were all the people she saw every day. But what was the point?

"We're doing a loop," the observer said.

Lena wanted to go back to bed. "Potato chip," she said.

"I'm sorry, but you can't eat yet."

They stopped outside a room full of people watching a movie on a big screen.

"It's still happening," the woman said to Lena.

"Should we have someone stop Madison?" a familiar voice asked.

"We can't interfere," Dr. Lisa said.

On the screen, a girl was pulling open a safe. Inside was a gun, what looked like a stack of money, and a brown box. Lena recognized her. It was one of the Madisons she had seen on the second floor. Madison didn't look at the money or the brown box, just reached for the gun. She stood still. It looked too big in her hands. She was wearing pajamas with a large whale pattern on them. Her hair was in two braids. She pointed the gun at the lamp. The curtains.

"She'll probably just put it back."

Madison walked out of the room with the gun. The camera lost her for a moment. The screen went dark, cut to many images of the house—inside and outside, from side and overhead angles. Then the back of Madison's head as she walked down the hallway, the gun visible over her shoulder. The screen cut to that view, following the girl. It was clear she knew how to walk around the house without waking up her parents. There was no sound. Madison pushed open a door.

"This might be too far," Smith said.

Dr. Lisa made a thoughtful noise, wrote something down.

"This is incredible," said the observer. She propped Lena against the wall. "You're okay."

In the room, a woman slept on her side, wearing a sleeping mask. A man, probably the girl's father, slept on his back, arms folded over his chest. It looked as if the woman was talking in her sleep. Madison kept the gun pointed at the bed. She walked to its edge, pointed it unsteadily at her mother. She squeezed the trigger once but didn't seem to get enough force behind it. Tried again, shooting her mother in the head. There was a kick. She fell back a little, hitting her arm on the nightstand. Madison's father sat up. He seemed confused. Reached out as if still in dreams, his mouth wide open as if screaming or yawning. Madison shot him too. A few people in the room gasped. Most were writing, scratching out furious notes.

Lena's mouth let out a sound. The rest she kept tamped down, though keeping all her emotions in check felt like holding in a sneeze. She would not cry. She would not put her hand over her mouth. She would not vomit, though rage and disgust were building in her throat.

Madison said something. She wiped her face, but she wasn't crying. There was spray on it. Madison put the gun on the foot of the bed and walked out.

"That was completely unnecessary," Smith said.

"We needed to know if it worked." Dr. Lisa sounded bored.

Most of the observers were looking at the screen, but a few were watching the two of them and writing notes. Dr. Lisa said, "We needed to see a full range of results from that study."

Smith stood up. Leaving behind his clipboard, he walked over to Lena and the observer. Lena opened her mouth. Shut it. Let her eyes focus on the wall behind him. "Broccoli," she said.

Smith put a hand on her cheek, peered into her eyes. She stayed focused on the wall, ignoring his gray eyes, the pale eyebrows.

"Why do you have her here?"

"She's walking."

"I." Smith sounded annoyed. "Come on, you know you shouldn't have brought her here."

"She's not going to remember anything." The woman's voice faltered. "I'm sorry."

"It's. Let's just take her back to bed."

They walked Lena through the hallways. People were talking loudly and with a lot of excitement about what had happened. It was like the end of a sporting event. People recounted the best moments—when the subject pulled the gun from the safe, when the subject shot her mother. No hesitation. Great results.

Smith said in a low tone that Lena was making excellent progress if she was already walking. She might be one hundred percent fine. He sounded relieved.

"Are you going to tell her?" the observer asked.

"She probably saw that you had this one with you," Smith said. "She's going to be pissed. It's our first round with this version."

"You're the one who told me to do the usual procedure."

"I know, but."

"I can't lose this job."

"I know," Smith said.

They helped Lena back into bed, tucked her in between the sheets, made sure her head and neck were supported by the pillow. Smith held a glass of water with a straw to her lips to see if she could drink. Lena took a small sip. Coughed.

"You're going to get better," he said.

Smith raised a hand, looked as if he wanted to touch her forehead, smooth her hair. Lena let her eyes flutter shut. She listened to Smith get settled into the chair, send the other observer away. He said she should go talk to Dr. Lisa now, apologize, and maybe it'll be okay. This subject is fried, the odds are low she'll remember anything in the morning. And the doctor is probably in a great mood right now, probably the best mood she'll be in all year. He would stay and watch Lena until the night shift came.

20

"Do you know what this is?" Dr. Lisa held up a picture of a fork.

"Fork." Lena was propped up on three pillows. Several people in lab coats were in the room, taking notes and watching Lena's face, her hands, her feet. More flash cards. CAT. STOVE. ARMCHAIR. BLENDER. They had her do math. Answer hypotheticals. They removed her cast, as if that would help her remember things. Lena's wrist felt weaker than before, but it was a relief to be able to scratch the skin underneath. Then they had Lena walk in a straight line without help. Hop on one foot, touch her nose.

"I'm not drunk, guys," Lena said, but no one laughed.

After two hours, Dr. Lisa said it was fine to stop. There was some soil in her hair, beneath her fingernails. Lena wondered what everyone in the office was doing, maybe it was like the Bethany situation and they were all having the day off.

An older man with a snow-white beard was standing with his arms crossed. He was giving Lena the kind of prolonged look that she equated with seeing someone with a smear of food on her chin or a chunk of oozy yellow sleep in the corner of her eyes and wondering if it was more or less embarrassing to say something. It was hard not to start feeling her own face, seek out the mess.

"Your last name is Johnson, right?"

She nodded.

He pursed his lips. "Did they feed you yet?"

Lena nodded again.

"Do you look like your mom or your grandma?"

"People say I look more like my grandma. But I think I have my mom's facial expressions."

The man nodded as if he knew exactly who she was talking about, not as if he was looking at her motor functions, listening to the way she spoke.

"Do you remember anything about last night?"

"I was dizzy. And I had a dream that I saw. . . ." She touched her chin. "What are those monsters? The ones that look like men, but big?"

"Centaurs?"

"Do centaurs live in mountains?"

"Oh—yetis." The man touched his beard a lot like he was unused to having it on his face.

"Yeah. That. The yeti was driving a lawn mower. I told my grandma about him and she said I was being rude. People can't help their faces."

While she spoke, the man seemed not to listen. He had a look on his face like he knew her from somewhere and was trying to figure it out. Lena waited for him to ask how often she was forgetting her words. Or if she was having muscle spasms or how strong her legs felt. She noticed that no one was interrupting, their eyes were mostly on him.

"You're close with your grandma?"

His question surprised Lena so much that her voice trailed up. "I was. She died."

The expression on his face was genuine sadness. He took a step closer to the bed. "What was she like?"

Lena adjusted herself so she was sitting completely upright. "If you don't want to talk about it, I understand."

The kindness in his voice made her exhale. She kept her eyes on his face as she spoke, ignored everyone else. "I think the thing I miss most is hearing her laugh. Though I guess that's not really about her."

"No, it tells me a lot." His eyes crinkled as he smiled. "It was nice to meet you, Lena Johnson."

He turned and walked out, pausing in the doorway to gesture at Dr. Lisa and say, "Let's talk again in fifteen."

Most of the observers began to gather their things and followed him out the door. Lena sank back into the pillows. The little girl's bare feet on the carpet. Her small hands on the gun. The way almost everyone in the room took notes, unfazed, as this girl killed her family, murdered her own life. Lena's brain kept clasping the image of the mother's head right after the shot had been fired. The sleep mask, her mouth open. Pink and scarlet and gray on eggshell walls and the charcoal pillows. Lena's eyes watered. She hoped if they noticed, they would explain that away as another side effect.

After Dr. Lisa signed off on Lena's health, Smith drove her home. He told her to get some clothes, some books. She was going to her mother's house.

"Do you need help going up the stairs?" Smith asked.

"My legs are tired, but I think I'm okay." Lena coughed.

Up in her apartment, everything was cleaner than she had left it. The carpet in her bedroom had fresh vacuum lines. All her dishes were washed. The tub and bathroom sink were sparkling. The medical power of attorney form she had filled out with a small note to Tanya had been opened.

She gathered books, checked to see if the other letters to Tanya had been found—they had not. She picked up her phone charger and some clothes. It wasn't yet 6:30 in the morning, but Lena didn't know what day it was. There are times in your life, Lena knew, where to think actively about what was happening in the moment, what had recently happened, would shatter everything. You could only focus on the small tasks, let them link together to build a chain to pull you through the day and hopefully toward the necessary distance needed to survive.

When she got in the car, there was coffee waiting in the cupholders. Smith said it was also okay if Lena wanted to sleep, not to worry about giving directions.

"You know, we don't know why people need to sleep," Smith said.

"Because we get tired?"

"It's not that simple." He took a sip of his coffee. "Sleep does so many things."

"How are we going to explain to my mom why you're there with me?"

"I'm not staying with you."

"Am I kicked out?"

"Oh, no. No. You're just getting a break. You need to recalibrate."

Fog seeped off the rivers and roads, thickening the air. One of the things that made this part of Michigan different from home was how foggy it was. The locals said it was because Lakewood was in a valley. That's why all the tornadoes avoided it too. Just the week before, Lena had heard an old man in one of the donut shops talking about how the government was learning how to control the weather now, because climate change was going to be a true crisis. His friends nodded. Lakewood was one of the test stations. No tornadoes. Blizzards miss us. You think that's all because of a valley? The hiss of tires on the road. Rubber telling pavement gossip that shouldn't be repeated.

Smith was driving fast. The car smelled of gas station coffee: burned, yet almost delicious. On the back roads, the car's headlamps did little to cut through the fog, only seemed to emphasize how thick it was.

Lena pretended this was going to be an ordinary visit. They would go to the casino if her mother felt well enough. Go to the cemetery. They would make dinner together. What if her house was being observed? What if they had done to her whatever they did to Madison? There were no guns in the house, Lena reminded herself. Small cameras that looked like smudges on the ceiling. Her mother's cell phone being used to listen in on all the conversations.

Smith drove past a car pulled over on the side of the road. Its hazard lights blinking in a 2/4 rhythm. They owned so many knives, Lena thought.

"Do you like science fiction?" Smith asked her.

"What?"

He told her that he was writing a sitcom in his free time. Aliens were planning to invade and conquer the Earth. But their plans keep getting delayed or messed up because the boss keeps telling jokes and pulling pranks, or making people mad in different ways. Stealing credit for ideas. Saying the wrong thing.

"Why wouldn't the boss just get fired?"

"Because he's the son of a big-time admiral in the alien space force. Nepotism. Sexism. And maybe the twist is they don't really want to invade Earth, but aliens need to be kept busy, so."

"Doesn't it make you sad to think aliens would have all the same problems we do?"

"That's why the joke works."

Lena leaned her head against the car window, made a show of yawning. She shut her eyes.

Smith touched her shoulder and said they were at her mother's. Despite everything, she smiled. Their little yellow house. Across the street, Miss Cassandra's hibiscuses were bright pink. Lena got out of the car. Smith popped the trunk and she pulled out her backpack. She was caught between a desire to be polite and say goodbye and the urge to run into the house and hug her mom. Lena put up her hand like a crossing guard telling someone to stop. He took it as a wave, returned it, and drove away.

Lena pulled out her keys, unlocked the front door. The house smelled different, like popcorn and violet soap. Her mother was awake; she could hear her singing loudly along to the radio in the kitchen. The living room was mostly clean, with some kicked-off shoes on the floor. A cooking magazine drooped off the couch.

"Mom."

Lena's mother dropped the coffee mug she had been holding and hugged her. They were laughing and crying and Deziree was saying, "This is the best surprise." In the flurry of hugging and emotions and I-missed-yous, Lena could see how her mother had changed. She was standing straight, her voice was clear, her eyes bright.

"Oh baby, you look rough."

"I'm getting over a virus," Lena said. "And I was feeling burned out, so."

"Let me make you breakfast. Coffee."

Her mother let go of her to pull out pancake batter, eggs, milk. The wall closest to the kitchen table had a long, forest-green streak on it. The rest of the wall was still painted cream. Color cards were taped to the wall: jade, eucalyptus, malachite, cactus,

Joshua tree, fig, sea glass, sorcerer's mist. Deziree heated butter in a pan and turned down the radio. The coffeemaker blew steam out its top. In the chair that used to be her grandma's place at the table were two shoeboxes stacked on top of each other.

"What color are you thinking?"

"I was thinking perfect chameleon."

It sounded gross, but it did look nice. A softer color. Although Lena preferred English cottage ivy.

"If you want, we can paint the kitchen while I'm here."

Her mother laughed. She was wearing a robe Lena had never seen before—floral pinks, silky—over her usual sweatpants and tank top. Deziree poured batter into the pan.

"I like your robe."

"It was a gift."

Lena pulled out plates, silverware, mugs. She went to the refrigerator, found some bacon. She fried it on the burner next to her mother. Deziree kept pausing to touch Lena—the top of her head, a squeeze of her arm or her shoulder, a small hand in the middle of her back. Home was the sounds of them cooking together, their voices harmonizing when a song they both knew and liked came on the radio, her mother's deep laugh. Lena pushed herself to be present, not to let her mind whir to why she was allowed here. Not to think, they're only letting me see my mom because it will make me want to stay in the studies. I am being manipulated. Deziree made a pancake in the shape of an "L."

After breakfast, Deziree carried the shoeboxes from the kitchen to the living room. Set them on the couch, patted the spot next to them.

"These are filled with some of Mom's papers. I think she would have wanted you to have some of them."

The top box had journals, loose sheets of paper, notes,

letters, recipes. The other box had pictures of Lena when she was young. Second grade: a peony-pink dress with a frilly white collar, no front teeth. First grade: a pair of black overalls with a long-sleeve white shirt beneath it. More pictures, more papers.

"There are other boxes in her room," Deziree said. "I'm just taking my time."

"Mom, I can do it, if it'll be easier. It's not a problem for me." It was, but she couldn't stop herself from offering.

"I like it. It's why I'm taking my time. I get to see her better. I'm not purple to let her go."

Deziree paused. "I meant yet, not purple."

"I know."

"So." Deziree leaned forward. "I have a date tonight. I can definitely cancel it."

"What? Really? The same guy?"

"Yes. Miguel." Deziree smiled as she said his name. "He's very nice."

"You should go." Lena knew she sounded polite to the point of being passive-aggressive, but her mother didn't—or didn't want to—notice.

"But."

"No, no, go."

"Okay." Deziree looked at her phone. "I've gotta get ready for physical therapy."

Lena nodded. "I'm exhausted."

She stood up, took the top box, and went to her room. Her side ached. She already felt the effort of pretending everything was fine. They hadn't said how long she was going to stay here.

In the box was a picture of Deziree from before her accident. She was 22. Cupping her belly, though there was barely anything there to cup. First picture with baby was written on the back.

Her grandma didn't have handwriting like other people's

grandmas. She was too forceful for flowery cursive. Every letter could be a sword. She wrote with a heavy, excited hand, as if everything she thought needed to be engraved on the page. Pick up coats for the charity drive. Talk to insurance. Milk, bananas, chicken thighs, spinach. Lena's English paper is due.

The next page was filled front and back: My daddy called them nights and I always thought I could come up with a better name than that. But I've been sitting in this bed for at least 10 minutes and everything I think up is worse than the last.

Nights were creatures he warned me about. In the daylight, they could disappear into the world around them. Make themselves invisible. Some would sleep. Their snores sounded like machinery in the distance. Others would take things from your house, especially if you were messy, careless. They could make themselves seem ordinary. And some seemed to fall in love with people. They couldn't stop watching them, following them around. They wanted to know everything there was about people.

When the sky started to turn navy, the nights couldn't hide themselves. Their eyes shined in darkness. White, yellow, or green. And their eyes seemed bigger. If they crouched low, they could be confused with a large cat or possum. But most were man-tall. Imagine seeing a pair of shining green eyes walking toward you in the night. My daddy would make his eyes wide when he said that part, spread his long fingers to make them look like claws. Somehow, doing this made me truly see them.

"Miss Shaunté is here," Deziree called through the door. "Be back in a few hours."

"Have fun," Lena replied, too distracted to remember that her mother was going to physical therapy. She was trying to remember if her grandma had ever told her this story. Lena could remember being in her bed, her grandma's arm around her, a stuffed toy snuggled between them—a floppy brown dog named Eddie. Her grandmother's voice was slower at bedtime than it was during the day. But it was all the times merged together.

Nights became endangered. Men were killing them. Children were throwing stones. One bold woman figured out how to set one ablaze. Daddy said they learned the only way to stay alive was to learn people's secrets. "You're a sinner: I see you gambling, drinking, chasing women. I saw you pretend not to hear your child fall." There were still some who attacked a disembodied voice and eyes that spilled out their ugliness to the world. But most people learned to ignore them. Some took it further and left out gifts, food.

My daddy said when he was a boy, the nights would still come into towns, sniffing out secrets, offerings. One day, the biggest night anyone ever saw walked into his town. It said they were gonna learn everything there was to learn in the entire world. And then they disappeared. No more offerings, no more voices whispering secrets. The only times people saw them anymore was in the evenings, when they were places they weren't supposed to be. The nights are still gathering secrets.

When I was a little girl, I took this as a truth. Every time I did something wrong, I would imagine a large pair of eyes opening wide, sucking in my badness. I would take long blades of grass, braid them into rings, and leave those by my bed as gifts for the nights. When I was older and understood a little more about the world, I thought maybe my daddy was trying to tell me something about the way people treated each other. I might be giving him too much credit now, though. He was a direct man, someone who didn't like talking about things sideways.

Lena read it again. It was like having her grandma sit next to her, cups of tea for both of them steaming in their hands.

If you hadn't been sick, if you hadn't died, Lena thought.

She didn't let herself finish. That path was filled with the thorns and snakes and loose gravel of life's deep unfairness.

She touched her grandma's handwriting. It was nice to get a glimpse of her great-grandfather. He had been a character, Miss Toni often said about him. He was one of the biggest, strongest men she had ever seen. He worked his farm, taught himself how to make the best butter around. The secret was the sweet grass he grew. It had a smell when it was wet, she used to say, like a mix of warm strawberries in the sun and freshly cut lawn.

Lena's grandparents had divorced when she was young; her grandfather was still alive but had not come to Miss Toni's funeral. What Lena knew of her father was his people were from the East. It was a phrase she loved. It made her sound as if she came from a long line of fairy-tale witches. Deziree's people were mostly from Michigan. Although with her grandmother now gone, stories about them could only be found in these boxes.

Lena put the boxes down by her bed and tucked the story carefully back in. She slid between her covers, looking up at the ceiling. A dark spider was centimetering its way across the ceiling. Outside, the neighborhood was completely awake. Cars backing out of garages. Miss Claire and Miss Cassandra loudly talking and probably power walking up and down the street. Miss Claire in her old pink tracksuit, Miss Cassandra dressed as if heading to church, in a long, conservative floral skirt. They had been doing the same rotation for the last six years. Up and down Lena's street for four blocks, one block up and over, then turn. Three blocks to the left and three blocks to the right, they knew, it was unsafe now for two older ladies on their own. In Lakewood, everyone bragged about how safe it was. People kept their doors and windows unlocked. There hadn't been a murder in 30 years.

"Are you okay?" Deziree whispered. Lena opened her eyes, rubbed them. Her mom was wearing bright-red lipstick. Her skin looked dewy.

"How long have I been sleeping?"

"All day."

"Oh shit, I'm sorry."

"Don't be. You needed the rest."

"You look great," Lena said. She sat up. Her mother was wearing black jeans and a navy-and-white-striped T-shirt that was Lena's. Her grandmother would've hated Deziree's lipstick color.

"I want to wear heels, but I know if something happens, I'll probably get hurt worse if I fall."

"Does he know?"

"He knows about almost everything. He knows that sometimes I have to use a wheelchair. But there's a difference between me saying the wrong word or having to ask him to repeat himself and, you know."

Lena nodded.

"You should fix your hair," her mother said. "Brush your teeth."

Before Lena could say she didn't think she was ready to meet Miguel, her mother had turned and headed back to her bedroom. Lena went to the bathroom, brushed her teeth. Tried to ignore the dark circles under her eyes.

In her dream, she had been on a playground. Kids had been throwing dodgeballs and plastic ponies at Lena. Every time one hit her, she died. Exploded. And then was re-formed slightly different. The kids laughed every time it happened. Didn't care when she tried to talk about the excruciating pain or tried to get them to see her as a person.

Lena moisturized her face. Tricked her hair into getting into a low side bun.

Out in the living room, her mom was excited and buzzy. She must really like him, Lena thought, and told herself to be cool. What if he was gross? What if he was too hot—so attractive as to make her uncomfortable all the time? What if he was super-young or super-old?

There was a knock at the door. Deziree opened it, and in walked Tanya, Kelly, and Stacy. They were holding bags of Chinese food, bottles of wine. "Surprise," Deziree said. All three of them were grinning.

21

It would have been easier if Lena's friends held grudges. But every time Lena apologized for how distant she had been or asked a question to catch up on the missed time, they smiled. Tanya said stop apologizing. Kelly talked about how he sent money home to his family. Said things that should have been corny, like "Family takes care of each other," that made Lena look at the ground and feel tears gathering. And Stacy was laughing and dishing out plates of food for everyone, pouring wine, telling a story about being at a recent drag show that made them all laugh and gasp. He was clearly exaggerating to make them all comfortable, but it worked.

And Lena was drinking wine, glass after glass. Tanya kept pouring. "You're on vacation."

Kelly told her, when they were alone, that he couldn't stop thinking about her. He leaned forward.

"Then why haven't you said anything?" Lena asked, spilling drops of wine on the table as she gestured with her glass.

"I was being smooth." Kelly pulled out his phone, took a picture of Lena and showed it to her. She was laughing and her eyes were half-closed. Lena's impulse was to take his phone, delete it. The photo wasn't unflattering; it was too intimate. It was a photo you took of your girlfriend, not the girl you sent pictures of sneakers or Chinatown or a sunrise.

"I look drunk," Lena said.

And then she and Tanya were laughing and talking in the living room while the boys put the food away, wiped down the kitchen. Lena noticed she was occasionally saying the wrong words: camping instead of work, list instead of missed. Tanya didn't comment on it. Lena hoped it was because of the wine, how exhausted she was. It was something that happened to people all the time.

"I might be in love." Tanya sounded embarrassed. Her lips were wine-slapped.

"You should be happy," Lena said, adding five extra A's to the word.

"I'm twenty-one. It's a year of my life and then we'll have a fight, or we'll get bored and one day it'll be embarrassing that I ever loved him."

"Do you really feel that way or do you want to feel that way?"

Tanya put her feet up on the coffee table; her toenails were painted antique gold. Her hair was flat-ironed. A small hoop earring in one ear, two diamonds in the other. She was wearing a light-gray tank top and her hot-pink lace bra kept announcing itself. Lena set her wineglass down on the floor. It felt important to take all of Tanya in, make her a real person again. I missed you and who I was around you too, Lena thought.

"I'm not sure," Tanya said.

"Why not try?"

"Well, what about you?"

"He's in California and I'm. . . ." I'm in a government-

sponsored research study that I have to keep secret. Lena cleared
her throat. "I'm in Lakewood."

"Let's play a game." Stacy plopped onto the floor next to the
couch. He took a sip out of Lena's wineglass. "If you could make
a movie about anything, what would it be?"

"I would make one, a good one, about Marian Anderson,"
Tanya said. "My dad can't stop talking about her."

"I would do one based on the life of Janet Jackson," Stacy
said. "*Rhythm Nation* era."

Kelly said he was making a movie right now for an exhibition. It involved paint, and light, and this really cool DJ he had
met. He put his legs over the side of Lena's grandma's chair. His
socks were tie-dyed, green-yellow-blue. Kelly said he was really
into textures right now. Like crushed ice. Cement.

"Stop, you're making me hate you," Stacy said, clawing at
his brother's feet.

"Don't. Touch. My. Feet." Kelly rearranged himself in the
chair, tucked his feet away.

"I think I would make a movie about . . ." Lena picked up
her wine, drank it in one long gulp "research studies in America.
Like, I would make a movie about Tuskegee, or I read about this
one in the 1950s that was about mind control. People love mind
control."

The front door swung open. Her mom was back from her
date.

"That sounds like a Chadwick Boseman movie. They make
him take LSD and he has a psychotic break. Something about
civil rights. He wears a suit."

"I would watch anything with Chadwick." Lena held her
wineglass out to Stacy. He poured more.

"It could take place in Russia now. Have you been following
the news?" Tanya said. "It's wild."

"What are y'all talking about?" Deziree kicked off her shoes. Her lipstick looked smudged.

"Research studies," Kelly said.

"Oh." Deziree frowned.

"Movies," Stacy said. "Your daughter wants to make a movie about a research study."

"I would make one." Deziree put a hand on her hip. "That's just a nice comedy. No gross stuff. A comedy with manners. No pee or poop or vomit or butt stuff. Just funny black people."

Her eyes were on Lena's face, but Lena couldn't tell what her mother was thinking. Lena raised her eyebrows to ask if she was okay. Her mother tilted her head to the left. That meant don't worry. But there was thoughtful concern on her face. Maybe Miguel had done or said something.

"Let me get you a glass of water." Deziree looked around. "Let me get you all a glass of water."

They ate more, put on a movie. Deziree excused herself, saying she had to work at the church early tomorrow.

"We'll keep it down."

Lena woke up halfway through the movie. Went to her room to get blankets, pillows. Her bag was on the floor, the contents spilled. Someone had gone through it, looking for something.

"I'm being paranoid," she whispered. No one here would go through her bag. The house was too small and loud for someone to have broken in without them hearing. Lena shook her head. Took all the bedding out to her friends. Covered Tanya's feet where she slept on the couch, gave Stacy a pillow, paused by Kelly. Looked at him in the white light from the television, his face gentle with sleep. Kelly's eyelashes were long, his lips looked—were—soft. She put a blanket on him. He took her hand, laced his fingers between hers. Lena exhaled. She relaxed, tried to focus only on his warm hand, how much bigger it was.

On the edge of everything was the terror Lena felt when she fell. She remembered the sounds her mouth made, the way her body refused to do anything she said. The girl walking into the bedroom, the way it still hurt to breathe because her body was bruised from the fall. The three seconds, bullet out of gun, bullet into mother, the spray, the sound of pens on paper. Wasn't it ridiculous, she felt, how something that had only started in May was crumbling and rearranging so much of who she was, how she was. How could almost three months be so big in proportion to 21 years? Kelly's breath became slower. Lena let go of his hand, went to her room to sleep.

Her friends left early the next morning. Alone in the house, Lena went back to her grandmother's shoeboxes. She found a photo, yellowed and square, of her grandmother as a teenager. Miss Toni was holding a book in one hand, a small handful of wildflowers in the other. Long grass obscured her knees. A tree in the background looked familiar. Her grandmother was smiling big enough that you could see the gap between her front teeth. She rarely did that. Lena's eyes kept cutting to the tree, the grass, the wildflowers. It was a guess, but Lena was almost certain her grandmother was in the meadow near Long Lake.

It wasn't impossible. Her grandmother had grown up only 30 miles away. It was probably nothing. A trip to the country to see a lake, a meadow crowned in purple clovers and the August wildflowers worth having a picnic in. Maybe she had known—or maybe they were distantly related to—someone in the area. And it was probably nothing: Lakewood was probably just a small mid-Michigan town then. A lot of churches, a lot of donuts, bad winters. Lena's hands shook as she set the photograph down.

PART 2

22

D^{ear} *Tanya,*
    Yesterday morning, my mom told me to quit my job. She said stay here, we can figure it out, we have savings now. Deziree showed me some research she had done about negotiating medical debt. There was still time, she said, for me to register for classes. We have a cushion. She didn't know how much we really have. I had only put four thousand dollars in her bank account, and I have a new, separate account that she couldn't see or access. My mom said she could try to find something real. I take calls and do appointments now in the main office. I have a system that keeps me and everyone else organized. Deziree was talking to me like I was my grandma, like I needed to be convinced. I drank some coffee, ate some fruit, found it in me to say that I liked working at Great Lakes Shipping Company, I liked living in Lakewood. My voice, bordering on content. I don't want to do it forever, but it's a good life change. And we'll be in incredible shape if I can do this for a year.

    Your job pays a lot of money, my mother said. I waited for

her to continue. I felt suddenly that she knew what I was doing in Lakewood. It was her tone. The slow way she spoke. I kept my eyes on my food because I knew to make eye contact would mean we would have to be honest. We would have to have another conversation: this pays for your pills. For the first time in over 15 years, you get to have an ordinary, boring life. I can give up a year for you to have that for forever.

But that was probably paranoia speaking. Because she said next I might never want to leave. I'll get comfortable.

I told her when she gets a full-time job, we'll talk it over again. My voice was not as kind as I meant for it to be. My phrasing was completely wrong. One of the reasons why I love my mom is every feeling is on her face. It makes me trust her. She looked ready to shake me, she looked like she understood my point.

I'm writing this back in Lakewood. I start doing studies again tomorrow. This afternoon, I had a follow-up appointment with Dr. Lisa. We did shapes, colors. I told her who the president was, what day it was, how long I've been gone. I wrote things down. We looked it over together. My handwriting looked different before—straight up and down, not leaning, less connection between letters. I had written some words down wrong. Pirple instead of purple. Brownie instead of cereal. Lint instead of drove. So, she assigned me to write in a journal every night. I decided for 20 minutes each day, I would write the boring things down for them to see. Then I would write you a letter.

You probably know this—the schools you went to were much better than mine—but when a person performs an experiment, they're supposed to have a hypothesis. Something they're attempting to prove. With Madison's experiment, the only hypothesis I can assume is: What can we do to make a child completely turn on her parents? With mine, they claimed they're testing a medication. But what does it do? It was just a pill to help us memorize words? Well, why?

Lakewood is isolated from all major highways. You have to drive 15 miles south to connect to the interstate. The closest town is 10 miles away, but it's really just a few streetlights, a party store, a bar called JJ's, and a gas station surrounded by a cluster of ranch-style homes. The roads here are redder than other places. It's mostly farmland outside of town, but there's the woods behind Great Lakes Shipping Company, a small state park six miles outside of town, and Long Lake. The water here is terrible. I've become a bottled water person when I'm home. I know it's irresponsible. And the people here are different. They're so, so mindful. I don't mean in like a meditation way. I mean, they're always aware of each other, the people around them. There's the usual Midwestern judginess, but everywhere I go I feel noticed. Some of it is the I-only-encounter-black-people-from-watching-conservative-news-stations look. But.

Could it be possible that the entire town is somehow not real? There were so many people working in the facility I was in. Is it like some sort of fucked-up Disney World? Everyone except us, the guests, were in on it. But what about Charlie, his friends? When I did a street view of Lakewood, there were the donut shops, the Methodist and Lutheran churches, the gas station where I filled up, my apartment. Maybe it wasn't that widespread.

But my phone doesn't let me search for research studies.

My apartment is still very clean. Someone had gone through my refrigerator when I was away, threw away all the rotting food. They bought me new produce, fresh milk, and eggs. A sticky note on the fridge where someone had written Welcome back! with a smiley face below it.

Do you remember that city in South America that was

in the news, maybe six months ago? They had changed their name to McDonald's. I think it was maybe in Peru. There was a crisis there after an earthquake, and someone had convinced the town's leaders that changing the name might help them get some sort of corporate sponsorship. They painted every house red and yellow. People started dressing in those colors, but some took it further: Ronald McDonalds roamed the streets. A man dressed as the cheeseburger robber guy. People were writing op-eds and blog posts about whether it could possibly be real. It seemed like a fucked-up corporate stunt. Some offensive attempt at advertising. Another theory is it was for a movie. But it was real. I think of it now as proof people are realizing governments can be absolutely worthless. The only dependable way to survive today is to put your faith in the power of other people wanting to give you money. Online fundraising. Corporations that still pretend to care what consumers think. They want to be able to say, See, look how benevolent we are, think about this instead of how we're polluting the ocean and not paying our workers enough.

At the time, I had only thought of how strange it must have been to be there, to walk down a street and see red and yellow houses next to rubble. People in bright wigs and painted-on smiles next to those suffering.

23

*D*ear *Tanya,*

I've been back a week, and every day they have me take different tests. Vocabulary, identify pictures, look at gradients and arrange them from darkest to lightest. I'm still being asked to memorize words—tuxedo, baseball bat, cinnamon—but I haven't been given additional doses of the medication. Almost everyone has been out of the office doing separate studies or taking breaks. It's quiet and has almost convinced me in its slowness that I can make it another four, another eight months.

Tom and I eat lunch together, we talk about his garden. He showed me a picture of his tomatoes—they're a fancy kind that I'd never heard of, Cherokee Purple—and they're big. Lena, he said, they're the size of both of your fists already. He had to set up special cages because of their weight. But he said the ripe ones so far have tasted like garbage. Literally, garbage. Like when you drive past a dump and the air gets in your car and your mouth and nose.

This town is cursed, I said. Tom said I sounded like a local. You would love the way they talk about this town. Whenever something is weird, something is wrong, they talk about how a great chief once lived and loved this land and cursed it for all white men. Yes, it's racist. But I've heard old white men in the donut shops using it as an explanation for why there are bad cell signals, an increasing divorce rate among young couples in the area, drugs. Why a girl was murdered here in the early 1970s. No blame on the man who did it, the father of a child the girl was babysitting. And for "the mysterious illness going around town." It sounds like a bunch of people have summer colds, some rashes, they feel weak, headaches, and it's all been conflated into one big illness. People here are wild.

Today, after work, I went running for the first time since the—I don't know what to call it—I guess the experiment. Downtown, near the courthouse steps, people were protesting something. They were holding signs and yelling. When I got close enough, I could see one sign that read STOP HUMAN RIGHTS VIOLATIONS IN THE USA. They were all wearing Sharpied shirts that read Freedom from Government Tyranny. Human rights, Human dignity, they yelled. If you're in a study, we can help you, a white man with dreadlocks yelled.

The longer I've been here, the better I've gotten at making my face a mask. I keep it polite: never react too much, especially if someone is doing or saying something that is annoying me. Whenever I'm listening to someone speak, I force myself to make my eyes a little wider. I know it makes me look younger, more innocent. And I rarely wear makeup for that reason too. Especially as a younger woman who is also a very small person, I already know most people don't think of me as a threat. But I add to it. Smile a lot. Apologize for things I don't need to acknowledge. Laugh often. And I make sure not to do that forced, giddy laugh people do that can sound too desperate. I try as hard as possible to laugh like I'm delighted. The cuter

I am, the more agreeable I appear, the less people notice how much attention I'm paying.

It's changed me. I can't just be any longer. When I was at my mom's, I noticed I was watching her, and trying to anticipate what she wanted from me. In some ways, it wasn't that much different from when I was growing up. I realize I've spent most of my life watching someone, making sure I was doing everything possible to not upset her in some way. Pushing my reactions down so I didn't add stress to the situation. Maybe that's why college was such a relief for me. It was the first sustained amount of time I could remember when I could think about me first. When I could know who I was when I had some space.

When the protester, the white man with dreadlocks, yelled the "word" study, my eyes instantly darted with fear. My mouth started to open. I looked at their faces, hoping I would recognize them on second glance. I thought they might be observers trying to see if someone would break. I had never seen these people before in my life. One of the women shoved a flyer into my hand. I kept running. Waited until I was two blocks away to stop and read it.

Written at the top of the flyer was Stop operation lightbox!!! Below it in a much smaller font was: They have been testing on us since the Cold War. This is a human rights violation. They are tricking you into making your body trash. They are rounding up the meek and turning them into murderers. The poor, the sick, the queer, the black, the small, the victims of the great credit scam, the natives, the disabled, and using them for experiments. Wake up, America!!!!!! We are eating ourselves! Go to stoplightbox.net.

Stoplightbox.net was blocked on my phone.

Below that a drawing and a comic strip featuring Uncle Sam. The drawing showed Uncle Sam eating a person, which looked like it was modeled after Goya's *Saturn Devouring His Son*. I hate that painting, but this version of it made me laugh. The comic strip had Uncle Sam hitting either a husky child or a very short man with the American flag. Progress, he yelled. Next panel, the child burst like it was a piñata. After that, Uncle Sam gathered the organs. Then he labeled them. A heart was $1776. Intestines were only $74. Skeleton, $1.50. I did not understand what was being said here or Uncle Sam's value system. On the back was an all-caps rant. I skimmed it, but the highlights were the US government is sewing the heads of dogs onto men. Women were being given pills to make them more subservient. New lab meat was being grown only for the rich, and the grocery-store meat was making everyone shorter. Facilities were all over the world.

Three of their flyers were taped to the lamppost next to me. Another flyer taped above that: IF YOU'RE A SUBJECT IN A RESEARCH STUDY, YOU CAN BE RESCUED. Around campus last semester, some kids had done—I guess I would call it an art project? A prank?—where they put up posters claiming squirrels weren't real. ALL SQUIRRELS YOU SEE ARE ROBOTS! You probably remember seeing one. The website said they were vehicles for tiny aliens from a distant galaxy. I told myself it could be the same style thing. The protesters I ran past were a little too old, though, to be doing fake internet hoaxes.

I threw my flyer on the ground and ran on to the closest donut shop. Sweaty and tired and gross, I sat in a booth, ordered a glass of water and a chocolate donut. How long have you been in research studies? a woman's voice asked. I shook my head, sure that paranoia and anxiety were making me hear things. A man said that he wasn't in them, he just was sure they were happening in this town. He had been hearing rumors for years. I know I should've left immediately. But I was too curious. I wanted to know what he meant by years.

The average person is most interested in someone who might give them attention. They would notice me if I turned my head or was obviously eavesdropping. I pulled out my phone, opened the notes section. The man said he had heard stories since he was a boy: You don't ever go to the basement of the old hospital. He said colored people were always coming and going. The woman said Colored? in an I-beg-your-pardon way. It made me like her. I always like anyone who hears something racist and can immediately react, not get caught in the processing loop of what-the-fuck-did-I-just-hear. I wanted to see who they were, so I posed and took a selfie. Took another.

The woman was wearing a black blazer and small red reading glasses. The back of the man's head was balding, a little sunburned. He could've been anyone. The woman looked like a television show's idea of a reporter: a cute white woman with dark hair that was a little messy, like she was too busy hunting down stories to get a trim.

In the past, they've always told me whether or not I was in an experiment. But when I was in the facility, I saw notecards that sketched out things we would do outside of work. Things that had happened, like Charlie's party. The woman could have easily been an actress. The whole situation could have been engineered for me to open up to her. I could see the neon-pink notecard: Lena acts as an anonymous source for a reporter, violates her NDA.

The man rambled about other things: the illness going around town, a man found dead in a car. His hands were blue. He still hadn't been identified by anyone. The protesters, huge bats in the woods, ones that looked even bigger than fox bats. He said they were an evil corporation using people as slaves for these studies. I ate my donut quickly, got frosting on my lips, crumbs stuck in the corners of my mouth. The restaurant smelled like fryer grease and sugar, nothing-special coffee. The booths still stunk from the thousands of cigarettes people had once smoked there. I thought about how we used to stay up late studying, how I would take a hit off your vape pen, and for a few minutes after each puff my thoughts would run so clear. I could figure everything out, know the right path, if I could walk and talk with you honestly for an entire night.

I hate being alone.

The only thing the man said that made me think he was on to something was the bats. So much else was wrong. I'm getting paid, I'm getting excellent health care. The splatter of blood on Madison's cheek. Mess on a wall. Her eyes blank. How much did she, her family, get paid to be in a study that made her do that? They've said I could leave.

So, this morning, I took one of the flyers in to work. I got Haircut to take me upstairs to Dr. Lisa's office. There was a new plant hanging above her desk, its leaves neon-green. She was talking to the old man I had seen before, the one who had asked me about my grandma. When they saw me in the doorway, they stopped talking. When I showed them the flyer, Dr. Lisa raised her eyebrows, but the old man laughed.

He said people say small towns are boring, then told us about how, when he was in college, someone was sure Stephen King was the Zodiac Killer. They put up flyers all over the city with how the killer's crimes lined up with things in his novels. He said the weird thing was that Stephen King didn't live there. I couldn't figure out who he was or what he was doing there. It was as if a well-liked college professor had stumbled into the observers. He had to be someone important. Dr. Lisa let the old man talk, listened to him attentively.

They asked me how this flyer made me feel. Scared, anxious, mostly, and parts of it were kind of funny but I couldn't think of the right word for that. Then I asked them what would happen to all this if people found out. They asked me what makes me think people don't already know about this, and then laughed. I wanted to ask them, Since when do you all have a sense of humor? Instead, I went back downstairs.

There was a Get Well Soon! card on my keyboard, though I had been back for so long already, and a new person in the cubicle next to mine. Taped over the STRESSED IS JUST DESSERTS SPELLED BACKWARD! poster was a new one. This one had a photo of a pineapple upside-down cake, with a bright-green background and words in all caps: STRESSED IS JUST DESSERTS SPELLED BACKWARD! I could still see the purple edge of the other poster.

The woman was probably in her fifties. Green eyes. Hair dyed a static dark blonde, so you knew it wasn't completely real. But she was short and in good shape, like the last Judy. I introduced myself and she laughed as if I was joking. Then stopped, looked concerned.

You know me, she said, I'm Judy. It was already starting again.

Throughout the morning, Judy sent me six emails. A forward about the dangerous chemicals in the food we eat. Each bite takes us one step closer to cancer. There is only so much yoga mat a girl can swallow before there are consequences. A short email written with no punctuation that told me to eat more fish, but not the salmon, because there was a disease in it. People who ate the salmon sometimes found worms growing in their arms and legs. The salmon wasn't heart-healthy, as people wanted you to believe. Sales of the salmon were funding foreign governments.

Judy linked me to an article that was on a website I had never heard of called GreatHealthVibes.net. There was a picture of a man who had to have 17 worms pulled out of his forearms and a close-up image of one of the worms. Shiny, black. I turned slightly, so I could watch her emailing me. Judy was so intent on finding all the ways to fix me. She was reading a site about drinking a special kind of ground-up grass every night before bed, muttering some of the points out loud to herself.

After the sixth email, I knocked a pencil off my desk, and as I leaned down, I checked to see which observer was watching us. But the only one in the office was Haircut. He was eating a power bar and looking at his phone. This Judy turned to me, looked at my face, pursed her lips. Her eyes on my skin tone. I could feel her noticing the puffiness of my eyelids from lack of sleep. Cut all fermented foods out of your life, she said loud enough that her voice startled Haircut and he dropped his phone. They're super death foods.

Later, Haircut handed me a pill and a glass of water. He said it would cut down the stress I was feeling. Another email from Judy popped up. It began, Per my last email that you have not bothered to respond to. I took the pill, drank the water down. I almost spit it out. The water tasted worse than I remembered.

24

Day 63: One of the warehouse employees was caught smoking a joint in the parking lot. You spent the rest of the day taking Great Lakes Shipping required online training about drug use in the workplace.

Tanya, Charlie's still not here. Every morning since I've come back, I've been worrying that sitting at his desk would be a man who kind of looked like him. The man would tell me he was Charlie. The observers would watch and see if I was willing to argue that he was not the Charlie I knew. At lunch, I stole a yogurt in his honor, and asked Mariah and Tom if they knew what was going on.

Mariah stepped on my foot, gently, said he was on vacation. Tom looked around and started talking about sourdough bread. How you had to keep it alive, like it was a goldfish. They spoke to each other with growing excitement about yeast and starters. Bread bowls. Pancakes. I ate my yogurt, hearing the message that I should just shut up, behave.

After work, I went for another run. One of the most striking things about Lakewood is how clean it is. No graffiti, no pop cans or cigarette butts lingering on the grass. The sidewalks are uncomfortably clean. No birds or dogs have dared to poop on it, not a stray piece of spat-out gum. It was hot out. The humidity and the past weeks of not-enough sleep made me heavy. As I ran, my feet argued with my brain. They kept trying to turn in. It had never taken effort like this before to get my body to obey me. My left leg was going limp, and I had to stop. I flopped on a bench. The flyers were gone. Not a scrap of hot-pink paper on any tree trunks or lampposts. I was on the verge of panicking but was telling myself over and over: my legs were just tired, it was normal, it was fine. How long does it take for lying to yourself to work? I held my sides. I walked down the street. Turned the corner and went back to the donut shop.

The biggest table in the restaurant was filled with old-timers. In the middle was the woman who might be a reporter. She was taking notes as the old men argued about Lakewood's history. They started up with the curse stuff again. One said it was from the Ojibwe. In this version of the story they had cursed the white men who had forced them off these fields. Their last acts were to pray retribution befell everyone who dared live here. There was a flurry of men interpreting each other: dead girls in streams, unusual amounts of cancer. Their fathers had grown up talking about a man with a dog's head terrorizing the woods. One said, Maybe these stories are still around because it's the only way we can talk about the consequences of the past without feeling responsible for our present actions. The rest ignored him.

I got a glass of ice water, went to an empty booth in the back. The drink was so cold it almost made my throat close. I coughed. Pressed it against my cheeks and forehead to cool down. The older waitress there brought me a chocolate donut without asking, put down a carton of skim. I remember you, she said. I smiled at her, though I knew I would have to stop coming back. She would start asking me about my life. Maybe tell people around me.

The old men had stopped talking. They and the woman were looking out the large front window. Some were half-risen out of their seats. I set my water glass down, paid, and went to see what was happening outside. Standing on the sidewalk was the man with dreadlocks who had been protesting two days ago.

His shirt was off. There was a large hole in his torso. His intestines were pink, blood was circulating, there was a yellowish thing visible, maybe his stomach or gall bladder. The top of a bone, light pink and gray. He was shouting, They did this to me, they did this to me. Stop letting them control this town.

I felt faint. My brain was split between fighting my nausea and wondering how it was possible. How did his organs not flop out? How was he alive? His intestines reminded me of hot dogs. And in most contexts, I find hot dogs disturbing. It's the way they shine, the way they look like human meat. There were more flyers at his feet. His stomach was quivering.

As I'm writing this, my fingers are shaking, my eyes are burning. The anticipation I felt that his organs would fall out onto the sidewalk, that I would see him collapse into a pile of mush or start bleeding out keeps rushing inside me.

I signed up to be in a "memory experiment." But it's been so much more than that. We were simply told it's a small town and people like to talk. The pellets. The cabin. The girl. The pills. My brain. The way they're making me doubt myself, reality. The secrecy.

It's torture.

When I got home, I texted you. I called my mom. She didn't pick up either.

25

*D*ear *Tanya,*
I'm in my apartment here after a long evening walking in the meadow with Charlie and Mariah. There were bruises on his arms and feet. He kept saying that he felt great. He showed me his arms and legs. They're completely hairless now. A pill, Charlie said. I'm so smooth.

It's a full moon. In the park, Mariah told us she was in these studies because for years she had ruined her life. Stole money from friends and family, ran up credit cards. She was addicted to Adderall, liked uppers in general. When you take enough of them, they can make your hair fall out, your teeth start to get loose, but you can get yourself to do things. I couldn't stop asking questions, I was amazed at all the things that she said those pills can do. She's making the money to pay people back. Mariah's hoping that maybe the money will help rebuild her life in the way apologies couldn't. Now I realize I was probably being super-rude, but at the time, I couldn't stop asking. She said she got into crystals, oils, the nature of it all—though these things could be expensive too—because there was so much you had to know. The fiddly details, the focus it took, gave her brain something else to focus on.

Charlie said he was doing the studies because he wanted to go back to school, but his parents couldn't help him.

We walked in the meadows, in the moonlight the flowers Charlie promised would show up in August were tiny ghosts. I asked them both if they had been tempted at all to tell someone what was going on here.

When I was growing up, my grandma said that full-moon nights are when Earth and heaven touch. Miracles are more likely to happen. You might hear or see a loved one, or God's voice. There was a feeling as we walked along that my grandma was 10 steps behind us, walking at her own speed. The pull of her made me feel distant.

Charlie ignored my question, instead tried to distract me by telling me another Lakewood myth. The old graveyard, the one near the sunflower field, was haunted by the spirits of two competitive sisters. A statuesque sister who tried to kiss you, tried to convince you that your love could bring her back, and a plain sister who would tell you jokes but say that to kiss her sister was to condemn your soul to hell.

Mariah said she had been tempted to tell her sister. They hadn't spoken in over a year and then, a few nights ago, for no good reason, her sister had called her hoping to reconnect. Mariah knew if she told her sister about Lakewood, she would get quieter and quieter. Until finally, in the small disappointed voice that Mariah hated hearing, she would say, "You're high."

Charlie cut her off. He said his grandfather had told him Long Lake wasn't carved from the same glaciers that made this valley or gave the soil its unusual composition. It was made by men in the fifties. It became the town's water supply and made visitors stop asking where the lake was.

It's hard to lie to my mom, I said.

Charlie talked about how in a town about 50 miles away, they had found the world's largest mastodon skeleton. I was getting more and more fed up as he talked. He had far less to lose than us. I doubted, as he spoke, that he would ever go to school. If Charlie made enough money this year, he would probably talk himself out of it. Find another excuse that wasn't money for never leaving this place. It was the most I had ever disliked him. I turned and walked away without saying goodbye.

I went to the tree I thought was in the photo of my grand-mother. Long grass, small flowers. The big tree cast a shadow, the blades moved with the wind, and my brain convinced me for a small gorgeous moment she was there. The moment after, when it was clearly only a tree, the shadow of its leaves in the bright-lit night, was one of the worst for me in a long time. It was as if I had lost her again. Feeling like that is why I try as much as I can to not think about her. I have understood since I was a child that life is deeply unfair. Life's meanness is nothing. I've spent years now convincing myself that although something is unfair, it can still be worthwhile. My mother is healthy. Her laugh is different now. There's no hesitation, no sourness. But this year has been a test.

I haven't been religious in a long time. The god my grandma spoke about, the god I heard about in church, never spoke to me. I don't mean that literally, like I was waiting to speak in tongues or to have him appear as a burning bush and order me around. There is no pleasure or comfort for me in the idea that an omni-potent being made a world like this one. Lately, I've been wish-ing things could be different. Having faith would mean I truly believe I could see her again.

My grandma wanted me to be a good person. I used to resent it when she told me to be a helper, to be kind. I would always wonder if I were a boy would she say the same things to me? Or would she tell me to be brave, to provide for my family, some other crap like that. She said to be brave was to be kind. I remember rolling my eyes. It felt like a social media daily affirmation. Too nice, too easy to mean anything real.

I walked back over to Charlie and Mariah when I felt less like I might start crying. They had pulled out the food we had brought to snack on. Blueberries, extra-sharp cheddar, crackers, beers. I asked them what they thought was the point of the studies, what were they truly trying to learn. Mariah said probably a lot of things. Charlie said it was a memory study. He didn't look at me. He focused on using his pocketknife to cut the cheese into manageable chunks.

Maybe, I said, it's like what's going on in other countries. The doping, the experiments on soldiers and athletes. Maybe the United States was more cautious than other countries. They were using nobodies like us first, so they didn't accidentally damage someone important. Charlie made an attempt at a joke, something about him being a very important person. I did not smile; we were not on good enough terms for me to pretend there was merit in his attempts at being funny. Mariah said she didn't read the news. She kept asking me questions, kept patting her body and saying, But I don't feel special. Why would they choose someone like me?

I wished again that these were people I could absolutely trust. It took two months, living together and having a class together, for me to know we were really friends. Tanya, it was the time we stayed up all night freshman year, trying only to speak Spanish to get ready for our exam. You snorted when you laughed and didn't try to hide it. You didn't care that I had to keep reminding you about the gender of certain words. You just kept laughing. I knew we were friends then because in public, you keep yourself polished. You always dress well, you think before you speak. Everything you do with most people gives off the sense that you are thinking deeply.

Would I feel as lost here if I trusted these people?

And doesn't trust lead to love? And wasn't loving my mom, my grandma too much the reason why I was in Lakewood?

Mariah said, Sometimes I think they're just torturing us.

I feel that way too, I said. Like they're trying to see how much they can take from us, mentally, physically, emotionally, before we break. I cracked open my can of beer, looked up at the moon. Maybe the hypothesis is how much do people value money over themselves? I told them how I had heard an older man say that he thought studies were going on here since he was a boy. I turned to Charlie. Made eye contact, tried to look soft as I asked if that could be true.

Charlie said we should talk about something else. We were making him uncomfortable.

26

D^{ear} *Tanya,*
  It's very late. I haven't been able to sleep. Today was
Day 66. The fake-life me found a bat in the warehouse again.
I complained to Charlie and said if he wasn't going to take
this seriously, I was going to take this to corporate. What
happened is Judy, Mariah, and I all came in early. We were
given pills whose side effects might make us feel very sick,
we might have painful, excessive bowel movements after they
wore off. Headaches. Nausea.

  I told them that sounded miserable. Einstein Eyebrows tried
to make some joke, but the gist of it was just do it. Do you
think people really believe another person's pain exists? Do you
remember that white girl at college who said—and she was so
proud and it made us both furious—she liked to go to cities in
the aftermath of a police shooting? She didn't bother to lie about
standing in solidarity, bringing needed resources, or in any way
hiding the fact that it was all about the spectacle, about being
able to see she was part of something big. The girl had done it
twice; stayed in hotels, watched the protests, kept herself safe

and distant. She said over and over she had been there, as if that alone warranted someone handing her some roses and a fucking tiara. I had asked her what the point was of going there just to watch. The girl shrugged and left quickly after people started asking her further, meaner questions.

The way the observers were acting reminded me of that fucking shrug.

After we each took one, Pancake Butt said, Oh shit, I forgot to ask. Are you menstruating? When we said no, all the observers acted super-relieved. Internally, I screamed. I saw myself knocking over all their coffee cups while reminding them this is our health, our lives. Instead, I went to the vending machines and bought myself, Mariah, and Judy candy bars.

At lunch, Charlie and I sat outside at the picnic table. He told me when he was finished eating his sandwich that it looked like something was wrong with my car. I was about to ask what it was, and then we made eye contact. It was clear he wanted to talk privately. As we walked over to it, Charlie told me there were blank spots in his memory. But he remembered being in a room filled with gray plants. They had him eat one that looked like parsley, but tasted hot, like chili pepper. It made him throw up. Then he got very jittery and excited as if he had drunk too much coffee. At my car, he pointed to the back tires and said loudly, I must have been mistaken. He looked around and said, I guess maybe what I'm trying to say is I didn't know there was a whole facility underground. Maybe it's possible this has been happening for longer than I thought. I would've been happier if he had apologized for doubting me or if he hadn't looked so pleased with himself. But it made me a little less angry at him. I squeezed his arm.

Then he surprised me. Charlie squeezed me back. He said I had to promise not to talk to anyone about this. That it could hurt me, my mom, but also everyone else in these studies. We all have good reasons for being here, Lena, he said. His voice cracked. He sounded 16.

I was about to remind him I had signed an NDA just like everyone else. That I had great reasons for staying here. But I noticed something moving out of the corner of my eye. It was Smith, watching us from the sidewalk. He was smoking a cigarette. I pushed Charlie's hand off my arm and walked back into the office.

The rest of the day was a literal mess. I couldn't focus on what Charlie had said to me because I started experiencing side effects. I had felt no different after I had taken the pill but by 3 p.m.—and I want to be funny here, to act like it was nothing—I was experiencing a poop emergency. I've been eating crackers and drinking Pedialyte, nothing else will stay in my stomach. Miss Shaunté texted me to let me know my mom wasn't feeling well; it was the worst she's felt in a long time. I slowly ate another cracker, then called.

Where is she, where is she, Deziree kept saying on the phone.

I asked her who, hoping it wasn't what I thought it was. My stomach was making death-metal sounds.

Mom, Deziree said. When is she coming home?

My grandma told me never to lie to Deziree when this was happening. Lying to her wasn't kind and in fact would make things worse. But I didn't want to do this. I put my phone down for a second. Clutched my stomach, trying to find the right words, but there was no way to tell her that would be right and kind.

I told her in my bluntest, most matter-of-fact voice that Grandma had been sick. Remember, she had cancer. She died months ago. We had the funeral. You spoke at it. I was crying, but I don't think she could hear it in my voice.

Deziree was quiet. I hoped that maybe it had gotten through. She told me all bees were aliens and that was why they were disappearing now. Then she made a high-pitched sound, started sobbing, and asked me again where her mother was. I'm sorry, I said over and over. I wanted Grandma to come home, arms full of groceries, wearing her sandals with the coins on them. She would soothe Deziree, hop on the phone and order me home. It's childish, but I pretended all our problems would be solved if she was alive. But there would still be the medical bills, she would still be recovering from surgery, from chemo.

My mom hung up. I sat up and rubbed my face. I called her multiple times, but she didn't answer. I texted her. No response. I texted Miss Shaunté. Nothing. I was sure in those moments that something truly terrible had happened. She was walking the neighborhood, trying to find Grandma. She had fallen and hit her head. I started packing my bag, sure I would have to drive home, stopping to relieve my stomach agony at every rest stop and 24-hour restaurant I could find. The trip would probably take most of the night because I was so sick. I changed into sweatpants, drank more water. Then Miss Shaunté texted me. Deziree had a seizure, they were going to the hospital. She would be back in touch. Everything was probably fine, but they wanted to be safe. And I should be calm, she was there and taking care of things. Lena, I have this, she said twice.

I tried to force myself away from worrying. I texted you some boring lies about work. I scrolled through an art blog that was featuring a series of photographs I usually would've liked. A group of models—black people of all different shades wearing body suits—in poses. Sometimes they were superimposed on each other and they looked elegant despite the rat-king grossness of seeing several interlocking arms and legs. I got sick again and again. Online-shopped for a new hypoallergenic pillow. Miss

Shaunté called me. My mother was fine. It was just a little worse for everyone because it had been so long since she had felt so bad.

Lying on my bathroom floor writing this, I can't stop thinking I have to stay here. I can do this. I can do this.

But what I also keep thinking—in the voice in my head that doesn't sound like me, the one that sounds like my grandmother—what will happen if I don't make it out of here all right?

27

*D*ear *Tanya,*

It started on Day 68 of the experiments—an ordinary day according to the sheet they gave me, nothing special except my new headset had come in—and they announced this morning that we were beginning another phase of the memory study. We were in the conference room, all of us were given two pills. When I held them up to the light, they were a shimmering gray. Fog trapped in a bottle.

What are the benefits of this, I asked.

Dr. Lisa looked up from her clipboard and raised her eyebrows at me. If you're uncomfortable doing this, she said, you can always leave. I know last time was rough on you.

Everyone else had stopped talking. They were watching her face. No one had swallowed their pills. She paused. You could see she realized her reaction had been a mistake.

What are the benefits, Mariah asked. She was sitting with her face resting in her palms. Everyone else had their arms crossed. I was so grateful to her for backing me up that I wanted to reach under the table, squeeze her arm, find some way to say thank you.

Faster mental processing, increased memory clarity, faster reading comprehension and retention, less risk of developing dementia or Alzheimer's when you're older, Smith said, keeping his eyes down. He spoke quickly. Charlie, Tom, and Judy relaxed. But Ian, Mariah, and I shared a look. It was too good to be true. How could one pill do all those things?

Dr. Lisa asked if there were any other questions. Her face was relaxed, but her voice came out clipped.

I had so many, but the situation felt that if I breathed the wrong way, I would be thrown out. Now I wish I had kept asking questions, talked and talked until they got fed up, sent us all home for the day, sent us all home for forever.

The day before, Day 89, I'd come home and made myself dinner. I pretended that I was tired, not from a morning spent running and an afternoon when I gave blood, but from having my fake job at Great Lakes Shipping Company. Spreadsheets, tracking routes, worrying about shipments. A job where I said things like This is such a Tuesday. Flirting with a non-creepy truck driver, the type of guy who said things like I know you're fine, but how are you. I could call my mom at any time and tell her exactly what had happened during my day.

What else did ordinary people care about? A house. Paying off student loans. Finding someone I liked enough that I was willing to see him every single day, that I was willing to build a life separate from my mother's. From there, kids. But I'm not ready to think about those things yet; it felt too fake and was starting to break the spell.

So, I searched online for adoptable cats and dogs. A pit bull mix named Snake Plissken. I distrust all people who say bad stuff about pit bulls. All dogs can be bad dogs. I seriously considered adopting a one-eyed cat named Star War. The people at the closest humane society are so bad at naming animals. Blackie 2, Blackie 4, Colon, Vodka Cat. After reminding myself there was no way I could be responsible for a cat in the middle of all this, I brainstormed vacations.

Deziree and I in Paris. Going to a restaurant and eating a plate of brightly colored vegetables in butter sauce. Walking through the Louvre. Being a basic and crying when I saw the Mona Lisa for the first time. Going to the Pompidou. Drinking wine. Seeing so many wonderful things, being somewhere so different that my brain aches from how exciting life can be. Eyes liquid with emotion, having to attempt to communicate with gestures about how big you're feeling in that moment. The only place outside of the country either my mom or I have been is Windsor. I promised myself that when I was done here, we would go, we would see everything.

We took the pills. Each tasted like nothing. Dr. Lisa gave us words to memorize. I waited to drift off again, for my arms and legs to quit. They didn't dismiss us. The observers kept writing notes. Someone made a noise like they were choking. I looked up. Mariah's eyes were rolling back in her head, blood was coming out of her nose, she was having a seizure. I ran around to the other side of the table. I helped stabilize her, got her on her side, with Smith's help. Charlie was still coughing. I was tired and weak, but I kept whispering to Mariah that she was okay, she was okay.

Everyone was watching. She kept bleeding. It was coming out of her nose, out of her mouth. She went limp in my arms. I stopped whispering.

Mariah died.

Smith kept trying to help her, but I knew she was dead. I let go of her hands, ran out of the conference room. I wasn't a person any longer, I was shock and anger and fear. There was a moment when I was sobbing by the vending machine, the chip bags shiny navy and matte red. I went into the bathroom, tried to barf, but it didn't work. Then the old man was there. He took my hands, guided me up the stairs.

We went up to Dr. Lisa's office. The old man said he had something for me to take, it would calm me down. He pulled out a box. It contained golden pills, like something a witch offers a dumb peasant in a fairy tale. If you take one, your life will be filled with riches. If you take one, your life will be filled with riches because everyone you touch will turn to gold. The old man's eyes were shining with excitement.

Where would you be, he asked me, if you could be anywhere right now?

I would be 7, I said, and riding my bike.

He laughed as if I were joking, but I wasn't.

NPR played out of the laptop speakers. A woman with a serious voice was speaking about how several nations had collaborated to make a kind of super-steroid in advance of the next Olympic Games. There were severe repercussions: sanctions against all the participating nations, health issues for the subjects. Liver damage, high blood pressure, weakened bones. One had died while lifting weights, skeletal collapse.

Can you believe people care so much about the Olympics, the old man asked.

Not really. The Olympics are boring, I said.

He told me that it's all a cover story. People want to believe these research studies are about something simple that they can relate to like winning a contest. They don't want to think about why a government would want to experiment on its citizens.

They do it because they can, I said. Because you don't see us as people.

He didn't like that and handed me a pill, a big glass of water. It looked cloudy, as if there was some soap in it.

Take it.

I did. After I swallowed the pill and water, I started coughing. I coughed harder and harder. My eyes squeezed shut. When they opened I was outside. The sky and clouds were moving quickly, blurring as if they were in a race. Cumulus shape-shifted into diamonds, the blue folded around them, so it looked like art deco wallpaper. It all kaleidoscoped: diamonds, crosses, squares. I understood I was crying, but I couldn't feel it on my cheeks. The world felt fluid, holy. I turned, and Smith was there, watching and writing. The clouds continued behind him. I watched him turn and follow my gaze, but he didn't react. I understood that to him everything was ordinary. He wasn't beyond reacting to a spectacle. If it had been a dream, he would have seen it too.

Smith said my pupils were a little too big for how bright it was. I might be risking damaging my eyes. He pulled out sunglasses, handed them to me. I couldn't feel the plastic in my hands. My fingertips were dulled, maybe. Or it was like whatever I had taken had somehow made it so my brain could no longer process tactile sensations. I put the glasses on.

I asked him for water. He nodded, got up, and walked about 30 paces away to a small cabin. It was like the one they had locked me in.

My heart was beating quickly, as if I had just run up and down steps for 20 minutes. There was a figure in the distance. At first, I thought he was dark because he was standing among the trees and I was wearing dark glasses. But it looked cut from ink. And the sun was shining. I could see it coming closer, between the branches, a sludge among the green and lush. Darkness spilled and pooled over roots, looped between trees, closer. I held my breath. It continued slithering. I could feel a sort of ache coming from it: a longing to be near me. I touched the grass, tried to focus on it to calm myself. Don't look. But I couldn't feel the soft blades. There was no heat from the sun on the ground. There should have been smells too: grass, soil, woods in the distance, my deodorant fighting against the heat. Nothing.

Right before my grandma died, she told me knowing about her cancer felt like a bird that was constantly on her shoulder. It refused to go away. Sometimes it chattered at her. Its feathers were always brushing her cheek, its sharp claws digging into her flesh. She was never alone ever again because it was always with her.

I had thought that was terrible. I couldn't imagine how it felt to always know you were dying. There were times where I wanted to ask her: Did you wake up each morning and have to tell yourself, this could be it? How did you stop being afraid? How did your brain cope with the stress of thinking each day could be the last day? Are you scared to go to sleep? It would have been selfish and immature to ask her those questions. I held her hand, told her I loved her every time it came up.

I was going to die when it reached me. It was the most certain I'd ever been in my entire life. This is some unfair bullshit, I thought, with my eyes shut. I knew in a few seconds the shape would unfurl, cover me, drown me. Something poked my arm.

I screamed.

A thump as the water bottle dropped. I opened my eyes. Smith stared at me, tense and afraid. It's just me, he said. I looked behind him toward the woods. The darkness was gone. I pushed the sunglasses up, rubbed my eyes. Little red flecks floated in the corner of them, but the world pushed mostly back to normal. Why did you yell, he asked.

I said it was black like tar. A shape that wanted me dead. My voice was flat. The sky was beginning its distortions again.

Tanya, the only time I had felt close to this was when we had gotten high at that co-op party. We had walked home together. I was scared and holding the back of the frilly blouse you'd worn to the party. Did someone slip you something, you kept asking. But I was monumentally stoned, and we came upon a tree and it was covered in so many crows. In the night, it was a monster with many heads. Its 50 mouths were screaming at me. But what scared me was the world was completely different than I had ever known before. I tried to explain it to you, and you said in a very sweet voice, You'll be home soon and I'll make some popcorn. Think of how cozy you'll feel.

You're too stimulated, Smith said. If I had been less scared, I would have said That's not how people talk to adults. It's how they talk to dogs and children. He took my hand. Led me to the cabin. Because I couldn't feel his fingers, it was more like a force—gravity—was pulling me there. I couldn't fight it.

The cabin's wood was mesmerizing. I could see it coming back to life, becoming a new kind of tree. It interlocked, with clear leaves growing off every space. Inside the cabin was a trapdoor. My heart is going to fucking explode, I said.

Smith went first and helped me down into a stairwell. He was sweating. He told me to touch the sides to get steady, to tell him if I was light-headed. We walked down a flight of stairs carved into the earth. It smelled like peanut butter and rain. He pulled me forward, though I wanted to touch the walls, the stairs. The darkness soothed me a little, made everything move closer to ordinariness. A millipede scuttled on the wall, growing longer and longer the more I watched it.

We came to a door, heavy and new. Smith had to key in a code. When the door swung open, we were back in the facility. I realized I was still wearing the sunglasses. I tried to take them off, but he said it was still bright. Keep them on.

I meant to ask him, What did you do to me? But it came out as Why would you do this to someone? My mouth said it multiple times. I didn't mean the drug, I meant the experiments. But Smith took it to mean the drug and said he knew it wasn't ready. Why do you do this job, I asked him. We walked past the room where everyone had watched the video, and Smith led me to a room that was set up for medical work. There was a man sitting in a chair alone, his mouth open. A blue goop was oozing out the sides of his lips. Below his nose was tinged with it too. His expression wasn't concerned or upset, it was closer to a Jesus-Christ-I-can't-believe-I-have-to-wait annoyance.

Smith drew curtains around the area, so I couldn't see the man any longer. Then he helped me onto a medical table. The paper clung to the backs of my legs. Sweat ran down my forehead. Smith pulled out his cell phone and started texting.

Five women appeared, all wearing lab coats. One took notes while one removed my sunglasses and looked in my eyes. Another one checked my reflexes while her colleague listened to my heart. The woman looking at my eyes muttered something about it being a little soon to make me do something like this. Then she looked at Smith and I couldn't tell if she was looking to see if he agreed or if she was afraid of his reaction.

The women left, and Smith and I were alone.

He grabbed my shoulders, pressed the top of my head into his chin. I could feel and count every hair that made up his stubble. He smelled like coffee and cigarettes and mints. The ceiling lights shimmered in my peripheral vision.

That sounds almost romantic, but it wasn't. Objectively, Smith is not an unattractive person. And I did feel the small attraction that can come from spending a lot of time around a person who is paying attention to you, but there wasn't a hint of sex in what he was doing. He was listening for my breath, feeling the warmth of my skin, but it wasn't about connection or an upswelling of feelings. He was reminding himself, This is a person. Lena is a person. It became more and more disturbing. He had to feel my hair, my skin, to actively remind himself I was someone. Still, he was touching me, and I didn't want him to. It was another chipping away of my boundaries.

I told him I was going to barf. My voice sounded 9 again— high, almost squeaky. I opened my eyes. My grandmother stood behind him. Not as she was when I knew her, but as she was in the photograph. She told me my life was cracking open. Sticking out of her left arm were—I don't know the precise medical name for them—needles used to inject vaccines.

Hello, I said to her. Tell me. I'm not sure if I said this aloud or thought it. Tell me that I'll have my life back.

She took my hand but didn't smile. Tell me, I thought I said to her, to go home. My grandmother took a needle from her arm and put it in my own. It's just a pinch, baby. Look at me. Together we can get through anything.

I reached for her hand, but there was only air.

28

And then, Tanya, I woke up and I was at Long Lake. Across, on the other side, was the meadow with my grandmother's tree. But I was near the docks, where people could launch canoes and have picnics. I watched as the observers threw metal containers into the water. It smelled like a mixture of cotton-candy perfume and cleaning supplies burning on a stove. The air hurt my nostrils, my lungs. I put my hands over my mouth and nose, but my fingers stunk of it. The containers sank into the water and I had a coughing fit. I bent over from the force of it. There was an empty pop bottle near my feet, and I picked it up when I was done. I threw it in the recycling bin and coughed again.

I walked back to a car and Dr. Lisa was waiting for me. The night was so clear. I asked her if I was going to be stoned for eternity. She turned on a song and started up the car. The song was about being on fire or asking someone for fire. Or maybe it was about being a match and begging to be struck, to crumble, to die. I was sure the song had been written for me. I opened the window and stuck my head out. The wind was sprinting to keep up with the car. A bug smashed itself on my forehead. I howled at the clear skies, the stars that didn't give a shit about anything. They were just light. Dr. Lisa laughed, told me to put my seatbelt on.

Sacred is an anagram of scared, I said.

Being high is so embarrassing, the doctor said. I miss it.

I don't know how much time passed, but the next thing—and I'm not sure if it was before or after being at the lake—was I was wearing a wig and red lipstick and a black dress. I was paying close attention to every conversation that was happening around me, while pretending all my attention was on the crab cakes I was eating. I knew everything I heard I was expected to discuss later. I wiped my hands on a tablecloth. I was a white woman's date and she kept asking if I was having fun. You're being so quiet and polite. She had three braids wrapped around her forehead like a crown. I wondered who she was. We were wearing matching bracelets, thin and gold, that clacked together when we moved our wrists. I asked her where she was going next week, and she said back to the oil. I laughed a little, hoped she couldn't tell I was so confused. There was a gun in my handbag. A list of names next to it, some red lipstick, and a small sprayer of perfume.

Another memory: I was binge-eating ice cream. Strawberry. I didn't care how it tasted. I needed the cold in my mouth. It hurts, I said. The darkness from the woods was standing in the corner. It came over and stood at my side. I refused to acknowledge it, shoved more ice cream in my mouth. It shuddered, as if it, too, was getting an ice cream headache. There was a frozen chunk of strawberry in my mouth. I held it there until it rehydrated a little. Plump and half-alive again with my spit.

Days or minutes later, Dr. Lisa was talking to me. I was on a treadmill running faster than I ever have before. She sounded almost envious. Do you feel great? You have so much energy. And I was telling her in a strained voice that my brain and heart are moving faster than ever before, and it is fucking terrible. I am also feeling great because running is fucking fun. And I think I was supposed to start menstruating four days ago, but that hasn't happened yet. The small part of me that was still Lena was so uncomfortable at the rapidness of my speech, at the way it seemed I must at least be having some kind of manic episode. It's the only possibility I could think of. And don't a lot of mental illnesses really get going in people's twenties? Then I thought, Oh, maybe it's because of the drugs. The closest I can come to describing how I felt at that moment was I was sentient champagne. I loved the feeling of being exposed to the air, fizzing over my bottle's edge. I was doing what I was meant to do and was sure that soon I would be all used up and that was okay. Everything dies.

I was sitting in a room and a man punched me in the eye. He said something like, Tell us, tell us, and this will all stop. I had no idea what he was talking about. The inside of my mouth was tender. I remember saying, I don't care if you do this to me. He stopped, shook his head. I threw myself at him. Hit me, I said. Hit me. I don't fucking care. Do it. He was much bigger than me. I was slapping him and screaming. I could tell I was scaring the shit out of him. Do it, I said. My voice suddenly quiet, calm like I was answering a question in a classroom.

Last night, or a week ago, I was sitting in a room filled with animals. They were all speaking in human voices. They were talking about celebrity gossip. A celebrity was caught cheating with the maid. Two of her kids were his. One of the animals was Bigfoot. His teeth were yellow. Leaves were caught in his face fur. You look much more authentic, I told him. There were different raccoons. A bat. I wondered if they were all robots

I had seen before. My nose was bleeding. It stained my shirt. You've gotta take care of yourself, one of the raccoons said to me. I laughed. The blood ran down my nose and chin, but I stayed and listened to them talk.

Then today, I woke up in my bed. Looked at my phone and was surprised by what day it was. It was Saturday, September 5th. I had lost weeks in August and the beginning of this month. It was late in the day, 6 p.m. I went to the bathroom, undressed to take a shower. There was a scar near my breast, close to where my heart lives. I took a breath. Thought about how I was seeing, breathing, hearing. Took my heartbeat. I felt like me again. There was a small, healing bruise beneath my eye.

I showered, dressed. Wrote the beginning of this for both of us. As I wrote, I tried as hard as possible to feel nothing. I needed to be objective. I needed to be as clear-headed as I possibly could.

First, I went to the closest emergency room. I wanted a doctor to look at my scar. Maybe they could tell me what had happened.

The ER was packed. There was a child with a cloth pressed against her head. She kept trying to take the cloth off, wanted to touch whatever was beneath. A man was lying on the floor, while two other men tried to coax him up. I can hear everything, he said. I can hear your blood moving through your veins. I can, I can. A woman whose skin was tinged yellow, so that her hair and flesh were almost a matched set. Multiple people saying they could see a black sludge following them. It was seeping beneath the door. It was glistening on the walls. Couldn't you see? It sounded exactly like what I had seen, and I looked around, but all I saw was white walls and scared people and cheap televisions in the corners.

I think I really hurt my eye somehow. A teenage girl said, I keep seeing these neon diamonds. She had a paisley print scarf wrapped around her eyes. Her mom was holding her hand.

Some teenagers smelled familiar. Sweet, like cotton candy, fire, and, maybe, vitamins. One of them had a long cut on his palm. His blood looked closer to blue than red. A man with a nail sticking out of his foot. He was saying, It doesn't hurt. I could live like this forever. Let's go get a milkshake.

Despite the cold, I was sweating. A mother walked in holding a baby. Its skin was bright red. The baby had a scream that sounded like it could melt glass.

The news broke in with a special report. The anchor said we weren't supposed to drink the water in Lakewood and the surrounding areas. He listed off the small towns nearby. There was widespread contamination, and not boiling, at this time, would help. None of the people waiting seemed to notice. A nurse came out and taped a garbage bag over the drinking fountain. On the intake station, she put out a line of water bottles. It's going to be a three-hour wait for anything not life-threatening, someone yelled.

I left and drove the two hours home. When I opened the door, my mom screamed. She dropped the glass of water she was holding and ran to me. Are you okay? she asked me. What happened? Did I do something to make you mad at me? I haven't heard from you in days. She said she had called my office to make sure I was okay, and they said I was still coming in.

Deziree was grabbing my hands. Tell me what's wrong. Tell me. Tell me.

I took a deep breath. Another. And then I told her everything. How the letter came in the mail inviting me to be a part of the Lakewood Project. And no, I didn't have it anymore. I had torn it up and thrown it out after signing the NDA. The tests during orientation, what I could remember about Lakewood, how I was sure this wasn't about some sort of advancements in medicine, it was about torture, about control. It felt like I spoke for hours. My voice was getting raspy, I spoke without interruption for so long.

Deziree didn't let go of my hands. She looked thoughtful, her eyes were on mine. I kept checking to see when she would stop believing me, when I would see her start to think I was having a mental health crisis, that I was talking about something that was impossible.

She told me to take a break. She went to the kitchen and came back with a glass of water. Drink this, she said. Then she went into my grandmother's room and returned with a slip of paper. It was very faded and had been folded several times. Dear Deziree, it began, you are invited to participate in a research study about memory and perception. The Mineral Hills Project was designed to help future generations understand the most mysterious place on Earth: the human mind.

There are three years of my life, my mother said, that I can't remember. The year I got pregnant with you and the two years before I had my "accident." Your grandma and I were fighting in those years, so we barely spoke. She thought I was on drugs. And I thought her thinking that was offensive. She pointed at the piece of paper. I was there. I don't have any proof. But I know it.

I believed her.

When I was young, my grandma took me up to Mackinac. The first time I saw the Straits, where Lake Michigan and Lake Huron join, the water was so blue. I knew it wasn't the ocean, but I asked if it was anyway. I felt overwhelmed by the beauty of it. People talk about how large expanses of water can make them feel insignificant. But there was something for me in it that made me feel larger. Maybe it was the mixture of the joy of loving something so immediately and the fear I felt knowing I loved something I should never touch. That's because I couldn't swim. I would die quickly if I ever went into the Lakes. I don't know. But seeing the piece of paper, feeling that here was an explanation for why no one could figure out what had happened to my mom, I felt that same mixture of joy and fear.

29

Dear Tanya,

Deziree and I spent the rest of the night talking. I reminded her that this is how I was affording her health care. I began to offer to stay in, to keep her well, but she held up her hand. If I had known this is what you were doing. Lena, this is my life. The only time you get to make decisions for me is if I'm truly too sick to do it. You need to talk to me. I thought you knew better.

And I promised I would never do it again, but deep down I knew I would do anything to take care of her. In the middle of everything else, it's overwhelming to know truly how much you love someone, how much of yourself you would destroy because of that. I went to the kitchen, searching for some alcohol to drink, but I had to settle for a kombucha.

We talked through the NDA. My mom said we should talk to a lawyer, not rely on internet searches. We put that on our to-do list. We talked about leaving the country. Would that make us both feel safer if we did figure out how to talk about this? I told her about the reporter, thought it was probably worthless because I probably couldn't go on the record. We talked our way into a labyrinth of possibilities. Around 1 a.m., we decided to go back to Lakewood in the morning to get my grandmother's shoeboxes, which I had left behind. We decided that based on how we felt—if we felt remotely unsafe—we would just leave and in the morning we would decide again.

There were things I wanted to ask her. Did she have any idea who my father was? Was it possible that somehow my whole existence was because of one of these studies? And if so, why? But she said she didn't remember the entire year she got pregnant with me. I thought of all the bits and pieces of father I had tried to put together over the years. She had said my dad was taller than her but would not be considered tall. Once, when I was laughing, she said, You sound more like him than me. And then there were all the things I inferred about him: how I was good at math and she wasn't; the difference in our hair, my ears, my ugly toe; that I like cilantro; and how I liked to be alone because it didn't make me sad to be in my room, talking to no one for hours. I had built an idea bit by bit, but now there was this. I think I might never want to consider who my father is ever again.

The sun rose as we drove through the outskirts of Lakewood, my mother napping in the passenger seat. Orange, purple, pink reflected on all the windows. The sky was candy. An old woman wearing a gas mask was clipping her hedges. Families were loading up their cars, taking things as if they had all been given notice to be out by noon. There was a wind of panic, growing stronger and stronger. It was shoving around children and grabbing the hair of all the people in Lakewood trying to leave.

There was trash on the sidewalk. Most of the downtown shops were closed. We went to the donut shop. All the old men were still there, eating donuts, drinking coffee. They were all reading different newspapers. On the front of some were head-lines that read Small Town Water Emergency. Another: Area Hospitals Apologize for Role in Research Studies.

We bought papers from the woman at the counter. Hello again, she said to me, handing me a chocolate donut with white frosting. In a booth, my mom and I spread the papers out. There was a story about a hospital system across Michigan apologizing for its role in research studies on African Americans in the late 1960s, early 1970s. In one paper there was a letter published next to the official report.

My mama and daddy were some of the most suspicious people on Earth. When my mama saw me smile or look at a boy for what she thought was too long, she would give me a pinch. And then say, This is a reminder of all the pain any man is gonna give you, especially this early in life. She was saying that since I was six.

This was when we were living in Flint. They would tell me about two towns to never go to: Lakewood and Otter Pond. I was never, ever supposed to go to either of those places. My aunt and uncle were farmers and lived near Lakewood. We had heard rumors. They had seen pickup trucks with black boys being brought in. Seen them around town too. Fresh from the South. They felt like they were on another planet because white people were treating them with a hint of manners. My parents said they were studying death. They were killing these boys, loading them up with different diseases, seeing if we died from them slower or faster than white people.

Stories like that had been around my whole life. I wasn't allowed to visit a friend's house when it was dark because it was too close to a hospital. My parents said people from the hospitals rounded up black kids to use for their experiments and most never came back. And the ones who did come back, people would say, "They ain't right." Those kids were always seeing what happened to them. They couldn't sleep good. They tended to die young or disappear again or be taken away.

Some people said Lakewood wasn't about death, it was about making a new kind of slave. They were testing obedience. The men who were brought there were given drugs. The kind that made you feel as if you were in a fairy-tale land. Some of them were kept isolated, or would be hurt in different ways. Electricity on their feet. Water over their heads.

I was 17 and I wanted to feel like myself. To feel important like the adults around me. Some of my friends were already getting married.

So, one weekend, I went to Lakewood with my friends. We were in the town for probably only two minutes when an old white man came over to us. I felt the trouble coming out of his pores. I thought he was going to call the police on us. But instead, he smiled and asked if we wanted to make some money.

Yes, I said.

He told us to go to the hospital and tell them we were there for the vaccine study.

We went, and they sent us to the lower level. We walked past the morgue with the smell of the dead, the chemicals they used to keep them fresh. There was a small room we took turns going into. A doctor gave me two injections in my arm. I was surprised that it didn't go into my stomach or thigh or butt. But if it had been one of those places, I probably wouldn't have done it. They gave me 10 dollars. I had to give them my name, my social security number, and a written promise that I would return next month for another injection. I would get 15 more dollars for that one.

A thing I never anticipated about getting older is feeling ridic-ulous about how much things used to cost. I don't feel proud I was alive at a time when I could get coffee for less than a quarter. Maybe I would feel better about it if the coffee had been any good.

One of my friends said that what they were doing after that was testing vaccines. They were trying to find a way to make you immune to STDs, chicken pox, cancer. Most of my people died of cancer. Sometimes young, sometimes old, but all of them had it. It felt better to think maybe this vaccine would pass on to my children and my children's children. A way to avoid that early death.

I did this for six months. I never told my parents. I'm still a little proud that I made so much money and kept a secret from them. There is a part of me that is always going to be 18, I think, and a little afraid of my mama.

My arm hurt bad after each visit. My friends and I would laugh, though, and say it's the price of living to a hundred. We would be sitting in rocking chairs together, playing cards still.

But if they did give me their vaccine, it didn't work. I'm not surprised anymore. How could they keep a cure for cancer secret for more than 40 years? Like two of my aunties, my grandpa, I'll die before I'm 70.

I became used to the idea I may have been given those shots like how Catholic ladies use those saint medals. I smoked cigarettes, I drank, avoided going to the doctor, breathed in chemicals, ate poorly, ignored the pain growing in my stomach. A part of me thought a little, Well, it's fine. I'm immune.

Tanya, I was sure Grandma had written this. The letter was scanned in, blurry, hard to read at times on the thin newsprint. My mom said I was seeing what I wanted to see. Your grandma didn't make T's like that. And her handwriting leaned to the right, my mom said, also she preferred cursive. But I thought about everything she'd had me give out and mail after the funeral. The letters in the shoebox.

At the end of my grandma's life, she was calm. No regrets. It would be like her to tie as much up as possible, find a way to make things a little better without hurting either of us. It would be why the older man from the studies liked to ask me about her. Wouldn't it be something to have research on three generations? The samples they'd taken of my blood, my urine, my skin. Were there lasting effects that could be seen in my genes?

Deziree and I decided to go somewhere private to talk.

Have you seen the lake yet? the waitress asked me while bringing me a to-go cup of coffee.

No.

She told us if the cops weren't around, it was worth seeing. And Tanya, it was.

We drove toward it. Past the cabin with a satellite dish decorated with an image of Jesus holding a glass of wine in one hand and a fish in the other. He is the truth was written in papyrus font beneath the image. I thought the person who owned that satellite dish might be the pastor at Tom's church. I had gone with him a few times, but it hadn't done anything for me. A family was standing in the backyard, no masks, looking dazed. They were all wearing bathrobes and pajamas. The mom threw up in the yard, the rest of the family didn't seem to notice. Their eyes were on the dirt road.

This is a bad idea, my mom said. But she didn't tell me to turn around.

Parts of the lake were covered in bubble-bath foam. It looked like magic. Small rainbows appeared in some of the white clumps. Other parts were iridescent, like gas on pavement. A low-lying bike path near the lake was covered in the foam. It was so high that if I rode a bike through it, it would be up to my neck. My eyes were tearing as I parked the car. The area stunk of gross lake scent mixed with rot and sweet and gasoline. I was relieved that the woman from the diner told me to go, that my mom was next to me. If they hadn't been there to confirm what I was seeing, I might have thought I was still high.

I got out of the car and walked to the beach's highest point. The people who were there seemed to be taking samples of the water, of things along the shore, or calling to a small boat. They were wearing hazmat suits or rubber gloves and ventilation masks. My mom handed me a scarf from the car. She had my spare sweater tied over her nose and mouth. Deziree tied the scarf as tight as she could around my nose and mouth. Raised her hand up and pointed at her fingers to indicate we should stay for only five minutes at most. I peered out, trying to see what was happening with the boat. The light reflected off the water. The foam was almost blinding at that angle, but I thought I saw a lone woman sitting in a canoe.

My eyes were stinging by that point.

A man in a dark suit noticed us and came over. He recommended that we leave. The government still doesn't know how toxic it is, he said. In a few hours they were going to start a mandatory evacuation of everyone who lived around the lake. They were giving them time to pack up and make arrangements if they could.

What does it do? I gestured at the foam.

Exposure leaves a rash. It can induce neurological symptoms, he said. Two men were here earlier taking pictures and one got too close. He said it made their hands bright red, felt as if they were burning. There could be permanent nerve damage. He sounded almost giddy. There's a woman out there who apparently sleeps only in that canoe and now refuses to come back to shore.

I shook my head. I was having a more visceral reaction to the idea of someone preferring to sleep in a canoe than to the polluted lake right in front of me. Maybe it was about boundaries, or context. The lake was so strange. My brain didn't—and still doesn't—know how to make a big reaction, how to completely understand it. I took photos of it on my phone. Then a short video. I made sure to capture the way the foam moved with the lake's small waves. Did a slow panoramic of everything.

How did this happen? my mom asked.

Chemicals, the man replied, as if that was enough of an answer.

I walked a little farther down. The man didn't stop me. The dunes were shifting and pulling at my feet. I was on the verge of tripping, rolling down the beach and into the lake. I paused. There were no news cameras around. This is real, I told myself. Real, real, real. Cigarette butts, a shiny gum wrapper. Some gulls were circling above the lake; people were trying to chase them away, encourage them not to land or go after anything they might want on the shore. You'll die, they yelled, as if the birds could understand English. You'll die.

The woman still refused to come to shore.

The foam probably felt like bubble bath. It would feel soft until it started to burn.

30

*D*ear *Tanya,*
      When we got to my apartment, everything they provided—the couch, the bed, the bedroom dresser, the dining room table set—was gone. My clothes were thrown on the bedroom floor, scattered on top of the boxes I hadn't bothered to unpack. Books everywhere, with letters to you still sealed inside them. They had taken my plates and bowls. I kept focusing on that fact as I went through the rest of the apartment; I think it allowed me to pretend the stakes were lower. It was easier to act like I had just broken up with someone petty who would take things that were obviously mine than think about what this really meant.

      Well, this isn't what I was expecting, my mom joked. She was holding the framed photo of me, her, and my grandma. It was steadying to have her here, to have someone else confirm yes, this is happening and yes, this is not normal. I tried to make a joke. Something dumb about the year's biggest decorating trend is flee-the-country chic. She didn't laugh. Instead, she looked around at the walls, the white cabinets, and said that she was getting major déjà vu.

I texted Charlie what felt like a million times. He didn't respond. I tried to call him. Nothing, not even a voicemail box. Maybe he got a new phone, my mom said. Neither of us felt convinced by what she said.

Online, more and more outlets were covering the hospitals' admissions to performing studies on African Americans. There were concise reports. Somehow, people had already cranked out op-ed style posts about how experiments like these were a reminder about the United States' history of racism. Seeing the discussions gave me hope. People cared! And this was about studies done close to 50 years ago. People would keep digging, keep paying attention, and they would find out it wasn't just hospitals, it was the government. They would find out this wasn't just once, this wasn't just in the past, but it had happened over and over.

People were talking about what an outrage this was. But they were already creating dumb jokes and memes. There were already several accounts saying this was all faked. It was just more lies by the blacks. It's what they do. People asked what they can do to help. There was genuine rage. I knew nothing could be solved in a day or a week or a month, but I hoped, I hoped.

We took a risk and drove to Great Lakes Shipping Company. The gate was wide open, so was the front door. There were no cars in the parking lot. Inside, everything was gone—cubicles, vending machines, computers, the blinds off the windows. There were echoes as we spoke. I held my mom's hand as we went into the warehouse. It smelled like someone had recently dropped and cracked open several large jars of pickles. But the only things in the space were sparrows flying around and hopping on the ceiling beams. They were ordinary birds.

This happened, I said.

We went up to the second floor, the third. Everything was empty. Every step I took, I expected someone to jump out or round a corner and I would see someone I knew holding a gun. But it was quiet. Clean. Where else have you been, my mother asked me when we were out in the car. I told her about the cabin in the woods, but really, I didn't know if those were the woods behind Great Lakes Shipping Company or the woods in the state park north of town. We drove to Charlie's house. In the yard was a FOR RENT sign. I knocked several times. I called his name. Then we peeked in the front window. Nothing was inside.

We drove to Tom's. A different family was living there. A woman and a man who were watering a garden using jugs of water. A little boy with bright red hair who was chasing a dog around. I wanted to go to Mariah's house, but I had never been.

Do you still believe me? I asked my mom.

She squeezed my shoulder. I will always believe you.

You have to, though, I said, you're my mom. Deziree shook her head, reminded me that a lot of parents are not like that. People feel more loyalty to how they think things should be than to other people, including their family. I thought maybe she was talking about Grandma, but I didn't understand the context. There was so much between them that I didn't know, don't want to know. But now, I think maybe Deziree was already seeing things clearer than I was.

Is there anywhere else, anyone else you can think of who could give us proof? my mom finally asked.

I shook my head.

While we went back to my old apartment, started gathering up my things, my phone was blowing up with texts about Lakewood. You, Kelly, Stacy, people who hadn't spoken to me since April. It was all about the water. Was I okay? What are you going to do? How do you feel? Are you scared? I sent the three of you a picture of the lake. The foam, the people in hazmat suits. How can I help? you all asked.

When I used to go to service, the preacher loved to talk about how to be good in today's world. He would use generic, often corny, situations. When you're in the club. When someone sweet from your past sends you an email, but you booed up. He didn't usually speak like that and I always thought it was condescending when he said things like booed up, lit, wildin—but with the "g" pronounced. The way a cop would say it. Gambling, sex, violent movies, violent video games, opportunities to do violence. He steered all these situations toward the dads in the room. You will blow up your family if you make the wrong decision. Your kids will never look at you the same. Do you want to be another ain't-crap dad in this world? Mothers, you are angels. Kids, listen to your mothers.

Everywhere taught me to think about things in the simplest ways. School told me that anything could be summed up and have conclusions drawn from it in five paragraphs. This = good. That = bad. But now I think a lot about context. I think about what I owe the people in my life and what I owe people I will never see, never speak to. Can I make anything better? And if I did break my NDA, would anyone listen?

It's been six weeks since I've been in Lakewood. Deziree refuses to let me talk to any reporters. She says that I have done enough. Every time this comes up, it's the closest we come to fighting. She says if one of us has to take risks, giving things up, going to jail, it will be her. She says I have somehow forgotten—and the way she says it is so passive-aggressive it makes my teeth clench—that she is the mother. That she is the person who makes decisions for herself, our family.

What we know and don't say is that reporters might have an easier time thinking I'm more credible than her. She's reached out and talked to a few. Each one made scans of her invitation letter. They told her what she has to say is interesting. But she's come back grumpy and defeated from each meeting. There's no hard evidence. And Deziree says there are so many red flags that she doubts they take her seriously. Her health problems including her unreliable memory, her limp, her high-school-level education, her dark skin. She thinks they see her as someone trying to cash in. Or worse, someone who has read the papers and tricked herself into thinking this was the answer to why she was sick. I went to a good college, I speak confidently, but the times my mother has told me not to do something I can count on one hand. For now, the right thing feels like listening to her.

I think a lot about everyone else in the experiments, especially Charlie. Where was he? Was he okay? Sometimes, late at night, I wonder if there was ever a Charlie. Maybe he was just an actor pretending to be my friend, taking notes to report back to them. There's now no proof on the internet that a Charlie Graham from Lakewood ever existed.

Deziree says it takes time, but one day, you'll get used to living without certainty. You'll accept here are times you'll never get a clear answer to. Instead of it being the center of your life, eventually it'll be something you rarely think about. It'll be in the margins of your life. I want to believe her. I watch as she sips her tea, as she makes soft kind-mom eyes at me, a gaze that makes her look the most like Grandma, and hope she's right.

I want to tell Mariah's family what happened to her, that she was trying to repay them when she died, but I never knew her last name.

The other day, you asked me why I hadn't re-enrolled for winter semester. I said maybe I will and tried to change the subject. Here's the real answer. My mom and I haven't been sleeping well. Every sound could be them coming to take one or both of us back. Coming—and I wish this felt melodramatic to me, that I was able to laugh—to kill us. Miss Cassandra's nephew is staying with her. She broke her hip a few weeks ago and he's helping out. When I see his shadow at night, when I smell his cigarettes but don't see him, all my organs feel like they're congealing, becoming a heavy mass inside of me. My feet are desperate to run. My mom's new nickname for me is Squirrel. She is trying to tease me back into feeling okay.

There are hours where I am not scared. I talk to you on the phone. I try to think about my future. There are times when someone asks me how I'm feeling, I don't think about every glass of water I drank in Lakewood or the scar on my chest.

On Monday, my mom got a new job. She now has health insurance. Every orange, red, and yellow leaf felt like applause as she nodded and smiled while talking to them on the phone. Her eyes were so big. She was tearing up a little when she hung up. Deziree yelled, I got the job. Did it again. We danced like she had just won $500 playing slots.

Every day, she tells me I need to go back to school. Not just because I need an education, but because I need to feel like I'm moving in a different direction. And I want to. But then there are days where I can't leave the house at all. I try, but I can't get myself to put on shoes. Or I can't turn the knob and go out there. They could be anywhere. Anyone could be one of them. Or at night when I'm in the space between awake and rest, I feel hands on my throat again. I scream and I thrash and my mom has to tell me things will be fine. She scratches my scalp, smooths my hair. I'm not ready.

Back in early September, there had been talks about lawsuits, congressional hearings, damages, further inquiries into the research studies. Then there was Lakewood's water. It was so photographable! And I don't mean just Long Lake. There was the large flock of Canada geese that died from landing on its surface. Old white men—men I was used to seeing stuffing cake donuts in their mouths, their cheeks dusted with powdered sugar, chocolate frosting on their teeth—had been transformed into a combination of regal and broken in black-and-white portraits.

On major news websites, Lakewood is withered crops and rotten pumpkins. A small town with lots of big trees and empty old houses that seemed to inspire people on TV to rhapsodize about the past, the middle class. And what was going to happen to all these little white kids who had been drinking the water? Their lives would be shorter, they would probably have lingering health issues. And how long had the water been on the verge of this? Why didn't the state notice? What had pushed it to the tipping point? Look, look, look at all these sad farmers. It is the kind of disaster people love to look at.

Tanya, the reason you don't have these letters already is because I don't want you to think I'm crazy or a liar. I don't know. Maybe you would say something like at least you got paid for this. It's not fair to you, but I hear every argument, every way to make this much smaller coming out of your mouth.

I did make copies of all these letters. My mom and I sat with your dad and did our wills. If something ever happens to the two of us, you'll get the copies then. I hope I'll be able to at least try to say something someday. And if I don't, I'm sorry.

Sometimes, I look around—drinking coffee in my kitchen, sitting in traffic, holding a package of chicken in the grocery store—and I say, "Is this real?" I rarely feel alone; there's always a chance someone is watching. I have to stop myself from rating how I'm feeling on a scale.

Since coming home, I've been going to the art museum a lot. The one my grandma took me to when I was a child; it's one of the few places I feel safe now. On a whim, I signed up to do a training course on how to be a docent. There are cameras everywhere. The times when I go, I see the same people who have been working there for years now. They say hi to me, ask me about my mom, my day.

There's a painting here that's part of a traveling exhibition that I keep coming back to. On one side is a mid-century-style bedroom. The room is bright, its furniture gray, the carpet and curtains June-grass green, and there's yellow lampshades. A black-and-white image is small and superimposed over the room. Honestly, this side of the painting means very little to me. If I was in a classroom or writing a response paper, I would have to talk about postmodernism, something about emptiness, and the many ways it tries to communicate absence and distance. I'm already tired thinking about it.

But the other side. It is painted in purples and blacks. Four people are looking decidedly at you. They force you to react. Two are perpetually laughing, two are judging. There is nothing you can do to stop them. I should hate it, but I can't stop getting sucked in. I dream about this one, Tanya. I think it is pushing toward ugly and there is definitely some meanness in it, but I love it. It's the first new thing that I have loved in a while. I refuse to learn anything about the painter. I will myself to live only in the painting itself, to love how it makes me react.

I decided that I will go there every day. Drink from the

same fountain I remember my grandmother's hands lifting me up toward. Have a cup of coffee in the coffeeshop and watch the water spill up and out of the fountain. I will look at the brushstrokes, the sculptures gleaming under the light like well-tempered chocolates, the golden frames, black and white images of the long dead. I will force myself to remember, despite everything I know now, people are capable of making something wonderful.

ACKNOWLEDGMENTS

This book wouldn't have been possible without Dan Conaway, Andrea Vedder, and Lauren Carsley. You kept me creative, thoughtful, and organized during this process. A special thank-you to Taylor Templeton, who helped me feel my way through several almost-there drafts.

Thank you to the excellent staff at Amistad—especially Patrik Henry Bass (you gave this book a home and you understood exactly what it needed), Amina Iro, and Paul Olsewski.

Thank you to Dr. Reed and Dr. Meyer, and their excellent staff at CORL. You modeled for me how a research study should work, answered all my questions, and always gave me more to think about and more things to read.

Lakewood in a much different form began in a novel-writing workshop. Thank you, Samrat Upadhyay, for starting me on this path. And thank you to that entire class, but especially Bix Gabriel, Scott Fenton, Cherae Clark, and Tia Clark. You all pointed me in the direction that brought me here.

Thank you to Indiana University's MFA program for the time and money to start this book. Thank you, Romayne Rubinas

Dorsey, Ross Gay, Jacinda Townsend, Cathy Bowman, and Liz Eslami, for making me a better writer.

Thank you for all the support I've gotten from Miami University—especially from Eric Goodman and Margaret Luongo.

Thank you to the excellent staff at *The Offing* past and present—Allison, Jax, Kosiso, Mary, Penelope, Reem, Shristi, Di, and Mimi—for expanding my ideas about good writing.

Thank you to the Barbara Deming Memorial Foundation. Your support helped give me the time to write, and the confidence to think I was writing something worth reading.

Thank you to all the literary magazine editors who published my work before this. You helped me stay on this path. Helped me find readers (Hello you-knew-me-when readers! Thank you for reading me in the past, thank you for reading me now!).

Hello, Audra, Scott, Paul, Laura, Aaron, and Bix. You all let me vent, made me think, made me laugh about all this when I felt discouraged. I love you all. You, too, Jennifer, Jeff, Katie, Mom, and Dad. And H, D, and N. And Grandma, too.

Jon, thank you for the dinners, the listening, the love, the conversation, the books, the wine, our life. Even when I couldn't say it, you have always made me feel like a writer.

ABOUT THE AUTHOR

Megan Giddings is a features editor at *The Rumpus* and the fiction editor at *The Offing*. Her fiction has appeared in *Black Warrior Review, Catapult, Gulf Coast,* and *The Iowa Review*. She attended University of Michigan and earned her MFA from Indiana University. The opening chapters of *Lakewood* received a Barbara Deming Memorial Fund grant for feminist fiction. She lives in Indiana.